To Bunt:

With appreciation for all
your support!

Mimosa
A French Country Mystery

Gloria Marshall

5/01

Mimosa
A French Country Mystery

Gloria P. Marshall

Northwest Publishing Inc.
Salt Lake City, Utah

Mimosa: A French Country Mystery

First Printing 1994

ISBN: 1-56901-147-8

NPI books are published by Northwest Publishing Incorporated,
6906 South 300 West, Salt Lake City, Utah 84047.
The name "NPI" and the "NPI" logo are trademarks belonging to
Northwest Publishing Incorporated.

PRINTED IN THE UNITED STATES OF AMERICA.
10 9 8 7 6 5 4 3 2 1

This book is in memory of my dear brother
and collaborator,
STANLEY C. POTTER,
who accompanied me all the way.

Chapter One

"The first thing I must do is buy a straw basket to hang on my arm, so I can skip into the village to buy *poisson*, freshly caught in the stream." Hildy grabbed the dashboard as Alex tested the passing ability of the gleaming new sapphire Porsche he had insisted on picking up at the factory in Munich.

"What stream?" Alex peered through his bi-focals.

"Every French village has a stream where you stand on the bridge and barter with the fisherman," his wife explained. "No more Lean Cuisine. We will live off the fruits of the land."

"You've been seeing too many French movies," muttered Alex, zipping past a Vespa that wouldn't give way.

As they drove deep into the countryside, leaving the foothills of Grasse behind, mimosa blossoms blanketed the roadway. Hildy rummaged through her Pierre Deux tote for her journal. "Would you say the golden mimosa looks fluffy as ducklings or more like confetti thrown across our pathway to herald a new chapter in our lives?" She uncapped her lavender pen and clicked it against her teeth.

"If you don't mind, I'd prefer to keep my eyes on this pot-holed road," Alex snapped back. "You'd think those damned French would repair it."

Why had she bothered to ask? Alex was always so literal, utterly unable to grasp the metaphysical. He absolutely detested Shirley MacLaine.

To celebrate his retirement, Alex had arranged to lease a Marquis' villa for a six week holiday in the south of France. It was located in La Roquette, a storybook village—the kind somebody lived in once upon a time—only *this* time it would be Hildy.

Over the years, Hildy had learned to brace herself for Alex's surprises. True, they often delighted her, but they almost always meant a major adjustment for Hildy—like a sudden trip to visit her mother on the Jersey shore during the hurricane season.

"I just wish you'd given me more time to research the riches of the region before we left," said Hildy, pressing one of the thirty-six buttons on the Porsche's digital dash to check the outside temperature. Instead, her window rolled down. "Oh, well, I can always put my arm out to check."

Alex gave her a stern look. "Close the window! You'll get the new upholstery dusty."

Hildy found it hard to reconcile this trim, grey-haired, still strikingly handsome husband with his snappish annoyance with anything he was unable to control.

In the distance rose the Maritime Alps, most recently conquered by Alex. Give him a road map with flying eagles to indicate where Napoleon halted with his troops, throw in a gorge or two, maybe a tunnel, and her husband was in heaven. Not Hildy. With Alex at the wheel, she tended to be more hysterical, than historical.

It was late afternoon when they reached the outskirts of La

Roquette. The countryside had dissolved into a fairyland of fuchsia cherry blossoms. "Once I get settled in our villa…" she could already smell the lavender-scented gardens, "I shall begin revisions on my novel-in-progress." She turned towards Alex. "Just in case I run into a vacationing film mogul who wants to option it for development."

"Why do you put yourself through this, Hildy?" He grabbed her hand. "We're on holiday now. I feel like a kid let out of school!"

While pleased to see Alex revel in the luxury of leisure, Hildy felt the humiliation return over losing the novel contest to Dorothy, of all people. She was an animal rights activist. "Can you believe she set her Candlelight Ecstasy Romance in Ketchikan, Alaska, of all places?"

"My God, Hildy, are you still dwelling on that damned contest? It's not that important."

"Not for you, Alex, but it was for me. You don't seem to understand. I'm in the autumn of my life when I'm supposed to reap the rewards of my harvest, and I haven't even finished sowing my seeds."

Several bands of gypsies had set up their wagons in an empty field just outside the village. "Gracious, Alex, did you see that?" A pair of small children with hard eyes and hoop earrings shook their fists at the Porsche as it sped by. "I always thought gypsies sat around campfires, strumming on mandolins."

"Look more like activists to me," replied Alex, bouncing over ruts.

"I hope that isn't an omen," said Hildy leaning back. She reflected on how her heroine, Consuela, might fare as a gypsy vagabond. Wasn't she a vagabond already stumbling about the Apache Trail? Not for long. She would emigrate to France, even though she was *enceinte* with Orlando's child. Perhaps she would miscarry in steerage. On a tramp steamer. "No, tramp steamer crossings take months, don't they, Alex?"

Alex did not answer. He concentrated on his chariot of fire as it raced into the village. Roosters ran, calling.

"You really don't need to take the town by storm, dear,"

Hildy reminded him. A terrified townsman leaped aside to cling to a stone wall.

Alex screeched to a halt in a village square dominated by a bronze war monument. Shutters popped open as curious faces peered out to view the new *étrangères* in town.

"Quick, Alex. Get a picture of those quaint peasant ladies," said Hildy, jumping out of the car. Cloaked in black, the women chatted while they laundered their clothes in a stone washing trough fed by a fountain.

The women stopped their scrubbing to watch Alex, leaning on the roof of the Porsche to focus his Pentax. Glancing briefly at the dark clouds moving across the sky, he adjusted his camera.

"*Excusez-moi*, everyone," called Hildy. "*Bonjour!*" She offered her most dazzling smile. Silence, except for the gentle tinkling of the fountain. The women stared back at them. "Could you resume scrubbing just for one minute," Hildy pleaded, "so *mon mari* can take your picture?" She turned frantically to Alex. "Take it! Take it!"

Alex dutifully snapped.

"*Merci*," Hildy shouted. "*Très bon* and all that. I'd love to tell them we'll be neighbors," she said, climbing back into the car, "but unfortunately, I can only conjugate in the present tense."

One of the more elderly ladies, her cheeks framed by a black kerchief, hobbled over to Alex, as he opened the car door. She was brandishing a limp chicken.

"Oh, Lord, Alex. I believe we've run over her *poulet*. Quick. Give her some francs."

"*Combien* a pound *ici*?" Alex joked, plunging a hand into his pocket. Without stopping to calculate, he handed her a fistful of francs.

Scowling, the woman stuffed the francs into her apron pocket.

"Ask her *donde* the Marquis lives," said Alex, producing a map from his blazer pocket.

Hildy winced. "We're not in Arizona, dear. Donde is

Spanish." She smiled politely at the woman. "*Où est la maison du Marquis?*"

The woman studied them carefully, then waved the dead chicken vaguely in the direction of a narrow lane which disappeared up a hill beyond the square. "*Dominus vobiscum,*" she muttered, crossing herself, then, turning, she shuffled away.

Hildy reached for her journal, uncapping her pen to write a quick note. "Isn't she wonderful? Right out of Grimm's fairy tales. I wonder if she casts spells."

Alex revved up the engine. "It's up that cow path, according to the wicked witch of the West."

"You jest, of course, but my characters are very real to me, Alex. Could you pause for just a moment?" Hildy continued to absorb the local color, convinced it would add texture to her novel.

Outside a café, a burly workman sat drinking wine beneath a spreading chestnut tree. Hildy wondered if he might be a blacksmith. Carefully, he tilted the bottle up to his dry, cracked lips, closed his eyes, and following a hearty gulp, he brought the bottle back to his lips and cradled it in his hands.

"Notice how everything looks weather-beaten here," commented Hildy, furiously jotting down more notes. "…That old Romanesque church with its crumbling arches…" She thought a moment. "Even that old peasant lady. Her cheeks glowed— like pink charcoals." Delighted with her simile, she noted it quickly.

Alex shook his head. "I must admit this town is a bit more medieval than I planned."

Hildy squeezed his arm. "It's extremely picturesque, Alex. More than I ever dreamed." She wouldn't let him spoil her delight.

A figure, waving a straw hat, appeared suddenly at the top of the hill.

"What's wrong now?" Alex demanded, slowing down.

"That lady wants us to stop, dear."

Alex braked, looking at the woman with suspicion. "What the hell for?"

"*Ooh-lah-lah!*" the woman exclaimed, thrusting her head through Hildy's open window. "You must be the Bigelows. I am Marie de Musset." Jamming her hat back on her head, she extended her hand to Hildy.

Hildy's chief impression was of the woman's really absurd hat with its single fuchsia-colored rose lying across the wide brim and dangling in its owner's face. "Enchanted to meet you," Hildy replied, fumbling for the proper response in her phrase book.

"La Marquise de Musset, of course." Alex offered her the continental smile he used, Hildy observed, only on state occasions. "How did you know we were here?"

"Ah, I hear the car when it zooms into the village. *Très* powerful, the motor, no?"

"Oh, yes. *Très*," Hildy agreed. "I cannot tell you how thrilled I am to be on level ground again and to have found this haven…" It would at least serve as a home for the next few weeks. Hildy's gaze traveled over the wisps of silver hair that refused to be confined by Marie's ridiculous hat. She had not expected to see a noblewoman in such a disheveled state.

"Follow me, yes?" With an encouraging wave, Marie hurried over to a small rusted European car and slammed the door shut several times without success. Finally, holding it closed with one elbow, she switched on the ignition and sputtered up the lane, a cloud of exhaust and dust rising behind her.

Alex hesitated, watching the dust haze over the immaculate surface of the Porsche. Then, driving slowly ahead, he muttered: "The hell with it. It's going to rain anyway."

A short way up the lane, Marie's car turned, her arm signaling toward a wrought iron gate. Thick shrubbery obscured the surrounding countryside crowding the entrance Marie had indicated. When she stopped her car, Alex pulled up to park a respectable distance behind it.

"This must be it," said Hildy, jumping out. The gate stretched between two heavy stone pillars. A length of rope looped around the latch, guarding the courtyard beyond. "Oh,

Alex." Hildy inhaled. "I think I smell lavender."

"It smells more like stagnant water to me," said Alex, wrinkling his nose with distaste. Waiting for Marie to slam the car door shut, Alex ran his fingers across the tarnished crest embedded in the grillwork of the gate. "Needs polishing."

"The Marquis and I, we come here to make sure all is in readiness for your arrival," Marie explained, fumbling with the rope. "Our villa is over there." She pointed toward an olive grove.

"And where would the fields of lavender be?" asked Hildy, hopeful they would be nearby.

"My husband Léon, he will show you the grounds. You will see." She turned to point again. "Lady Helmsley leases the villa down the hill, beyond the mimosas. With one hand holding her hat on, Marie grinned at Alex. "You will find her *très amusant.*"

Hildy could not help but notice the gleam in Alex's eyes. "Damn him!" she muttered, under her breath. Couldn't he just once relate to the culture instead of stirring up her jealousy?

A portly man of about seventy-five emerged from a thicket of shrub edging the courtyard and swung open the gate. "Welcome to La Roquette."

With his white, bushy eyebrows and mustache, he reminded Hildy of Charlie Ruggles, the former film star.

"*Voilà.* Your villa!" The Marquis gestured broadly toward a two-storied structure of ochre stone, mantled with fiery bouganvillaea.

Hildy gasped. "Why I'm sure I saw this in National Geographic." It's newer parts were stucco painted a tawny pinkish hue in an attempt to blend with what remained of the original tile roof. Other sections seemed older, built in odd-sized stones. "It's so *provençal*," Hildy sighed, not exactly sure what she meant. "Imagine Alex," she grabbed his arm, "a Marquis for our landlord."

The Marquis guffawed modestly at Hildy's comment. Beaming over his shoulder at her, he led them proudly ahead to the gardens.

Hildy turned to the Marquise. "I feel as if I've walked right into a fairy tale and been granted my three wishes."

Alex gave her a disbelieving look, batting away the branch of a bush in the jungle-like surroundings.

"One wish was meeting Alex, of course," Hildy continued, bestowing a smile of affection upon her husband. "And riding off into the sunset…"

"How *très romantique*." The Marquise looked enraptured.

Hildy would have preferred to lapse into native French to complete her tale, but hadn't the foggiest idea of how to say "faraway places with strange sounding names." She settled for singing "Fairy tales do come *vrai*, it could happen to *vous*…"

The Marquise looked bewildered.

"As Pat Boone once said," Hildy added in explanation.

"I thought it was Perry Como," Alex murmured, stomping ahead on the garden path.

"It's like the wild country gardens of England," said Hildy, stunned at the breathtaking profusion of blooms. Enormous flushed pink roses tumbled over the edge of garden walls.

"It is quite beautiful, no?" asked the Marquise. A surge of wind blew petals from the creamy copper flowers crowded below towering cypresses. Tiny yellow ramblers laced the palms. "Ah, can it be the mistral?" She put on her glasses to study the sky. "*Ce n'est pas possible*."

Hildy buttoned up her cardigan. "What exactly is a mistral?"

"It's fearsome wind that sweeps down from the North," she explained. "The Romans considered it a dreaded god that purified everything in its path."

"We desert rats welcome winds of any sort, even an occasional shower, don't we, Hildy?" said Alex cheerfully.

"We must prepare, yes, Léon?"

"The weather is of no consequence, Marie." The Marquis' voice was crisp, admonishing his wife to dismiss the subject.

"We truly love *tempêtes*," Hildy assured him, sensing his fear his new tenants might leave.

Marie seemed unperturbed. "This fountain is *très amusant*," she remarked, hiking up her cerise pantaloons to step into the water, after removing her clogs. She fussed to dislodge something clogging the fountain's spout. "*Mon Dieu!*" she cried, as a sudden jet of water shot forth, striking Alex in the face.

He tore off his glasses, dripping them at arms length, as he brushed away drops of water.

The Marquis immediately offered Alex a crumpled handkerchief from his breast pocket. "Marie try to make her garden look like Versailles," he chuckled.

"I can definitely see the possibilities," Hildy conceded, trying to be positive in what was so far a negative situation. With a worried glance at her partially drenched husband, Hildy tried to divert attention. "See how the breeze billows through the splendor of the grass, Alex."

"A machete would help," he muttered, dabbing at his collar as he circled the pool. A vacuum hose stood stalled in a layer of algae in the middle. Oleander leaves carpeted what little was visible at the bottom. Then, yanking the brochure out of his coat pocket, he took a menacing step toward the Marquis. "Sir, this is the pool we see here on the cover, *oui*?"

The Marquis glanced at the picture of an azure pool, graced by two striking tanned bodies reclining on chaise lounges. "Ah," he smiled with recognition, raising his hand in apology. "But we had such a gardener then. André, he was the best. He also tended sheep in the fields there beyond the stone wall."

Marie shook her head. "Poor André. He is dead."

Hildy was alert to the fearful look in Marie's eyes at the mention of André's name.

"The pump, it does not run correctly," Marie explained, "but you can swim nevertheless."

"You wish to swim before dining?" asked the Marquis, wiggling the vacuum handle to stir turgid ripples in the pool.

"We rarely swim in the evening," Hildy answered quickly.

"Tomorrow Edmund, he will fix the pump," Marie assured them. He has great *esprit*, this gardener."

Hildy noted the look of skepticism on Alex's face.

Léon snorted. "Edmund, he is a peasant." He flipped his

cigarette away in the overgrowth.

Strolling toward the villa, Hildy lingered behind with the Marquise. "You know, Marie, may I call you that? I am most curious about this André person. You see I'm a writer…"

Marie's face lit up. "You bring book with you to autograph for me?"

"Not really." Hildy bit her lip. "I haven't quite finished it yet. I must transpose my characters to a French setting."

"*Vraiment?*" Marie nodded toward her husband with a patient smile, then, whispered to Hildy, "André, he did some work here in the garden and the fields. His sister, Madame Lescaut, used to be our housekeeper. She beg us to hire him, but only to earn a few francs." Her expression grew serious. "He would rise at dawn to observe the wonder of the sunrise. He had great reverence for nature. What went on here," she tapped her head with her finger, "I cannot say. He prefer to make the stained glass window."

Hildy panted, trying to keep pace with Marie. "Might I speak to this Madame Lescaut?"

"*Mais oui.* She will come to assist while you are here, but do not ask about André. It is painful since his death. Only last autumn…" Marie's voice trailed off.

At the Marquis' suggestion, Alex drove the Porsche inside the gate and began to unload the luggage.

"I adore your frock, Marie," said Hildy.

The Marquise beamed, pirouetting in her fuchsia tulip top and the clashing cerise pantaloons. "Ah, you like? I buy it at the Monoprix in Cannes. I take you there."

"That would be lovely," said Hildy, surprised. She assumed a Marquise would wear high couture, not something from a discount house.

"We will need a key to open the door," Alex announced, trying the latch. "It's locked."

The Marquis stood by, puffing on a freshly lit cigarette. "Marie, *ouvrez la porte,*" he said, wheezing.

It had started to rain lightly, black clouds rolling across the sky.

Marie rummaged in an earthen pot full of dried up geraniums. "Madame Lescaut, *toujours*, *toujours*, she hides our key."

The Marquis' face reddened. "Peasants. They no longer serve. They exploit."

With pointed impatience, Marie retrieved the key and opened the heavy oak door, leading the way into the stone foyer.

For Hildy, it was like stepping back into the Middle Ages. Over an archway hung a pair of crossed swords, displaying the de Musset crest. A detailed representation of the family tree dating back to 1100, covered one wall of the foyer. Vivid splashes of color showed in four gold-framed paintings of soldiers in red tunics mounted on white chargers.

"Are these your relatives?" Hildy asked, straining to see the captions. Her mind reeled with the sense of history these awesome figures represented.

"My great-great grandfather," the Marquis declared solemnly. "He was a General in the French Revolution.

Alex handed Hildy his soft pack full of camera equipment. "Hold this while I bring in our luggage."

"You must excuse Léon," Marie confided to Hildy. "He forget we have no servants." She hefted a suitcase to the foot of the stairs.

"I have replaced all the wooden casements with *plastique*, he announced proudly, running a finger through the small puddle forming on the sill. A strong gust swept a torrent of rain through the open door, prompting Marie to race over to swing it shut.

"It is very difficult to pump water up the hill," said Marie, leading the way up the stairway, "so..." she removed a can from the cabinet in the hall, "we use the Drano regularly. Mostly to cleanse the shower drain. *C'est rien*." She handed the can to Hildy.

Hildy dared not think of Alex's reaction. In no way could he cope with adversity when it came to his morning shower. She followed Marie down the hall.

"I trust you will find this room most comfortable," said

Marie, ducking under a stone archway.

Alex prodded the sagging three-quarter bed, one end of which was tied to the bedpost with a rope.

"Digs on the up-side," Hildy whispered, hoping to lighten Alex's evident exasperation.

"Look, Madame Bigelow," the Marquise cried, opening the shutters at the window, "over there beyond the hills…"

Hildy stepped over craning her head into the rain to see. "Oh, yes, Alex, see that distant smudge of azure sea, still twinkling like a jewel, as the storm clouds move to obscure its radiance," she improvised, in love with the sound of her own voice. "And the rooftops below, dripping pink droplets as the winds dance an interlude on their tiles." Why was it her best metaphors emerged when she wasn't even trying? She pulled in her head, brushing the raindrops from her hair.

Alex lowered his bi-focals. "What is that?" He pointed to a small hut with a bulls eye window in the fields below the villa.

"An empty shepherd's hut," said the Marquis, wheezing as he snuffed out his cigarette. "Come, Marie, we must go before the storm worsens."

"Did André use it when he was alive?" asked Hildy, following Marie into *la salle de bain*.

"André make this for us." Marie pointed to a small stained glass window embedded in the wall above the toilet. "Madame Lescaut insist we put it there."

"It's beautiful," Hildy gasped. In the fading light, she discerned a shepherd leaning on his staff in a field, surrounded by his sheep. The muted colors were earthen ochres and umbers, except for a purple sash at the shepherd's waist. His face was raised to the heavens where a clear white star shone down to light the scene. "The star of Bethlehem," Hildy said. A wall of wind shook the room. She backed away. The cut glass segments trembled in a sudden gust.

Marie took Hildy's arm and led her back into the bedroom where Léon and Alex were deep in a discussion about the nude beaches on the Côte d'Azur. "*Très magnifique, non?*" The Marquis outlined with his hands a woman's curves.

Hildy's mind was congested with doubts and fears, but could not wait to jot down her initial impressions of what had all the makings of a mystery. Why were the de Mussets so evasive about André? A peasant with such extraordinary talent...yet only his sister seemed to care.

Chapter Two

By nightfall, the mistral had struck the countryside with its full fury, bringing lightning and sudden crashes of thunder. Rain lashed the villa in noisy waves, drumming against the windows and washing swollen rivulets along the lane outside and down the hill.

Watching the tall cypresses shaking in the wind, Alex monitored the Porsche from the bedroom window. "I have to do something about the car, Hildy." He raced down the stairs. "If this wind starts blowing down trees…"

"But what can you do?" she yelled. "Alex, it's dangerous out there!"

"Of course it's dangerous!" he lashed back. "That's what I'm worried about!"

A broken tree branch flew by the open doorway as he

stumbled across the shining cobbled courtyard to the car. He struggled to get in and start the engine, maneuvering the car against the side of a turreted building adjacent to the courtyard, where it would be shielded from the wind.

He returned to the villa breathless, slamming the front door shut. Water was puddling in the entrance foyer.

"Alex, darling, you're soaked!" Hildy hurried him up the stairs.

"I wish I had a tarp of some kind," he panted. As they reached the stair landing, lightning blazed through the window followed by cracking thunder. Alex started back down the stairs to peer out again at the car.

"It will be all right, Alex," Hildy assured him. "That building will protect it." She put her arm around his waist. "Right now let's get you dry. Come on." She led him up the stairs.

While Alex changed into his pajamas, Hildy sat down at the desk. "I'm just too weary to write a single word in my journal tonight." Lightning flashed and the naked bulb handing from the ceiling suddenly dimmed, then came back on.

"I'm truly sorry," he said, "this place is not at all the treat I'd planned."

"It's wonderful, dear. I feel a *Wuthering Heights* quality here, don't you agree? Old and strange, alive with romance." She would overlook the wretched dinner of wilted *niçoise* salad and unripe melon their landlord had thoughtfully placed in the refrigerator.

A torrent of rain lashed against the window, driven by a shuddering blast of wind. The closed shutters dislodged, banging repeatedly against the house. Alex rushed to the window, tearing it open to icy sheets of rain. He leaned out and grabbed the shutters, pulling them closed. "Here, hold these. I need something to tie them with."

Hildy grasped the handles with both hands, as Alex looked frantically around the room.

"A necktie!" He rummaged through his suitcase.

A new blast of wind tore the shutters from her grip. Hildy let out a cry and stared out into the blackness. "Alex! Look!

There's somebody out there!"

Alex was at her side with one of his neckties. He looked down at the rain-soaked lane beyond the wall. "There's nobody, for God's sake, Hildy." He reached for the shutters and pulled them closed, wrapping the necktie firmly around the handles.

"I saw him, Alex, really, I did! He had on a cloak, a long, black cloak and he looked right up at me."

Alex tied a final knot, closing the window against the storm. There was a patient smile on his face. "Hildy, my adorable writer, you are letting your romantic imagination rattle your senses."

A blast of wind tore at the shutters again. A simultaneous explosion of lightning and thunder made the house shudder. They heard tinkling glass.

"Dear heavens, we've been hit!" Hildy cried, clinging to her husband.

They followed the sound into the bathroom. A shiny wet tree branch had stabbed through the shepherd window and hung eerily rigid in the half darkness. Rain swept through the grotesque opening in the wall.

"André's window. It's destroyed, Alex!" She flicked on the light, and a wet spring of leaves brushed her cheek. She reached to push it away.

"Stay here, Hildy" Alex pressed his arms around her, pulling her gently away. "I've got to find something to cover this opening. Don't stand there getting wet!" He hurried away.

She bent to sort through the shards of colored glass shattered on the wet tile floor.

The dripping branch stirred over her head as another gust of wind swept against the crippled tree, showering her with fine raindrops. As lightning flashed again, she spotted the piece that must have been the star itself—a crystalline white nugget, somewhat irregular in form, but even in this gloomy room alive with light. She reached to take it, holding it almost reverently in her palm. "The Star of Bethlehem," she murmured, "illuminating the face of the mysterious shepherd, André Dupres!"

Chapter Three

When Hildy threw open the shuttered window the next morning, leaden clouds still hung low in the sky. Some fallen branches littered the lane, the only physical damage she could observe. The mistral had abated sometime during the night, but she had no idea how long such a storm was likely to last.

Glancing at the sagging bed, she marvelled that they had managed a reasonably good night's sleep. One adjusts, she told herself, if one embraces circumstance with a willing spirit. She smiled, hearing the unmistakable sound of the shower and Alex's undaunted baritone rendering a lusty version of "Stormy Weather". Apparently, the tree branch poking through their bathroom window was not interfering with her husband's morning ritual.

She rummaged through her Hartmann for the proper

pieces to wear in her role as an expatriate writer in the south of France. According to her index cards, her mauve blouse should complement her lavender skirt. Well it might, she thought, in Arizona, but in this weather, she would choose warmth over *coûture*. Shivering, she bundled into her beige cardigan.

Picking up her tote from the little desk in the alcove, she suddenly remembered the glass fragment she had salvaged from the broken window. She took it from the bag to examine it, unfolding the Kleenex in which she'd wrapped it. It was beautiful, much more than just a souvenir to her, for reasons she had not yet quite figured out.

Dropping it back into the tote, she sprinted down the stone stairs, eager for whatever her new environment had to offer. She hoped it would exclude further trauma.

In the middle of the entrance foyer, her momentum was abruptly halted by the kneeling figure of a wiry woman of about fifty mopping up the muddy residue of the storm. "Ah! *Bonjour,* you must be Madame Lescaut." Hildy assumed a stance she felt appropriate for a warm mistress of the manor. "I am Madame Bigelow." She extended her hand.

The woman stood up, her brassy hair standing out from her head as if electrified. "*Bonjour, Madame.*" She clasped Hildy's hand loosely, dropping it immediately to move her bucket and rags aside. Her features were frozen in a mask of restraint as she opened the French doors to the living room.

"You will like *le petit déjeuner ici*, in *séjour est*?"

"*Pourquoi* on earth not?" Hildy replied cheerfully, not at all sure what *séjour est* meant. She followed her into the drab parlor. "Isn't this lovely," she said without conviction.

The room was done in a uniform bile-yellow, with ivory tassels adorning couch, armchairs, pillows and lamp shades. A stone fireplace opened on one wall, the grinning figure of a devil with a pitchfork centered in its mantel. Flanking the fireplace stood partially filled bookcases. On an adjacent wall, a French window overlooked the storm-ravaged garden. If, as Hildy had read somewhere, the home is a person's autobiography, then clearly Marie de Musset suffered from emotional jaundice.

The room cried out for color. Hildy's imagination immediately supplied the decorative touches needed: perhaps floral chintz pillows tossed carelessly about—and the console table and mantle glorified with baskets of freshly cut *fleurs*. She wondered why the Marquise would wardrobe herself in vivid cerise and magenta and yet create surroundings of such unrelenting neutrality. One thing was certain. Marie, standing in this room, would be the only thing one would see. Perhaps that explained it.

She looked out at the garden as Madame Lescaut opened the *armoire* and gathered together a pink linen cloth and two napkins. From another drawer she withdrew silverware, then crossed back to a small oak table by the window.

"*La Tempête*," Hildy ventured, "*très formidable, n'est-ce pas*?"

The woman shrugged. "Is mistral, Madame. No *tempête*."

"Oh. Of course." Hildy stood corrected. "The storm," she waved an arm in the direction of the ceiling, "upstairs, a tree branch, *un arbre*." She struggled for a verb, then settled for a vocal sound she hoped resembled a branch breaking through a window.

Madame Lescaut winced at Hildy's improvised sound effect, then said, "*Oui*, I see the debris in the garden."

"This Edmund, he will fix? The window is..." It dawned on Hildy that Lescaut might be unaware that her brother's window had been shattered by the tree branch. She went to her, placing a hand on her arm. "Madame Lescaut..."

The housekeeper withdrew her arm from Hildy's touch and busied herself laying the table.

Gently, Hildy began again. "The window, *la fenêtre*, the stained glass, the shepherd your brother, André, made, in the bathroom, *la salle de bain*..."

Lescaut stood suddenly erect, her face contorted, and rushed from the room. Hildy heard her start up the stairs then stop. She returned slowly to the room, tears now filling her eyes.

"I'm so sorry," Hildy said. "It was a tree branch, you see.

The tree was struck by lightning, and a branch smashed right through the wall."

Lescaut stood motionless for a long moment. Then she resumed her task. "*C'est rien*," she mumbled. "I make Edmund fix it." She busied herself completing the table setting.

Inside her tote, Hildy's hand clasped the piece of glass she had tucked away, but she let it fall back. This did not seem the time.

With his customary morning energy, Alex bounded into the room, "*Bonjour! Comment ça va?*" He wore his navy blue jogging suit with white stripes down the arms and legs. His hair was still damp from the shower.

Hildy grimaced at his atrocious accent. "We're all just perfectly fine, Alex. This is Madame Lescaut."

"*Bonjour*," Alex repeated, nodding to the thin woman setting the table. "I'm starved." He favored the housekeeper with his continental smile, which, as Hildy thought about it, was exactly the kind of smile used by candidates running for office. "What do we have for breakfast?" He rubbed his hands together.

"I was just explaining to Madame Lescaut about the broken window, darling," Hildy shot a look at her husband, hoping he would read her warning of tension in the room. "How I had admired it. Remember, you were going to photograph it for me?"

Alex moderated his good humor. "Oh, yes, We wanted to catch it with the sun behind it. But," he smiled, extending his palms, "what can you do? It was an act of..." he trailed off.

"*Oui*," Lescaut turned with a mirthless smile. "It is done. *Maintenant*, you desire...?" She awaited instructions.

Plunging into her reticule, Hildy whipped open her phrase book to "food." "*Les oeufs*, scrambled, *pour deux*," she announced proudly, "*très sec...*"

"You're ordering wine?" Alex looked alarmed.

"It means 'very dry,' the eggs, the only way you'll eat them, Alex." With her brows raised to Lescaut, she clapped the book shut, "*D'accord, Madame?*"

Lescaut remained impassive, her hands clasping and unclasping in front of her.

Hildy looked at her husband. "She may not understand my Arizona accent." She fluttered an indifferent hand at Lescaut. "*Les* eggs, cooked any way at all. *Comprenez-vous* eggs?"

"*Oui,* I understand. Eggs. I make now." She disappeared out the hall door.

Hildy said in a low voice, "The woman is either devastated by the broken window, or she epitomizes the negative element of the great mother archetype, I haven't decided which."

"I wouldn't exactly call her bubbly."

"Not the giver, but the withholder," Hildy explained. "A perfect model for my antagonist."

"If you say so, darling. Maybe she's just in a bad mood." Alex examined a phonograph nestled in a bookshelf. "A little morning music?" he asked.

"Edith Piaf would be nice." Despite the grimness of the earlier moment with Lescaut, Hildy felt an excitement on this occasion of their very first meal, served by their own private servant. She arranged herself in one of the tasselled chairs. "You realize, dear, it's not going to be easy to go back to microwaving Lean Cuisines after this."

But Alex was absorbed in his search for morning music. "These records seem to be in the wrong sleeves. No Piaf, anyway." He held up a record, examining the label. "The overture from *Carmen*, maybe?" He slipped the record on the turntable, switching on the machine. A somewhat scratchy, hissing sound dissolved into silence.

Hildy sighed. "So much for working-out with my Jane Fonda record."

"Why would you bring that?"

"I asked Charlotte to send it along with my cookbooks. To make up for missing my aerobics at Forever Agile classes."

"I would think a daily walk to the village with me would serve just as well to burn off calories."

"It's important for me to exercise my limbs to music." Hildy demonstrated with a little jump, clapping her hands over her head. "It also helps rouse the muse."

Alex slammed the phonograph shut. "I'll try the radio."

A genial voice rattled across the airwaves in nonstop French. "What's he saying, dear?" Alex inquired. "Is it a newscast?"

Hildy waved away the intrusive sound. "Who knows? You think I can understand that babble, for heaven's sake? Just turn it off!"

"Right," Alex said, clicking the switch. "Screw it. We'll just sit and talk. Tell me," he chose the chair opposite and sat, "what impressions have you entered so far in your journ—" He stopped abruptly as the cushion slipped forward, placing him in a semi-reclining position. "What the hell kind of chair is this?" He slid the cushion back and reseated himself, clinging to the arms to prevent being ejected.

"It's probably one of those chaise lounges, for naps," Hildy said, sliding her cushion forward a few inches. "Like this one, see?" She slid it back. "We just have to get the hang of it."

An uneasy silence followed. "Let's bag this place and head for Paris," Alex suggested. "What do you say?"

"No, no, Alex! We must give ourselves time to extract the essence and distill the texture of our surroundings." She got up to examine the bookcase. "Be patient, darling. You haven't had your *oeufs* yet."

Alex looked at his watch, clicking a few buttons to ascertain the time in Arizona, New York and Tokyo.

"Look at this," Hildy said, coming to him with a book. She read the title from the bind: "*La Flora et Fauna de la Riviera*!" She had flipped it open and pointed to a picture.

"Why Alex, it's the tree that crashed through the stained glass window! *La mimosa*!" The picture showed a branch with a cluster of yellow flowers. "It says the mimosa is such a…" she hesitated with the translation, "sensitive tree that if you touch one of the leaflets, the others close, one by one." She removed her reading glasses. "It's like some sort of signal travels from one leaf to the other, and in as little as fifteen minutes, they all recover." She closed the book. "I find that remarkable, don't you?"

Alex scratched his arm. "What's remarkable is how the damn mosquitoes are swarming in the broken window."

When she closed the book, a piece of paper fluttered to the floor. She picked it up, holding it at a distance to examine it. "It's a design of some kind on graph paper. Look at these shapes, chalked in with sunshine shades of gold, bright yellow, topaz..." She handed the paper to her husband.

"Looks like one of the paint-by-the-numbers things," he declared, handing it back.

Hildy looked again. "These shapes and color samples," her voice rose with excitement, "are part of a sketch for a stained glass panel! I'll bet on it. Dupres used this book as a resource." She hurried to open her journal and, with a last look at the sketch, folded it inside. "Do you see what I've learned about this Dupres, in less than twenty-four hours?"

"I'm impressed, darling," Alex's voice humored her. "Do you plan to write about this Dupres, or what?"

"I'm curious, that's all. He seems to have been underestimated, wouldn't you say? I think our landlady knows a good deal more about Dupres than she's told us." Hildy's hand was still inside the tote. She leaned forward, holding the arm of the chair against any unexpected shifting of the cushion. "You know, dear, I've kept a little piece of Dupres' window, a superb white crystal, the star above the shepherd figure. Would you like to see it?"

"Sure." He straightened, taking the crystal from the kleenex tissue and weighing it in his palm. "Nice. Too small for a paper weight, though."

The rattle of dishes sounded from the hall, as Lescaut came around the corner, wheeling their breakfast into the room. Hildy snatched the crystal from Alex, wrapping it quickly in its Kleenex, and plunged it back into the tote where Lescaut would not see it. She stood, feeling Lescaut staring from where she had halted the cart behind Alex's chair. "Oh, smell that, Alex! *Les oeufs*. Isn't it divine?" She sat at the table, whirling her napkin into her lap with a flourish.

He sat and picked up the goblet of juice. "*À votre santé*." He clinked her glass, then turned to raise his glass to the devil guarding the hearth, "and up yours, too, Charlie."

Lescaut gave Alex a stony sidelong glance and rattled the cart from the room.

"Madame Danvers, *en français,*" Hildy murmured.

"Who the hell is she?"

"The murderous housekeeper at Manderley in *Rebecca*, remember?" Hildy smiled. "She wanted to push her mistress out the window."

Chapter Four

Alex pushed his chair back and stood to give Hildy an affectionate hug. "I've been putting it off, darling, but I can't stand it another second. I've got to check the Porsche."

"I'm sure nothing's happened to it." Hildy suddenly felt annoyed to be competing with this machine for her husband's attention. "Really, Alex, you read about men who treat their cars like a mistress!"

Alex kissed her quickly, "You'll admit she's got nice lines, though," he said, "but—"

Suddenly they heard the piercing whoop-whoop of the car alarm. "See?" He released her abruptly and bolted out the front door. She heard him bellow, "You! Get away from that car!"

A slightly built man of about thirty, with thick, black curly hair, huddled over the hood, trying to release the catch that would open it. He danced back at Alex's exclamation, raising his hands in a gesture of surrender. He inclined his head with an engaging smile. "I am sorry, Monsieur! I try to stop the alarm!"

A battered pickup truck with bags of fertilizer and pool chemicals stood parked in the courtyard. In the rear, the handles of garden tools poked over its sides.

Alex yelled to Hildy. "Tell that creep I don't want him messing with my car." He advanced on the frightened young man, as the alarm continued to whoop.

Hildy stepped into the courtyard. "*Bonjour, Monsieur,*" she shouted. "*Voici, Monsieur Bigelow.* This is his car. He *ne dèsire pas* for you to mess with it!"

The man shrugged and extended his hand to Alex, yelling, "I am Edmund! I take care of the villa. Also the car!" He looked at it with admiration, brushing a tiny twig from the roof.

"Please! Step aside!" Alex unlocked the car and shut off the alarm. There was blessed silence, as he straightened. "*Bonjour.* You are not to touch this car, understand? *No touchez-vous*!" He indicated the garden. "Just clean up this garden, and for God's sake, do something about the pool!"

Lescaut had appeared at the front door, and now rattled off a stream of French to the young man. He nodded his head and hurried to unload a rake and a trash bag from the back of the pickup. Grabbing a coil of hose, he flashed another smile at the new tenants and scurried off to the garden.

Alex walked slowly across the courtyard to join Hildy and Madame Lescaut. "Tell her to have him do something about that tree branch sticking in our bathroom, will you, Hildy?"

"Did you observe his eyes, Alex?" Hildy asked.

"I do not give a damn about his eyes, nor do I plan to spend our sojourn here overseeing that maniac."

"He's rather dashing, I thought," Hildy said. "A certain Robin Hood kind of desperation there."

"Probably on drugs," Alex grumbled, returning to inspect the Porsche more thoroughly.

A short time later, Hildy found Lescaut scouring her

already spotless kitchen counters. *"Bonjour, Madame,"* Hildy said, uncertain about how to start this conversation. "I brought you this." She extended both her hands with her offering.

The housekeeper looked at her without expression, then at the fragments of stained glass Hildy had arranged on some Kleenex tissues. She rationalized the piece of crystal kept for herself. Her eyes went wide, and she cupped Hildy's extended hands with both of hers, bending with a little cry.

"It is the shepherd's head," Hildy explained..."some pieces that were not broken. Perhaps with some glue, you can cement these together."

The woman looked up at Hildy, tears brimming in her eyes. There was a warmth in her face Hildy had not seen until this moment. *"Merci,"* she whispered. "It is..." Her voice trailed off, as she tenderly removed the memento of her brother from Hildy's hands, placing it carefully on the counter. She smoothed the glass, pressing the several vagrant pieces into position in the leaded slots where they belonged.

Hildy beamed at her, saying nothing. Lescaut pulled herself up and nodded, once again distant. Not looking at Hildy, she said, *"Je...*I am grateful, Madame. Thank you for your kindness."

Hildy took a breath, feeling her relationship with the woman had finally progressed. She realized it was the sense of *loss* for her brother Lescaut had felt initially, not anger toward Hildy. The shattered window had served to bring it all back again. But having this key portion of her brother's window might compensate her sorrow in some way, Hildy thought.

She took a step back. "Excuse me, Madame Lescaut. We will need *des serviettes*, more towels, please. Would you show me...?"

Lescaut immediately relinquished her cloth and lifted a key from the rack on the wall. Seizing Hildy's hand, she led her outside across the courtyard to a small storage room beneath the tower. The sun, breaking through the broken clouds, glinted off the wet tiles of its roof.

Where was this strange little woman taking her? Hildy

looked around for Alex, but he was nowhere in sight. She flinched as the door clanged shut.

"*S'il vous plaît, Madame Lescaut*," Hildy pointed to a narrow stone stairway that led to shadowed darkness above. "What is up there?"

A look of distress crossed the housekeeper's face. "*Rien*! Nothing! The tower is never used."

"Really? You see, I need a place to work. I'm a novelist," Hildy's fingers pantomimed typing. "*Une romancier*." She started up the stairs. "Perhaps the seclusion of this old tower would prove inspirational."

"No! No!" Lescaut pulled Hildy back. "It is not safe, Madame! The stones are old, and many are loose." She led Hildy away from the stairway.

Hildy cast a longing look up the stairs. "Isn't that a shame. It looks so promising."

The small ground floor room contained cabinets with drawers, standing against a stone wall. Gray daylight filtered through narrow windows. Lescaut unlocked a drawer and wrestled it open.

She picked out a number of faded towels and laid them neatly across Hildy's outstretched arms. Hildy ran her fingers across a texture reminiscent of kitchen Handi-wipes and frowned. Next, Lescaut produced two sets of muslin sheets and pillowcases. She stopped abruptly, retrieving the towels she had given Hildy and stuffing them back in the drawer. Without explanation, she replaced them with several thick terry towels in a bright shade of blue, bearing an embroidered crest.

Hildy smiled to herself as they recrossed the courtyard. She clearly had been given a major concession—a decent set of *guest* towels! For what Alex was paying for the villa, it seemed the least one might expect. Still, Hildy welcomed this apparent breech in Lescaut's wall of hostility.

Alex appeared, his grim demeanor betraying a new crisis. "Look at this!" he commanded waving a slip of paper at her. "It's his bill for those bags of stuff he brought for the pool." Hildy looked at Edmund's numbers, scribbled on a shred of paper bag. "I can't really make this out," she admitted. "Are we being charged for all those chemicals?"

"You bet I'm going to take this up with our landlord! It looks like the damned trade deficit!" He glowered in the direction of the garden. "That bandit!"

"Look," Hildy said brightly. "Towels! See the crest? Madame Lescaut has given us their best linens!"

"Peachy." Alex followed his wife and Lescaut into the house. "Would you believe that fool insists on watering the damned flowers? I mean—it poured rain all night!"

"Edmund, he is *fou*," Lescaut said over her shoulder. "Come." She beckoned them to follow her to the kitchen where she replaced the key, positioning herself in front of the two-foot long rack fastened to the wall.

"*Voilà*," she said, pointing proudly to the twenty-four keys hanging from metal hooks. She dispensed a key to the front door, then selected another. "And *celle-ci, pour votre chambre à coucher*." She gave the key to Alex.

"*Merci*." He glanced at his wife. "Why do we have to lock the bedroom, for God's sake?"

Lescaut shook a warning finger. "*Toujours*! Always the doors must be locked." She glared at them, lowering her voice. "There are gypsies here."

Hildy tensed. "Gypsies! Oh, dear. Are they dangerous?"

Madame Lescaut inclined her head ambiguously.

Hildy turned to Alex, grasping his arm. "That man in the cape last night standing in the rain. Maybe he was a gypsy." She tensed. "I just hate the idea of running into a gypsy right here in our own house, Alex. I would simply die, right on the spot. I really would!"

"I'm calling the Marquis right now to tell him about the broken window and the bugs in this place. Not to mention the bill for the pool chemicals. I'm also going to see what he has to say about these damned gypsies. This is not some summer camp, for God's sake! Haven't they ever heard of security systems?"

Hildy swallowed, reminded of the sophisticated electronic apparatus in their condo in Arizona. Installing one here, in this fairy tale setting, would be an unthinkable corruption. "Let's not rush into anything like that, Alex," she said. "We'll just remember to lock up. *Toujours*, as Madame Lescaut has warned." She nodded to the housekeeper. The thought crossed her mind that nothing was locked at this particular moment.

As he headed for the telephone, Alex said over his shoulder, "I also want to ask him about this idiot Edmund he's hired for us. I'd like the Marquis to know I'm liable to just flatten that brainless bastard!"

Hildy sighed, then pointed to an old iron key on the rack. "That one there?" It appeared to be the only one with no duplicate. "What is it?"

"No, Madame. *Jamais*. This key is for the hut in the field, not for any doors in the villa."

"Would that be a place I could work? The thing is, the little desk area in my boudoir is simply not terribly conducive, *comprenez-vous*? There's no space at all to spread out my index cards."

"I am very sorry, Madame." Lescaut shook her head. "The hut is closed now, no longer used. The Marquise fills it with boxes to store her things." She held up a warning finger. "And there are—you say it also in English—*les rats*, eh?"

Hildy gulped. "Oh, I could not possibly deal with rats, I'm sure." Was this woman telling her the truth about the tower, and now about this shepherd's hut? Hildy was not convinced.

There was a sudden peal of female laughter from the courtyard. Hildy hurried down the hall where Alex stood in the front doorway, watching an attractive girl of about twenty embracing the yardman.

"Can you believe this, Hildy? That flake dares to have his girlfriends drop in!" He stormed across the courtyard. "What's going on here, Edmund? Who the hell is this—*woman*?"

Hildy moved closer as the girl released Edmund, smoothing back her peroxide ponytail. "*Bonjour, Monsieur*," she said in a reedy voice. She handed Alex a small, blue envelope.

"My cousin, Yvette." Edmund bowed with evident pride. "She works for Lady Helmsley down the hill." He put his arm around the blushing girl and hugged her.

Alex's expression was one of pained tolerance as Yvette batted her eyes at him. *"Enchantée,"* she said, with a tiny curtsy.

"For goodness sake, I wonder who on earth Lady Helmsley can be," said Hildy, reaching for the envelope. She stared at the elegant, raised monogram. "An invitation to tea, tomorrow at four," she read. "The *favour* of a reply is requested. She must be British."

"I hate tea, Hildy. You know that." Alex scowled and started back into the house.

"You tell Yvette to inform her mistress we'd be delighted to accept her lovely invitation," Hildy said, with a determined air. Perhaps a nice civilized tea would distract her from the hopelessness of this household she was to preside over, to say nothing of her concern about the sinister gypsy lurking beneath their window the night before.

Chapter Five

Lady Helmsley was younger than Hildy had expected. A stunning woman of about forty with coppery hair swept back in a chignon, their hostess greeted them the next afternoon on the terrace. "You must be the Bigelows." She extended her hand. "I'm Victoria Helmsley." Her suntanned shoulders contrasted with the lemon yellow of her chiffon.

Alex's smile widened in approval. "I'm Alex, and this is my wife, Hildy."

"*Enchantée*," said Hildy, hoping to impress her with the French. She was glad she'd chosen the turquoise jumpsuit with contoured belt for the occasion, even though its snugness made it difficult to walk.

"Thank heavens those insolent winds have subsided," said Victoria, ushering them over to a pair of lawn chairs by the pool. She wiped them dry before they sat.

"Are the storms always this violent?" asked Hildy. Her chair sagged slightly sideways as she shifted to avoid the cracked wooden slats. "I don't know when I've been so petrified. A mimosa branch smashed right through our bathroom window!"

"How dreadful." Victoria looked up at the sky. "I fear there's more to come."

She sank into a wicker chair in a swirl of chiffon." Now tell me what brought you both here," she said, removing a cigarette from a slim gold case.

Alex struck a match and held it for her, as she inhaled.

"Um, thank you, Alex. May I call you Alex? But you do strike me more as Alexander."

"He prefers Alex," Hildy said firmly.

"And Hildy. What a sweet name. Is it short for Brunhilde?"

"Hildegarde, like the *chanteuse*," said Hildy laughing lightly to hide the hostility she was feeling. "I seldom wear horns on my helmet."

"Everyone calls her Hildy," said Alex.

"Is this your first trip to France?" Victoria tapped her cigarette into the ashtray.

"As a matter of fact, yes, but I'm sure not our last," replied Alex. "Now that I'm retired…"

"Retired?" Victoria looked stunned. "But Alex you look too young!" She placed a slender hand on his forearm, then turned to Hildy. "Doesn't he?"

Hildy concluded she did not like this woman.

Victoria leaned forward. "But, of course, you must be frightfully confused about all this. Forgive me."

"I must say we did wonder a bit," added Hildy, deciding she might as well be honest.

"I felt we Anglophiles should get acquainted. After all, we're to be neighbors."

"Isn't that a coincidence," said Hildy, attempting cordiality.

"As it happens, I come here each spring to paint. The colors in the south of France are so delicate, and then, of course *la lumière.* You see for yourself."

"An artist," said Alex. "Isn't that fascinating." His eyes traveled over Victoria's thigh, remarkably visible when she shifted position.

"I see you find time to acquire a lovely tan," Hildy observed. Then, feeling it important to establish her own credentials, she added, "In addition to being Alex' wife..." she paused the slightest instant, "I am also a writer."

"How extremely busy you must be. What sort of books do you write—saucy paperbacks like Barbara Cartland?"

"Mine tend to focus on metaphysical themes, more Ingmar Bergmanish."

A huge, long-haired cat materialized in the doorway of Victoria's terrace and stood malevolently surveying the Bigelows. Behind it, Yvette carried a silver tea tray, listing in her extended arms.

"Oh good Lord," Victoria said, leaping up to steady the maid to the wooden table. "Thank you, Yvette." She grabbed for the pot, as it began to slide dangerously across the tray.

Alex jumped up to help the apparently tipsy servant. "Here, let me get that."

Victoria glared. "You will put the wine away now, Yvette. Do you quite understand me? We will not be having any wine at all now."

Yvette executed a lopsided curtsy. "*Oui, Madame.*" She withdrew, using convenient handholds.

Victoria poured. "I apologize for Yvette's lack of aplomb, Hildy and Alex. She and cousin Edmund come as a team—the cream of the village crop, one supposes." She deposited the cat off her lap, where it had leaped the minute she sat down. "Go lie in the sun, Ariadne," she commanded. "You were saying about the storm, Hildy?"

"Just that we did have this catastrophe at our villa." Hildy reached into her tote for the glass fragment. "The branch shattered a charming window of stained glass created by our housekeeper's younger brother. Did you know him?"

"You mean André, of course. Totally unlike his sister, let

me hasten to say. A shepherd, really, but gifted."

"A shepherd? I've always wanted to meet an actual shepherd," said Hildy. "I don't believe we have any in Arizona."

"André fashioned some unusual stained glass, with my encouragement," said Victoria pouring their tea. "I prodded him to get proper tools and do some serious work."

"I do love stained glass," said Hildy. "My friend, Charlotte, creates windows for entrance foyers, kitchens, that kind of thing. She was going to design some panels for our condo, but Alex felt they would argue with its totally 'tomorrow' look."

"An enigma, André was," Victoria continued, staring through the layer of cigarette smoke. "Inarticulate, moody, but a kind of primitive visionary. He was fascinated with light." She smiled, tapping off an ash. "But aren't all artists, really? André actually traveled to Stonehenge, of all places, to study luminescence."

Hildy thought a moment. "But I've always imagined Stonehenge to be such a dreary place. I don't care for Druids, do you?"

Victoria laughed. "I really have no feeling about Druids, actually, one way or the other. Thank God, I don't believe I know any. Except possibly Jeremy, my ex…" She laughed again, a hand slipping to Alex's arm. "Interestingly enough, André did not work in the customary north light. He claimed the south light was more *radiant*, that the sun shining through the glass as he worked released his inner energies. Isn't that original?"

"I'm afraid art isn't my strong point, Victoria," said Alex.

"I lent him my camera for the trip, and he took pictures of the sun at solstice, rising over the heel stone." Victoria's eyes narrowed. "An incredible celestial jewel—his description. Not especially eloquent, but he was seldom even that forthcoming."

Victoria watched her. "Oh, don't mind this," said Hildy. "A writer must constantly record whatever strikes a responsive chord in her mental chambers—fodder for future development." Hildy scribbled a few key words. "The senses are, after all, but tiny watchtowers surveying the vast terrain of our existence."

"Hildy makes these observations all the time," Alex explained.

Hildy detected an apology. "One can scarcely comprehend the complexities of life without metaphors to give it meaning."

"Really?" Victoria slowly shook her head. "I know nothing of any of his works in your villa. The Marquise commissioned one some time ago, but I was under the impression it was for their castle in Beaulieu. Describe the design, Hildy."

"It was a shepherd with his flock." Hildy gestured a circular shape. "He was gazing up at what I'm certain was the Star of Bethlehem."

"We now have a big, circular hole in the wall," Alex said with chagrin. "And if anyone's interested, I definitely did not come to France to do home repairs."

Victoria looked puzzled. "I don't know this window. Could he have done it in some earlier period, I wonder, before he became so abstract?" She smiled reflectively. "I had imagined, after all, that I created André before André created anything!"

"Look at this," Hildy said, unclasping her hand to show the crystal fragment. "This is the star. I'm thinking of having it made into a pendant. My friend, Charlotte claims crystals contain a magic power. She tunes into hers when she meditates."

Victoria leaned forward to take it and hold it up to the sun. "Pretty, isn't it? A bit of quartz, I imagine." She handed the piece back to Hildy. "Alex, I'm sure the Marquis will see to the window." She shrugged. "Perhaps, not immediately, but…"

"Our incomparable houseman, Edmund, has tacked plastic over the hole," Alex said. "I have this terrible feeling that will be the extent of the repairs for the duration of our stay." He studied the clear turquoise of Victoria's pool. "Does that lout tend your pool, Victoria?"

"Edmund?" She laughed. "You are funny, Alex. He came early this morning to clean it for me. I told him I would be having guests." Victoria reached down beside her chair to pluck a camellia blossom. "But the ill wind does blow *some* good. Look at my flowers. Are they not a joy to behold?"

Hildy's eyes swept over the garden. A group of purple and mauve lilacs, lavender-blue bearded irises and deep pockets of blue pansies separated the manicured area from the open fields. Edmund clearly tended this garden with a devotion not evident at their own villa.

A breeze stirred bringing with it the sweet scent of lavender.

"Are you warm enough, darling?" Alex asked.

"Oh, yes. Comfy as can be." Hildy took a swallow of her tea. "So, tell us, Victoria, how did you ever happen to land in La Roquette?"

Victoria leaned forward. "You see, in England, I volunteer my services as a docent in the Ashmolean Museum in Oxford, not far from my home—my former home, I should say. I'm divorced now."

"How unfortunate," Hildy said, meaning it.

"My husband was a member of Parliament. The lower house, of course—because he was in it." She laughed wickedly. "Do forgive me. I try not to be nasty about dear Jeremy."

Hildy nodded encouragement to continue.

"The Marquis got in touch with the museum to consult us about some family heirlooms he wished to see—tapestries and things. Dreadfully dilapidated stuff, actually. In absolutely wretched repair."

"Why on earth would a Marquis be selling off heirlooms?" Hildy asked.

"The European nobility is not what it was, dear. Ask me. I should know." Victoria crushed her cigarette out. "What with Mitterand's taxes, the French nobility are simply flat broke! They've had to open their chateaux as animal preserves or museums and invite the public in at 500 francs a head to feed the menagerie or to view their tatty old medieval furnishings. It's bloody pathetic, really."

"Seems to me they could get jobs," Alex suggested. "I mean, forget about a fiefdom, try for the boardroom."

Victoria's laughter was melodious. "How awfully funny you are, Alex. But really! A titled aristocrat working? They wouldn't know how. It's been bred out of them." She extracted another cigarette for Alex to light, blowing a cloud of smoke over her shoulder. "No, once they had no wars to fight for the peasantry, the nobility became *de trop*, unnecessary. All over Europe."

Hildy thought about this. "Here I've imagined all this time these titled people were intermarrying and living in little fairy castles everywhere."

"In fact, the Marquis does have a castle in Beaulieu," Victoria responded, "not far from Paris. He and the Marquise summer there with their family. I've no idea how he's managed to hold on to it. The rents from our two villas, I suppose. They occupy the third one themselves."

"A castle?" Hildy's brows went up. She quietly slipped her journal from her lap under the table and began making more notes.

"I'm afraid you'll find the village frightfully, *dreadfully* quaint," Victoria continued. The people, all fifty of them, are, in the Marquis' words, 'true peasants'. You see, he still thinks of himself as nobility, which is rather sweet of the old dear. And these peasants do nothing but toil for their masters in the vineyards or tend the few villas. You may find it charming. One hopes so."

"I can easily picture Consuela in a provincial setting," said Hildy, looking up from her notes.

"Is Consuela another friend of yours?" Victoria inquired.

Alex laughed. "The heroine of her book. Hildy's alter ego."

"I see." Victoria continued, "Apart from the crumbling Romanesque cathedral, there isn't much in the village to stimulate one at all, culturally."

"I'm more interested in earthy subjects anyhow," said Hildy. "Bourgeois habits, things like that."

"Frankly, I find the bourgeoisie excessively dull myself," said Victoria.

Hildy folded her hands. "Possibly so, unless one has an

interest in probing deeper. After all, on the face of it, what incentive do they have to better their condition?"

"I admire your social purpose, Hildy," Victoria conceded, lifting her tea cup. "Your housekeeper will be a marvelous subject for your probing. Tell me, Hildy, how are you getting on with her?"

"She seems extremely troubled," said Hildy.

"A pathetic little thing, she is, really, in her plain, home-spun dresses," continued Victoria. "I suppose she keeps house well enough, though I, myself, would go bonkers around a woman of such a drab, unyielding nature."

"She does not know how to cook *oeufs*," Alex said, "that much I can tell you. And you need a key to get a clean towel."

"It is customary for these villa leases to provide maids and linens separately," Victoria explained. "I can't think why. I agree it's a bloody bother." She held up the teapot. "Where is that girl? As you can see, Yvette is no prize either. Her problem is simple incompetence. God knows where the de Mussets found her."

"We won't be spending much time at the villa anyway," Alex said brightly. "It's primarily our headquarters for travel."

Chapter Six

Hildy swallowed hard, trying not to reveal her anger. "Alex doesn't seem to realize one can hardly write a novel gallivanting about Europe in a Porsche."

"I thought you told me Shakespeare wrote a sonnet while brushing his teeth," said Alex, grinning.

"Things were less stressful during the Renaissance," said Hildy. "Naturally, I'll accompany you whenever my writing schedule permits, but one would hope the country atmosphere Victoria has described so aptly will be conducive to my creativity."

"Fair enough," said Alex, patting Hildy on the knee.

"I must say Madame Lescaut seemed terribly upset that her brother's window was destroyed," Hildy said. "They must have been very close."

Victoria sighed. "I think that woman was a stifling influence. Look what Dupres was able to do with this art, given the slightest encouragement."

"By you, you mean. You must feel gratified, Victoria," Hildy said.

"It was rewarding, of course. But, I'm afraid I allowed him to become too dependent on me. Perhaps he mistook my encouragement of his art career for...something else."

Hildy surmised that Victoria meant she was so irresistible that the poor shepherd became infatuated with her. "The de Mussets speak of André as if he barely existed, why is that, Victoria?"

"They thought of him as a common laborer, quite unworthy of aristocratic concern."

"Was his death an accident?" asked Hildy, toying with the lemon in her tea.

"I'm not sure anyone truly knows. The Marquise is convinced the gypsies had something to do with it."

"The gypsies!" Hildy exclaimed, setting her cup down. "Oh dear, do you mean he was murdered?"

"Who can be sure? Perhaps André killed himself. In that hut up there in the field."

Alex's eyes followed Hildy's to the small terra cotta rooftop visible above the ridge. "What did the coroner say?" Hildy asked. "Weren't the police involved?"

"I can't really say," Victoria told her. "His sister hurried directly to the priest and arranged for a private burial. No bloody service at all, and no investigation whatsoever. One supposes Lescaut would have insisted."

"On the other hand," Hildy reasoned, "if the death was suicide, his sister might not have wished it to be known. Perhaps she was ashamed."

"Nothing would surprise me about that woman. I've debated whether she might be marginally psychotic, to tell you the truth." Victoria rested her chin on her hand. "I've also wondered frankly, whether he could have committed some sort of sexual offense against the Marquise."

Hildy's brows shot up. "Marie? Dallying with her gardener? Heavens, like Lady Chatterley's lover?"

Alex said, "Our landlady does tend to find practically everything *amusant*, we've noticed. Maybe André amused her."

Victoria's laughter required that she put down her teacup.

"I doubt it was the least bit funny to these people, darling," Hildy rebuked her husband. "But such intrigue, Victoria! Quite a departure from the regal lords and ladies you mingle with in London, I imagine."

"Actually, when I was married to Jeremy, we would never have come to a place like La Roquette. He preferred Beechwood Lair, our lodge in Surrey. Quite lovely, acres of trees."

"It sounds like an Edwardian novel," Hildy observed.

Victoria gave them a meaningful look. "*Proper* gardeners and nurserymen, and servants, naturally. We had seven guest suites in all and entertained constantly. Rode to the hounds weekends, all of that. I must say, I quite enjoyed it myself."

"Is one born to all that, may I ask?" Hildy slipped her notebook from her tote.

"Perhaps you've heard of the Empress Eugenie? Eighteenth Century? Part of a royal dynasty in one of those tiny countries they seemed to have all over the place at the time. Jeremy is a descendant, or so he insists."

"Oh, I've heard of Empress Eugenie, I think, Victoria," Hildy said. "Wasn't she the subject of a mini-series with Stephanie Powers?"

"I really wouldn't know," Victoria said. "Can I pour you more tea, Alex?"

"Thank you, no, Victoria." He picked up his cup and saucer, barely sipping, and then put the cup down.

"Now, you must begin your travels with luncheon at the Colombe d'Or, in St-Paul-de-Vence," Victoria said. "It's *the* gathering place for writers and artists."

"Isn't that where Chagall painted his annual bouquet?" asked Hildy.

Victoria looked surprised. "You know about that?"

"I understand the ramparts have remained untouched

since Francois I built them," Alex commented.

"How informed you are, Alex." Victoria turned to Hildy. "There's a window in the cathedral there you must see, Hildy, *The Assumption of the Virgin.* Dupres did some restoration work on the Virgin's crown. The Bishop's commission were delighted to find a skilled local artisan."

"I should be most anxious to see it. Perhaps in the next day or two, shall we, Alex?"

"By all means."

"Could you show us your studio, do you think, Victoria?" Hildy asked.

Victoria put down the silver teapot. "Oh, heavens! I never take guests in there. It's an utter slum!"

"No one understands the messiness brought on by the muse better than I do, Victoria," Hildy reassured her.

Alex chortled. "My wife is lucky to find the phone in the room where she writes. But she never seems to lose anything, do you, darling?"

"Have you noticed, Hildy," Victoria said, putting a hand against Alex's jaw and turning his head slightly, "the line of Alex's jaw, that little depression in his cheek when he clamps it tight? It shows great strength, doesn't it? Very masculine."

Alex looked stunned at this unexpected attention to his manliness.

"I must do a sketch of you while you're on holiday, luv." Victoria got up, sending Ariadne, the cat, streaking into the shrubbery. "Come along, if you want to see the studio. Mind the mud."

"I wish you luck sketching my husband." Hildy followed her hostess. "The only thing he'll sit still for is the Dow Jones Industrials on cable TV."

The door to the studio was in the rear of the villa. Inside, Victoria opened a pair of shutters covering the casement window. "You see, a north light of sorts."

Alex loitered at the door, as Victoria skirted around a table cluttered with tubes, bottles and cans. A dozen brushes were jammed upright in a jar.

"I just love the smell of linseed oil!" Hildy said, breathing in the sweetish fragrance. She moved toward some canvases stacked against the stone wall.

A covered easel occupied the center of the small room, along with a chair and a stool placed a few feet away.

"And turpentine mixed with mildew, I'm afraid," Victoria added. "Gravity apparently draws the dampness into this dungeon, and keeps that bloody medieval pumping station at the bottom of the hill from functioning properly."

Hildy examined the display of primitively painted flower arrangements and village street scenes. She was uncertain whether they were abstract or simply bad art. "Oh, this one! A 'white on white,' isn't it? I love purism."

"Oh, that," Victoria giggled. "That's just the undercoating." She held it up. "Though the way I slathered it on, there is a certain Malevich quality, isn't there?"

Alex looked up at the sky. "We'd better think about getting along, Hildy. It's getting black again."

"I positively loathe the mistral," Victoria complained. "It depresses me, alone here in this dreary villa." She brightened, "So, I'm trundling off to Monaco next week to get away. The Grand Prix should take my mind off these bloody storms."

"Hear that, Hildy?" Alex said. "How would you like to see The Grand Prix?"

"The racing fans are completely insane!" Victoria said.

Unable to restrain herself, Hildy peeked behind the cloth covering the easel. "Is this what you're working on at present?"

Victoria rushed over to catch the cloth as it slid to the floor. "Oh dear, I hate to show a work in progress…"

Hildy gasped as she saw the face staring back at her from the canvas. "Mercy! It's Edmund." She could not mistake the mischievous dark eyes and black curly hair, though sketchily drawn. She glanced at the rest of the gardener whose naked body was perched on a stool. He was leaning forward against a garden hoe.

Alex stepped closer. "That's Edmund all right." He looked away, as if searching for something else to observe. "And this over here must be the hoe." He examined the wooden handle.

"What a lovely hoe," Hildy remarked. "Don't touch it, Alex. Victoria's probably got it arranged for her painting."

"Please don't be embarrassed, Alex." Victoria patted his arm. "Edmund's Gallic features intrigue me. He has that universal quality of 'everyman,' tiller of the soil, all that rot."

"At one with the forces of divine nature," Hildy murmured in the ethereal voice she reserved for philosophic moments.

"One would hope to observe Edmund tilling the soil in our garden sometime soon," Alex said, heading for the door.

"Well, there you have it!" Victoria covered the easel. "My desperation to find models in this wretched little village reduces me to pressing our gardener into service. Isn't that a hoot?"

Hildy paused at the door. "The tea was superb, Victoria. Darjeeling?"

"*Baj Navoor*, dear."

"What a nice surprise. I'm accustomed to the Chinese blends." In her attempt at urbanity, Hildy managed to step on Ariadne, sending the cat zipping away. Hildy jumped back, surprised. "I'm so sorry!"

"Quite all right, Hildy, Ariadne is always underfoot," Victoria said as they walked to the courtyard gate. "Do enjoy Colombe d'Or. Perhaps you can send your friend Charlotte a postal of Chagall's bouquet. They still put one out every year without fail."

As they trudged back up the lane, Hildy shrugged the collar of her jacket closer. A mist of light rain promised another tempestuous night of storms. "I hope you're not taken in by all that garbage about your jawline, dear."

"You don't care for my jawline?" He squeezed her hand. "That's just artist talk, for Pete's sake."

"Just remember, Lady V is not a whole lot older than your son's wife."

Alex said nothing.

Hildy shook her head. "Can you believe that portrait of Edmund?"

"Posing bare-assed might account for why he has no time for his job!" He put his arm around her waist. "What about taking in the Grand Prix next week?"

Hildy thought a moment. "No, Alex. You know how I detest car racing. Why don't you go ahead? It will give me time to work on my book." She snuggled against her husband. Perhaps Consuela would be persuaded to sit *au natural* for Orlando while he applied his chisel to the virgin stone to release her voluptuous womanhood. "You know, Alex, I wouldn't be in the least surprised to learn that Lady Helmsley managed a few nude sittings with our dead artisan too, the young Monsieur André Dupres."

Chapter Seven

On Monday morning the sun shone brightly in the first clear blue sky since their arrival. In celebration, Alex crawled out of bed early to jog into the village for a freshly baked *baguette* from the *boulangerie*. When he returned, he bounded into the bedroom and immediately broke off a crusty piece of the French bread for Hildy.

She inhaled its delicious aroma. "Hmm. Heavenly."

"It was warm when I got it," Alex mumbled through a mouthful.

But Hildy could hardly wait to share with him a disturbing dream she had been analyzing in her journal.

"I was walking naked down a snowy street…" she began as Alex stripped off his Côte d'Azur T-shirt.

"You should have awakened me." Alex leaned to kiss her.

"You'd already left for your jog." Hildy continued with her dream. "And I was carrying this bag of colored scarves which I discarded, one by one—all except the pink chiffon..."

Alex performed his deep breathing ritual at the open window. "I'll bet the boys are teeing off at Canyon del Oro right now." He glanced at his watch. "Oh, hell. It's the middle of the night in Arizona."

"Then—are you listening, Alex? I quickly wrapped the flimsy chiffon scarf around me to keep warm until I could go back to our condo where I donned my comfy patchwork robe."

Alex wiped a residue of rain water from the sill.

"You see the symbolism?" She walked over to the window.

"What I see is that fool, Edmund, adding more chlorine to the pool." Alex's jaw tensed. "We haven't even set foot in the damned thing yet, for God's sake."

"I read somewhere that when you travel, the spirit of the place remains with you to recall during the dog days, when you return back home." Hildy mused a moment. "So, why do the dog days seem to be happening here?"

She reviewed what she had written in her journal. "Clearly my dream was one of displacement."

His face brightened. "I have an idea. Why don't we displace ourselves to the Colombe d'Or to enjoy a nice leisurely lunch? I could do with a four-star meal."

"Wonderful! I can locate a jeweler somewhere and have my crystal set in a necklace of some sort." She pulled the tissue out of her tote and unwrapped it. "I feel certain this glass reflects the power of the mistral purifying my life."

"You sound like Charlotte."

"I know. Did you know she wears one taped under her left breast, to impart energy?"

"Is that why Fred's so pooped all the time! I assume you'll wear yours around your neck."

Hildy admired the fragment before folding it back into its tissue. "I think it will make a striking piece."

Alex sat on the bed to shed his sneakers. "We'll take a table near the entrance to the dining terrace. Victoria says that's the best way to see the celebrities."

"When did she tell you that?"

"This morning. She was in her garden when I jogged by. Searching for Ariadne, her cat."

"In something diaphanous, no doubt." Hildy slammed her journal shut.

"My goodness, darling. I just mentioned I thought we might try the restaurant, and she gave me a little advice. What's wrong with that?"

"Nothing is wrong with that. But, my Lord, she flirts with a man when his wife is sitting right there? I find that terribly common."

"A common noblewoman?" Alex smiled. "That's just her way, Hildy. Look, we'll have a great lunch, and we'll find a jeweler. With your 'purified mistral energy' or whatever, you'll out-dazzle our English Lady a thousandfold."

"No wonder the bread was cold. You stood there mooning over that harlot."

Alex patted Hildy's rump. "Get dressed while I take a shower." He bounded out of the room.

A few seconds later, Hildy heard water gushing and the first few bars of "On the Street Where You Live," then a scream from the bath, "God damn it, there's no hot water!"

When the Bigelows stepped out into the courtyard to get into the car, Edmund grabbed a grimy cloth and began furiously wiping off the Porsche.

Hildy made up her mind she would not let her resentment of Victoria spoil the joy of this trip to the Colombe d'Or.

"*S'il vous plaît*, Edmund," she inquired, wedging herself into the front seat, "could you direct me to a jeweler in St-Paul-de-Vence?" Her voice was drowned out by Alex's repeated revving of the car engine. "*Une bijouterie!*" she yelled, putting imaginary rings on all her fingers.

Edmund laughed with delight and playfully sprayed water on the windshield, obliterating her view of him.

Giving up her phrase book, Hildy fumbled for her precious

fragment wrapped in tissue. "*Voilà!*" She leaned out of the window and displayed the glass, grabbing a finger at her neck.

Edmund's dark eyes danced with recognition at Hildy's newly-developed art of mime. He cast the hose and rag aside. From his ardent gestures, interspersed with the familiar names of several towns, Hildy surmised, she should be so lucky as to find a jeweler in St-Paul. Cannes, possible. Paris, *mais certainment!* Edmund would be more than willing to undertake any such mission.

"If you give your crystal to that bandit," Alex warned, "you can kiss it goodbye. Trust me, Hildy. One way or another, you will never see it again, and it will probably cost me ten thousand francs besides." He spun the Porsche around in the courtyard.

Driving east along the *autoroute*, they left behind the modern condominiums poking their ugly cement facades out of congested new complexes. As they turned inland, the topography dissolved into gentle rolling hills and lovely terraced estates. The sun shone on the mellowed buildings, transforming them into shades of sherbet-yellow, peach and strawberry pink. Once more Hildy thrilled to the palette of subtle colors which had for centuries inspired painters to memorialize southern France.

St-Paul's attraction was of a different kind. Perched like an eagle's nest atop a terraced slope, the rustic, walled town emitted the more forbidding flavor of secrets hidden among dark winding byways.

Tour busses discharged a steady stream of tourists armed with cameras, who trudged up the hill toward the town's entrance.

With Alex leading the way, Hildy threaded into the crowd cramming itself through the narrow stone arch. "I trust all these people are not planning to dine at the Colombe d'Or," she said, anxiously.

"Look at this!" Alex fondled the muzzle of a cannon pointed directly at the entrance archway. "We're talking real history here, Hildy." He read from an inscription, "Fired in 1537 by Francois I."

Hildy nodded, attempting to share the enthusiasm she knew her husband felt for history. Spotting the sign of the golden dove, she hurried Alex across the cobblestone street to the tall, wrought-iron gate. Through it she could see the dining terrace, its tables interspersed with fruit trees. Vestiges of the mistral winds still moved in the foliage of the trees and ruffled the ivy covering the walls.

"Where is everybody?" Hildy asked in a plaintive voice. Indeed, there was not a sign of patrons behind the bolted gate of the restaurant terrace. An old woman in a knitted cap fussed with wind-blown orange tiger lilies, bent irises and tulips in a decorative old wooden well. "We must be early for lunch," Hildy told Alex.

He squinted to study the framed menu written in English script posted on the stuccoed gatepost. "What's a *fermé le lundi?*"

"It means 'closed on Monday,'" Hildy sighed, "which today, unfortunately, is. Drat! I was hoping to see some celebrities."

Alex was undaunted. "We can still view the ramparts," he grinned, consulting the guidebook. "'They remain virtually intact, despite the ravages of frequent military incursions.'"

"So Victoria told us." The unfortunate symbolism of Lady Helmsley's ramparts intruded into her thoughts. "I had so hoped to dine *al fresco*."

"There's nothing like a bold climb to get the adrenaline going, darling." Alex reached for Hildy's hand.

She hesitated. Never in her life had she seen so many steps. "Oh, Alex, I just remembered! I promised Charlotte I'd bring her some sorrel seeds to enhance her macrobiotic cooking. You run on ahead while I absorb the texture of the Rue Grande."

"Fine. I'll meet you at the south ramparts." Alex raised an imaginary sword and charged upward.

The walls of the buildings along the narrow street offered tawny shoulders to cut her off from the crowds. Glad to have some time alone, Hildy finally had a moment to consider her neglected Consuela in this Fellini-like setting.

There might also be the possibility of a jeweler here to counsel her about the Star of Bethlehem stashed in her tote. The notion brought an insightful flash: the crystal as a symbol. Its clarity would focus her own goals! Even as Alex descended from his triumphant career in business to sample the delights of early retirement, Hildy still had *her* mountain to climb. She would "follow the star!" Huddled in a doorway, she scribbled this meaningful revelation into her journal.

A convoy of nuns rounded a corner and moved up the street. As they passed by a fountain trickling into a giant earthen urn, Hildy saw one of the black-cloaked figures separate from the group and linger behind. How strange. Whoever it was, it was not a nun. Could this be the same figure she'd seen from her window during the storm?

Darting into an *herbière*, she pretended to sample soap fragrances from the delicious varieties of lavender, gardenia and lilac displayed. Keeping her eye on the street, Hildy saw the nuns finally move on. The black-caped figure was no longer there.

The idea of her heroine, Consuela, masquerading as a nun, burst upon her mind. Of course, it would have to be a masquerade. How could anyone of Consuela's nature contain her passions?

Hildy panted up the cobbled street, past quaint *ateliers* and *pôteries.* The spicy aroma of coriander, fennel and cumin enticed her into a shop where she discovered, to her delight, the sorrel seeds Charlotte requested. They were so hard to find in the States. She bought several packets.

Leaving the shop, she thought she glimpsed the cloaked figure again, slipping into a shadowy doorway behind her. This was becoming ridiculous.

Grateful to leave the milling crowd below in the Rue Grande, Hildy climbed the long hill to the Romanesque cathedral. She stopped to admire it for a moment, feeling the wind pull at the scarf she had knotted around her throat. The spire of the church was blurred by a gathering gray mist. Before her, carved figures stared at her with vacant stone eyes from their niches above the entrance. She pushed open the massive wooden door and entered the shadowy interior.

Light filtering through richly stained glass windows played on the silver and enamel statues, giving them a mystical look. As she moved deeper into the sanctuary, tortured limbs of several martyrdoms seemed to assault her vision, making her uneasy. She hurried down the dimly lit apse to the altar. As she ran her finger over the intricate designs, her eyes were drawn to the grieving figure of the classic Mary, glowing in stained glass against the diminishing outside light. The Virgin ascended into a radiant heaven in a molten swirl of cerulean blue robes.

Hildy moved closer. *The Assumption of the Virgin.* André's window! This must be the restoration he had done. The leading in the crown section could be newer than the rest, but to Hildy it still looked exquisite. She stood transfixed in the gloom.

Suddenly the lights went out. Hildy froze as someone bumped into her.

"Who…what do you…?" She hugged her tote to her side and pulled away in time to glimpse a robed figure disappear around one of the columns of the altar's sacristy. The rest of the church remained in darkness broken only by the jeweled colors of the stained glass windows.

A match flared at the altar, as a nun lit a votive candle. She must have been the one who jostled her, Hildy thought…No! Whoever bumped her had lurked closer. To grab her tote, must certainly. She had barely 500 francs—and, of course, her crystal—but no one would know what was in her tote.

"*Ici, madame,*" the nun said, pointing to an altar box. "*Deux francs s'il vous plaît.*"

Hildy stared, wondering what she meant.

"*Pour voir la Vierge,*" the nun explained, lighting another candle and placing it on a velvet cloth covered with wax drippings from a dozen others.

"Oh! I see," Hildy puzzled. "One must pay to see the Virgin. Of course." She groped in her bag for coins. "…or pay for the lights, is that it? *Vous payez* or *les lumières* go pfft! *Oui*?" She attempted a disarming laugh.

The nun wore a serene, noncommital smile, then nodded, accepting the jumble of coins Hildy held out. In a moment, the lights miraculously flickered back on.

"Was it you who bumped...*C'est vous qui*...?" Hildy paused to consider how best to execute her second major pantomime of the day. After a tentative try, she determined there was no way one could mimic being bumped into by one's self. The nun's disapproving look brought a flush of embarrassment for even having attempted it.

The nun clasped her hands together and glided away down the main aisle, mumbling a prayer.

Hildy stood for a moment reluctantly allowing her eyes to search the shadows of the silent cathedral for another visitor who might have jostled her in the darkness. There was no one. With a little shiver, she fled the church.

Chapter Eight

After another long climb Hildy found Alex on the rampart, shivering in his alligator shirt as he huddled over his Pentax. "How do you focus for fog?"

Hildy looked out across the rolling countryside. Below what had been the bright blue of the sky, a damp fog now filled the low-lying depressions and was floating toward them in yellowish layers.

The ascent had left her gasping. "I hesitate to mention it, Alex, but I think someone's following me. That same man I saw in the black cloak the other night."

Alex stood straight, with a skeptical look. "Please, darling. Would you stand over there so I can get my focus?"

Hildy moved to stand against the railing Alex indicated. "I first thought I saw him down on the little street, outside a store selling perfumed soaps. He was attempting to hide himself among some nuns."

Alex squinted through the camera's finder. "How could you tell?"

"It's not funny, Alex. In the cathedral, while I was examining the *Assumption of the Virgin*, the lights went out and someone tried to grab my tote. I feel sure it was the same man—possibly a gypsy person."

Alex gave Hildy his attention. "Are you serious? Somebody tried to rob you?"

Hildy felt uncertain. "It seemed that's what was happening, Alex. There was a nun there. I suppose she could have done it."

"A purse-snatching nun, for God's sake?" He looked through his viewfinder. "Smile, darling." The camera clicked. "And one more, to be sure." Click.

"Alex, I realize this sounds far-fetched, but still, I don't understand what actually happened. Except for the lights going out—and that was simply because I hadn't paid-up. Imagine having to pay for the lights to see an historical religious building."

"Let's get a flashlight you can keep in your tote. In case you run into that situation again. Come on."

Hildy scampered after Alex as he descended the parapet path. "Wouldn't it be bizarre if the nun has a mafia connection of some sort? Stranger things have happened, you know! They may not even be *real* nuns. Spy rings are always using fake nuns."

Alex guffawed. "Honestly, Hildy! I think you're hallucinating. The French countryside has put poor Consuela around the bloody bend."

That English idiom, Hildy thought. Damn. He didn't even realize he was imitating the way that woman spoke.

"What we both need is food," Alex took her arm, pulling her close to him.

They passed a schoolyard full of uniformed children frolicking with a red ball. "*Bonjour!*" Hildy called, waving to a young, cherub-faced boy in a bright red sweater.

The child stopped to stare, then ran laughing to his comrades. *"Une Américaine!"* he proclaimed as the others tumbled over to gather at the wall.

"Doesn't he remind you of our Tim, Alex?" Hildy caught the ball lightly tossed to her. She held it up. *"La balle est rouge!"* Thinking of nothing more profound to say to the children, she looked past the boys into the gathering mist. "I just realized how much I miss seeing our grandson. Don't you?"

Alex tightened his arm through hers.

The children's laughter receded into the hills. "I guess laughter is the same in any language."

"So are Big Macs," Alex pointed to a sign flashing below them through the fog. *"Voilà!* Sierra-burgers!"

Hildy looked at the sign with disgust. "How utterly non-provincial."

Alex jogged ahead, leading the way.

"Alex," Hildy called after him.

He stopped and returned to where she stood.

"Darling," she said plaintively, "I don't want to lunch at the Sierra Burger. I really don't. Can't we find something more indigenous?"

"Sure. What did you have in mind, Hildy?"

She took his arm, leading him back down the hill. "Well, since we couldn't have lunch at the Colombe d'Or, why don't we find a nice quiet *auberge* somewhere with a lovely *cuisine provençal*. We really don't need to eat hamburgers on the Côte d'Azur, do we?"

"Good. I'd also like to find a bank somewhere to get some francs." He hurried her to the parking lot.

"And maybe we can find a jeweler."

Accelerating the Porsche back along the *autoroute*, Alex read the road signs aloud. Hildy noted his pronunciation was becoming more and more like Charles Boyer's, the 1940's French film star.

"Ah, look, Madame," Alex said pointing. "Zere eez a sign for Mouan Sartoux. You lak to go zere *pour la petit déjeuner, eh?"*

"*Pourquoi* not?" Hildy replied chuckling. But Alex had already exited the highway to follow the route sign.

On the country road outside the village, Alex slowed to inspect a small café nestled in a vineyard. "*Grand-mère fait bon café.*" Hildy read. "That looks quaint."

Alex swung in to park beside a battered farm wagon standing near a rear entrance. A scraggly goat shied and whinnied at their arrival then continued to munch on hay from the wagon.

Alex jumped out of the car and stood, hands on hips, surveying the café. "I doubt this is a four star, but we'll give it a shot."

Hildy took her husband's arm and looked up at the weathered sign. "Oh, Alex, doesn't that grandma sign make you homesick for Tim?"

"No, should it? Our grandson doesn't even drink coffee." Alex led her into the café.

A white haired woman hustled over to greet them.

Hildy smiled. "A French *grand-mère*. How picturesque."

The woman nodded as she wiped her hands on her apron, then ushered them through a smoky kitchen to a dining area beyond. Gathered around a long table covered in oilcloth, a group of burly workmen conversed loudly as they ate.

Hildy inhaled. "Smell that rich aroma, Alex!"

"Oh, I do, darling," he murmured. "Like cabbage cooking in a locker room."

"Perhaps *Grand-mère* can put us by a window."

"There are no tables by a window." Alex's lips tightened. "Just this one huge communal table."

"Now don't get upset, dear," Hildy whispered. "You must let the culture dictate to you, not the other way around." She followed the woman to two empty spaces at the table. "*Bonjour, messieurs!*" Smiling, she edged herself onto the wooden bench as if sharing a church pew.

Alex surveyed the table. "Listen, will you be all right here for a few minutes?"

Hildy looked at the peasant faces surrounding the table.

Several of them smiled at her, nodding curious greetings. "Well, I suppose so. Where are you going?"

"I'm going to question *Grand-mère* to find out if there's a bank anywhere close by." He departed toward the kitchen.

"*Je suis Hildegarde Bigelow*," Hildy announced, nodding to her tablemates.

The ruddy-faced laborer beside her abandoned his spoonful of noodles to welcome her with a sticky handshake. "Could you *passez-moi le menu*?" Hildy asked.

Her seatmate stared at her blankly, then reached for a plate from the stack on a serving stand behind him.

Anxious to sample French cuisine, Hildy looked for a waitress. An olive-skinned girl in an embroidered peasant skirt picked up a tray and came over.

Hildy looked at her tentatively. She was certain the girl was a gypsy. "*Bonjour, mademoiselle*. What is your *plat de jour* today?"

The waitress shook her head, reciting what sounded like an apology in rapid French. She motioned to a workman at the end of the table to slide down the platter of sausage and noodles and moved the handle of the serving fork around to face Hildy.

Hildy gave her a polite smile, pointing to the girl's skirt. "What a *belle* skirt, dear. I don't suppose there's a shop—*un atelier*…Oh dear, I don't know how to say that at all." She smiled and waved the girl away.

She looked down at the platter. This dish I could have in Arizona, she thought, disappointed it wasn't more *français*.

Heaping a spoonful of greasy sausages on her plate, she called down to the end of the table. "Could someone please *passez moi du cafe*?" She gestured drinking from a cup.

The man beside her took a swig from a wine bottle then held it toward her with an inviting look.

Noting the others seemed to be sharing the communal bottle, she wiped off the green bottle's rim with her hand and gulped down a swallow, her first major concession to her new environment. "*Formidable!*" She smacked her lips.

While chewing a mouthful of gray sausage, she observed the workmen's roughly calloused hands. Perhaps I'll use laborers in my novel as well as the artisan, Orlando, she mused, a sort of French *Grapes of Wrath*. Removing the journal from her tote, she jotted down several notes.

The men watched with fascination. "*Journaliste?*" asked the man next to her, wiping his mouth on a thoroughly used paper napkin.

"*Noveliste,*" Hildy replied easily. "*Romantique.*" Satisfied she'd intrigued all within hearing, she closed her journal and elaborately tucked it away.

"*À votre santé, Madame Hildegarde!*" Her seatmate rose to toast her.

"My friends call me Hildy," she said, once more accepting the wine bottle. She closed her eyes and took a hearty swallow. Suddenly, there was a pause in the chattering at the table as she rose to speak. Gazing up at the rough wood beams, she groped for the French words to express her deepest feelings, then lapsed helplessly into English.

"I have so long dreamt of delving into the fertile loam of your forefathers—to drink of the perfumed nectar..." She paused to take another swig of wine and considered how best to couch her thoughts. "But meeting all of you," she made eye contact with an elderly peasant munching on a sausage held in his fingers, "has made me re-evaluate." Her voice rose dramatically. "Consuela will, indeed, find revitalization in France!" She banged the bottle down for emphasis, "*Vive la France!*"

The men applauded as she sat down.

"And what is—*votre nom?*" She placed a friendly hand on a workman's arm.

"*Non capisco.*" He shook his head and pointed to himself. "*Italiano.*" He smiled proudly.

"*Enchantée*, Mr. Capisco. Italian! How...international." Hildy put down her fork. "Tell me—*Dîtes-moi...*Ah," she could not think of a single Italian word. "*À quelle distance est Roma?*"

A man across the table spoke in an indecipherable tongue to his friend.

The Italian held up five fingers.

"Five hours?" Hildy asked.

The man mumbled in Italian.

"*En auto.*" Her seatmate motioned, "*En haut et en bas les Alpes.*"

"Oh, no." Hildy shook her head vigorously. "No up and down *les Alps. Formidable!*" She spread her arms and flapped her hands to simulate flying. "I travel *par avion. Seulement!*"

"*Regardez la poulet Américaine!*" one of the men exclaimed, the others joining in to laugh and cluck barnyard sounds.

"Nadia!" another called. "*Encore de vin!*"

The waitress flashed a smile and placed a fresh green bottle on the table.

When Alex appeared in the doorway, he stopped, bewildered.

"They think I'm a chicken!" Hildy explained, passing Alex a bottle of wine. "Try some. It's quite bold."

"Evidently." He looked around the table at the peasant feast. "What's that you're eating, for God's sake?"

"Sausage. It's lovely." She moved over to give Alex some room. "Darling, I've had the most extraordinary idea for the thrust of my novel," she said, her head pleasantly spinning.

The waitress, Nadia, appeared behind Alex to hand him a clean plate.

"No thank you, *Mademoiselle*," he said giving her a cursory glance.

"I love Nadia's peasant skirt, don't you?" Hildy asked Alex, then lowered her voice. "I believe she's a gypsy."

Alex scowled. "I'd go along with that."

"But I was saying." She patted the seat next to her. "Sit down, dear. I'm changing the thrust of my novel."

"Wonderful. Can we go now? I don't believe I care for any lunch."

"If you're not interested in sharing what can well be Consuela's salvation...very well, Alex. But first I must say my farewells." Hildy gathered her tote, then addressed the table. "*Au revoir, mes amis.*" She blew a kiss.

The man next to Hildy stood to give her a kiss on both cheeks, as his friends looked on with approval.

Hildy breathed in the fresh air outside. "My, but doesn't that fresh air smell good?"

"I'm afraid we're both going to smell like sausage for hours." He opened her car door. "Is that called getting into the culture, darling?"

"It's not the food I'll remember, Alex. It's the cultural ambiance."

He started the car. "I congratulate you. You seem to have made quite a cultural impact yourself on those fellows."

"But won't you be hungry, Alex?"

"I'll eat something later." He grinned at her. "Guess what?"

"You found a bank."

"They're closed on Mondays. I'll have to find a hotel that changes money. But guess what?"

"I can't possibly."

"I've been thinking about the Grand Prix, you know, and I decided to call Victoria to check it out. About tickets and the rest of it."

Hildy glared at him. "What's Victoria got to do with the races?"

Alex patted her knee. "Now just calm down, darling. I merely called to ask her how I make arrangements. That's all."

Hildy turned away.

"You knew I wanted to go." He put his hand on hers. "You'll come with me, won't you? I know you're not especially…"

"I've already told you I have no interest, Alex." She folded her hands over her tote. "You just do what you want. I know you will anyway."

Alex careened the car out into the country road. "Seeing all those incredible cars. Imagine, Hildy!" He grinned and pounded the wheel for emphasis. "The Grand Prix. Damn!"

Hildy had no idea why she suddenly felt so depressed. But of course she knew. Another dark presence was beginning to haunt her now. It wasn't an imaginary figure in a long black cloak. It was the specter of a bosomy Englishwoman floating in chiffon.

Chapter Nine

"Why are you packing a shirt?" Hildy asked.

"I might stay over to watch this Manzo fellow race his Ferrari." Alex arranged his camera equipment and a Grand Prix tour pamphlet in his shoulder bag, oblivious of Hildy's complete ignorance of anyone named Manzo. "To tell you the truth, I think I'll take a hotel room just so I can experience an honest-to-God shower and sleep in a bed that doesn't list to starboard."

"And not be bombarded by mosquitoes all night," Hildy added. "I can see your point." She handed him his shaving kit. "Just be sure to let me know where you're staying, dear, in case I need you."

"You could come with me, you know."

Hildy debated a moment. "It's sweet of you to want me

with you, dear, but I really must work on my book." She followed him downstairs. "I imagine you'll see Victoria there." She couldn't help raising the question.

"I'm not sure. Didn't she say she was planning to paint or do sketches or something?"

"Yes, but you're almost bound to run into one another. Monaco's not a very big place, after all."

Alex stopped on the stairs and looked up at her. "Hildy, darling, relax. If I run into the lady, I may buy her a drink, okay? No big deal."

"Why should it be?" Hildy considered this likelihood and made herself accept it. "No big deal."

"You won't change your mind and come with me?"

"No." She kissed him on the cheek. "But thank you for asking me." Hildy told herself she mustn't let her overactive imagination create intrigue where none existed. "You just enjoy the races. When is your train?"

"I'm having Edmund drop me. You'll be pleased to know he's going to look for screens for the windows on his way back."

"Thank goodness! But I can't believe you'd trust him with the Porsche."

"No problem. He drove me to the village the other day. Actually, he's a better driver than he is a gardener."

"That doesn't surprise me in the least."

Edmund stood in the courtyard eagerly holding the passenger door open for his master. For the occasion, the gardener sported a leather vest over his T-shirt and a beret cocked over his left eyebrow.

Alex hesitated, running a loving hand over his car. "I may be making a horrendous mistake," he murmured.

Hildy patted his shoulder. "Look at it this way, what's the worst that could happen?"

"Don't even ask." Alex slid into the seat as Edmund skipped around the car and slid in behind the wheel. Grinning, Edmund gave a majestic turn of the key, revving the engine to a roar.

"Goodbye, darling." Hildy waved.

Alex offered a limp wave, staring rigidly ahead as Edmund

inched the car snail-like through the wrought iron gate.

Actually, it was a relief just to be by herself. Ever since Alex retired it seemed they were together twenty-four hours a day. It was like having a permanent house guest. Sometimes she felt she would suffocate. Lord, that's why she'd signed up for the Writers' Workshop in the first place—to give herself breathing space.

It infuriated Hildy that Alex didn't take her craft seriously. He'd always considered it nothing more than a hobby, but for her it had been a continuing journey to discover herself.

Of course, she would be the first to admit that at times, the journey had yielded little more than a florid outline and a cast of characters with incredibly memorable names, but there were no dead ends in writing as far as she was concerned. It was impossible to arrive at one without having traveled—and the journey itself was an achievement. Furthermore, every dead end had one end open; the way in was also the way out.

Nestled in her writing alcove, Hildy reviewed the notes in her journal. Time for some serious writing about the irrepressibly carnal Consuela, last seen clutching her bodice together with trembling fingers following Orlando's assault. But the notes in her journal focused mainly on their arrival, the villa and gleanings from—and about—Victoria.

Hildy rolled a piece of paper into the rented Olivetti. Her chin tilted as she awaited the muse. Instead, Madame Lescaut charged into the bedroom with a green felt pad to place beneath the typewriter. "*Madame, faîtes attention.*" Her look made it clear that not a word should be typed without this pad in place. On her way out, the housekeeper gathered up two plastic bags of laundry.

"*Deux* bags full," Hildy quipped. "*Un pour master* and *l'autre pour moi!*" But Hildy's allusion to the nursery rhyme brought only an uncomprehending stare from Lescaut.

For the first time, Hildy noticed the protruding purple veins in Lescaut's legs, no doubt from long hours on her feet serving others. The observation prompted another entry in Hildy's journal:

Why do I always get the feeling this woman sees me as an ugly American with nothing better to do than to pen letters to my friends? She in no way understands I'm a novelist. Even after our moment in the kitchen with the glass from her brother's window, she's still a wall of resentment, What is there about this dedicated woman that makes me feel so guilty?

Hildy tossed her journal aside. The interruption had deadened her flow of thought, which, in fact, had not begun to flow at all. She wandered to the window and gazed out at the field and the shepherd's hut. That might be the place to work. A perfect time to investigate, while Lescaut was busy washing clothes. She snapped the lid on the typewriter.

Quickly jamming her journal into her tote, she seized the typewriter and hurried to the kitchen.

Lescaut was nowhere in sight as Hildy examined the iron key on the rack behind the swinging door. Pasted below it in almost unreadable script was the word *Berger*.

"*Formidable*," she murmured, marveling at the orderly array of keys and their duplicates. So intimidating! She reached for the forbidden iron key, uneasy about her violation of the housekeeper's sacred key rack. Still hadn't she the right to a conducive writing atmosphere, after all? Besides that, she was now impelled by a powerful curiosity.

The sun on the shepherd hut glowed pink against the olive groves as Hildy lugged her typewriter across the meadow grass still wet with morning dew. The smell of jasmine saturated her senses. Oh, yes, if ever she was to find inspiration, it would be here!

Standing on her tiptoes on a wobbly chunk of stone, Hildy tried to peek in the bull's-eye window, but she was not quite tall enough to see the interior.

When she unlocked the door and stepped inside the hut, a murky light illuminated the rough flooring. She shut the door and drew in a sharp breath as a cobweb brushed her face. Groping her way across the dimly lit space, she could discern stacks of sketching boards against the wall, some wooden frames and a large oil drum receptacle containing discarded lengths of wood and other trash. A wooden table near the window stood barren except for a candle in a waxy wine bottle.

She hefted the typewriter to the table.

Scanning the hut for an electric light source, she found none. She dragged a wooden box over to step up to the grimy window and after several futile tries, managed to jam it open, letting in a brilliant shaft of sunlight. She remembered Victoria's explanation of Dupres' strange practice of working in a south light because of its mystical power. Would the glass seem more alive to him against bright sunlight? Light is, after all, the essence of stained glass.

She ruffled through the disorderly stack of sketching boards. The colors were brightly drawn in bold designs. Her attention was drawn to a print of a Cézanne landscape tacked haphazardly to the wall above her head. Pinned next to it, a brown paper showed the design areas in abstract shapes, resembling a dress pattern. She studied the serenity of Cézanne's blue-gray mountains intersecting the olive hues of his rocks. What a stark contrast to the outrageous bold designs of Dupres whose reds were ruby, his greens emerald, and the yellows more luminous than Matisse.

So this was André's work. Victoria was right. The man had a strong sense of color and striking design elements, but his sketches evoked very disturbing emotions. Was Dupres himself disturbed, or was he merely struggling to create a disturbing effect?

Letting the sketches fall back against the wall in a whoosh of dust, Hildy coughed. Her eyes were drawn to the round window pouring sunlight into the hut.

How did this shepherd, Dupres, die? Would he end his own life so wretchedly? Might he have died right here in this hut as Victoria hinted? But what happened? Why didn't anyone seem to *know*? Lescaut! She knew, Hildy was certain.

She forced her attention back to the table where she sat. Pushing her typewriter aside, she wobbled the table's drawer open. Among the wine corks and fragments of colored glass, she found a small knife which was sharpened on both edges.

With revulsion she shoved it aside uncovering a yellowed piece of parchment in the back of the drawer. Unfolding it carefully, Hildy scrutinized a crude map of France with three crosses slashed across it in black. One cross appeared in the southeast corner, another slightly west of it, inland, and a third slightly south of Paris.

Hildy felt certain the parchment held a secret meaning, but even with her trusty magnifying glass, she could not translate the scrawled notes beside the crosses. She folded it carefully and placed it between the pages of her journal.

Moving her typewriter back in place, she poised her fingers over the keys, forcing her thoughts to Consuela's flight from Orlando's sordid assault on the Apache Trail. To start with, *Apache Gold* would no longer do at all as a title. But where would one most likely find gold in Europe—other than at Cartier?

Suddenly she heard a most alarming rustling noise. A rabbit? A *rat*? "Oh, God," she cried aloud, her creative impulse vanishing instantly. One of the sketches fell silently forward to the floor sending up a puff of dust.

The fallen drawing uncovered a circular design, depicting clusters of vivid yellow flowers against a vibrant background of cobalt blue. Hildy recognized the familiar mimosa blossom, segmented by feathery green leaves. In the center, a golden burst of light emanated from a single mimosa blossom, fluffy and yellow. She stared, captivated.

But even this radiant splash of color could not banish the dark decay Hildy sensed like a presence in this room. She hurriedly noted her impressions in her journal:

> *The dismal darkness enfolds me here, the void of an empty tomb. I feel shut away with Dupres' unfinished works arrayed like ghostly epitaphs to the dead artisan.*

Was this the extent of the writing she would be able to manage in this haunted place?

She hesitated, then packed her journal away in her tote.

Shutting her typewriter case, she took a last look around the gloomy room, her eyes stopping to fix again on the arresting mimosa design.

She locked up the hut and breathed deeply of the air stirring against her face. It bore the fresh smells of growing things, of life.

Anxious to put her depression behind her, she cut through to a clearing framed by towering cypresses. Converging into the distance before her lay lines of lavender, relieved by triangles of golden broom. Beyond, the ancient village of Mougins arched against a cloudless sky. Her spirit rejoiced in Cézanne's familiar cone, cylinder and sphere, the colors merging into shapes. What was it Renoir had said? She murmured the lines from memory: "When a great painter has lived a long time in the country…the country seems to become the work of the painter."

She thought of the mimosa branch, assaulting the artist's shepherd window, destroying it, and now the artist's depiction of the mimosa, itself a visual assault on the observer. Could this be what Renoir meant? If so then something got lost in the…abstraction.

Stumbling over a rock in the path, Hildy grabbed for a slender tree trunk, turning as she steadied herself. To the left of the path beyond a low stone wall stood a tiny graveyard, giving unexpected substance to the deathly pall she had felt in the hut only moments before.

Climbing over the wall, she found four weathered markers set unevenly in the soil. A fifth grave stone was marked by a small shrine with little pillars framing a photograph of a striking young man holding a lamb in his arms.

"André Dupres," Hildy read the name aloud. She knelt to examine a carved inscription below the picture

Je vois le sang sur la rose
Et dans ses yeux la gloire des étoiles.

She touched the withered bouquet that lay strewn beside the altar, translating, "I see the blood on the rose..." She felt a sudden rush of emotion, for the eyes of this shepherd not only reflected the glory of the stars but radiated an earthy passion. Hildy felt the intensity of the shepherd's gaze stir her unexpectedly.

She struggled back to her feet to gaze thoughtfully across the field. Was it a trick of the morning light or did she see Lescaut disappear quickly around the ancient tower?

Chapter Ten

The next morning Hildy sat on the terrace and, inspired by the heady scent of jasmine blended with *muguet,* filled seven notebook pages in longhand, referring to a revised outline of her novel in her journal:

> *Orlando will be a sculptor obsessed with capturing Consuela's tumultuous spirit in stone. He will not ravage her immediately. They will both be Spanish Basque and dwell in the Pyrenees. New title? Cannot decide, but am toying with Basques in the Sun. It has a nice ring to it.*

Exhausted by her productivity, she clipped the pages together and turned her attention to an idea she had for celebrating their wedding anniversary next Tuesday. She decided she would stage a French *déjeuner* as a surprise for Alex.

Fumbling through Julia Child's *Simple Country Fare*, Fed-Exed to her by Charlotte, she chose *Quiche Lorraine*, accompanied by a *salade niçoise*, to be climaxed by a *sorbet aux fraises*. She tried to convince herself the reason for this choice was that the menu was indigenous and had nothing whatever to do with the fact that it was the only one-pager in the book. And to make the luncheon doubly festive, she would serve it *sur l'herbe*, in the tradition made famous by the French painter, Manet. Except her guests would wear clothes.

Inspecting the terrace, she noted that the tangle of grape-vines, jasmine and honeysuckle not only threatened to over-whelm the area, but obscured the distant hills of Grasse as well. She would definitely need to have Edmund tidy up the luncheon setting.

Whatever the challenges, the vision she hoped would flicker back to her in the future was that of warm, stony, herb-scented hillsides rising out of her kitchen pots, mingled with the aroma of crisply cooked bacon and *fromage*.

"*Bonjour*! *Bonjour*!" The Marquise waved gaily from her car as it sputtered into the courtyard. "I go to Mouans Sartoux to market! You like to come with me?"

Hildy tripped over the abandoned garden hose, hurrying toward the car. "Oh yes, Marie! How fortunate you stopped by. I've decided to have a luncheon *sur l'herbe*, and I'll need to gather my ingredients." She grabbed her tote from the terrace table, suddenly remembering another item she would need. "*Un moment*," she said, rushing to the kitchen and returning immediately to climb into the Marquise's car with the basket Madame Lescaut had found for her.

"*Ah, bon*!" The Marquise patted the basket on Hildy's lap with approval. "So, you will have your luncheon outdoors? Beautiful! The garden thrives, no?"

Remembering that Marie fancied the garden an incipient Versailles, Hildy agreed, "Oh, yes. *Magnifique*. It just wants some thinning out. I mean, everything grows so abundantly, thanks to your climate here—and Edmund's incessant watering."

"I think the weather will be fine for your luncheon, Hildy. When will you do this?"

"Our anniversary is on Tuesday. You and Léon must come."

The Marquise clapped her hands together. "*Ooh-lah-lah*! *D'accord*! I tell Léon we will postpone our departure for our castle at Beaulieu." She shifted into first and the car lurched into a turn to exit the gate.

"You're not leaving us?" Hildy was instantly wary of losing the safety net of their landlord's presence in La Roquette, to say nothing of Marie's daily visits to supply Drano.

"Just for a few days. We go to ready our castle in the Loire for the summer. It can wait a week." She put her hand on Hildy's arm. "You and Alex will come visit us when you go to Paris, yes?"

Hildy tried not to seem too awed. Nobility did, after all, live in castles. "Oh, I'm sure we could manage it. We hoped to tour the chateaux region in any case."

The Marquise groped briefly with one hand in the purse beside her, handing Hildy a crested card. "*Voilà*. You must telephone us there when you will come."

Hildy examined the flourishing script. "How lovely. I just adore castles! We don't have all that many in Arizona."

Marie's car crept down the lane. "Edmund fixed your *fenêtre* satisfactorily, Hildy?"

The sagging plastic Edmund had nailed over the hole in the bathroom wall hardly qualified as satisfactory, but Hildy did not really want to express her grievances with Edmund at this particular moment. The friendly outing was at last her chance to traipse through the marketplace with her straw basket to collect the special items she would need for her luncheon.

But she could not resist remarking, "Unfortunately, Edmund has had no luck at all in locating screens for the windows. The mosquitoes have been quite fierce."

"*Ah! Les moustiques! Formidable, non?*" The Marquise pumped her brakes as she rounded the curve leading past Lady Helmsley's villa.

A sapphire vehicle in the courtyard sparkled in the blazing afternoon sun. "Stop the car, please, Marie."

"Ah, but that is your car, Hildy, is it not?" Marie's car jerked to a halt, and Hildy strained to listen from the open car window. A tinkle of laughter sounded amidst noisy splashing from the pool beyond the stone wall, further obscured by a mantle of bougainvillaea.

"Edmund!" Hildy leaped out of the car, slamming the door furiously. A silence immediately fell inside the wall. Hildy marched to the garden gate and pounded on it, while Marie jumped out, shouting for Yvette.

In a moment, the servant opened the gate. She was dripping wet, clad in a tiny bikini and clutching a towel which she fumbled to wrap around her torso. "*Oui, madame.* There is something the matter?"

"Where is Madame Helmsley?" Marie demanded.

"Madame goes to Monaco to the races."

Hildy needed no reminder of the Grand Prix.

Marie barged through the gate, bumping into Edmund, dressed in swim trunks.

He bowed cordially. "*Bonjour, mesdames.*" Strutting to the edge of the pool, he seized the skimming net to forage for leaves in the pool. "*Voilà!*" He smiled widely, scooping up a little clump of oleander leaves.

At that moment, an olive-skinned girl in a halter top and wraparound darted from the French doors to the terrace and began furiously wiping off the deck chairs and tables with a cloth.

"Who is this, Edmund?" Marie pointed to the girl.

Hildy recognized the girl from somewhere. The gypsy waitress at the café! Hildy had admired her peasant skirt. What an odd coincidence, she thought.

Edmund colored fiercely. "Ah, that is Yvette's friend, visiting from Spain. Do you not remember Nadia who once lives here, in the camp outside the village? She helps my cousin to clean everything for Madame Helmsley. *En désordre, non*?

Messy was right, thought Hildy. The pool area looked very much as if it had been the scene of an impromptu swim meet, with refreshments served. Yvette was frantically arranging a towel to hide an open wine bottle. Hildy wondered if the gypsy girl recognized her.

"I do not remember this Nadia, Edmund, but she does not belong in Madame Helmsley's villa when she is away." The Marquise braced her shoulders, raising her chin to the young man. "You try my patience, Edmund." Marie looked at Hildy and shrugged with a tolerant half-smile, apparently willing to accept the pool party as a minor lapse.

Hildy knew what Alex would have done: fire both cousins immediately and tell the gypsy girl to pack herself off to Spain. She remembered Alex's uncharitable reaction to Nadia and the café where he wouldn't even eat the food and felt a sudden surge of anger that he wasn't here to deal with what ought to be done. Irrationally, she found it intolerable that his car was parked in Victoria's courtyard. "Edmund? What is my husband's car doing here?"

"I clean Madame Helmsley's pool on the way to market for Madame Lescaut." He gave both women a soulful look. "It is not a problem, *n'est-ce pas*?"

"It is indeed a problem!" Hildy made no effort to control her fury. "First of all, I am doing the marketing today, not Madame Lescaut. Furthermore," she took a step toward him, "Monsieur did not—I—did not give you permission to drive the car on your errands. You will return it *immediatement* to the villa!"

"Errands?" Edmund blinked his bafflement at the word.

The Marquise muttered aside to Hildy, "He comprehends what he chooses to. It is a game he plays."

"I drive the Porsche like an angel," Edmund assured Hildy. "Monsieur, he will be very happy with me."

"I gravely doubt that, Edmund." Hildy could only imagine

her husband's apoplexy when he learned of this. Even she would want Alex's blessing before driving off in his brand new, most precious possession. She felt her anger collapse into a feeling of hopelessness. She needed the mimosas trimmed, as well as the relentless country garden thriving on the terrace walls. Who else could she turn to but this rogue, Edmund? Certainly not Alex. He wasn't about to play gardener in his rented French villa.

As she climbed back into Marie's car, she fought off her uneasiness about Alex in Monaco. Had he arranged to meet Victoria there? If not, Hildy could vividly picture the English, so-called Lady, literally panting at his heels!

Chapter Eleven

Half an hour later, the Marquise honked her way into the center of Mouan Sartoux, eliciting continuous shouts of disapproval from her fellow countrymen. Makeshift vending stands under striped umbrellas crowded the square for market day.

"The flea market here is *très amusant*, Hildy."

"I love it, Marie!" Hildy looked around at the pulsing excitement of the square. "It reminds me of scenes of the French Revolution. Remember? When Errol Flynn storms the Bastille?"

Marie catapulted the car over the low curbing to the sidewalk and shut off the engine. "*Voilà!* We park here."

"It's all so French!" Hildy struggled to open the car door against the surging crowd of pedestrians. The crowds were so thick among the stalls and twisted trees, it was impossible for Hildy to follow Marie at a normal walking pace.

Feeling the warm sun on her head, Hildy stopped a moment to absorb the alien tumult about her, forgetting completely about her mission. Barkers hawked copper pans, old wine glasses and paring knives that cut everything from dress patterns to sweet Valencia oranges.

"*Un moment, Marie*," Hildy called, making her way to a stall displaying junk jewelry. Maybe she would discover a lovely antique chain for her crystal.

"You need a *poulet* for your luncheon?" Marie shouted from several stalls away, removing a chicken from where it dangled, impaled on a hook. "Very good bargain!"

Hildy recoiled from the headless poultry still bearing its scaly feet. She recalled with an unpleasant twinge the old woman in the square in La Roquette the day of their arrival, brandishing her dead *poulet* and demanding compensation from Alex. "No, no, Marie," Hildy called. "What I really need to find is a measuring cup I can comprehend. The one in Lescaut's kitchen is labeled in *grammes* and marked to measure out *riz, feçule, cacao* and *semoule*. I won't be using those ingredients, you see." Hildy had recognized that these markings would be convenient if she were planning *semolina* with rice, but not at all useful for measuring *gruyère* for a *quiche*.

"Ah, first you must have a new French *chapeau*." Marie dragged Hildy to a table where she fingered the manila straw hats stacked in rickety piles. She removed one with a lavender ribbon trailing down the back and plunked it on Hildy's head. "*Voilà*! To protect you from the sun." Marie fumbled in her purse as Hildy protested, grabbing a handful of French coins from her tote.

"I do wish I could understand your money, Marie. *Centimes* sound like they must be 100 somethings, but they're only worth a few cents." Hildy thrust out a palm full of money, but Marie had already offered the gold-toothed proprietress some francs.

"Twenty-three francs we pay," said Marie with seasoned

authority, toppling a pile of hats as she thrust the money at the woman.

The woman narrowed her eyes coldly and shook her head.

Marie then removed the hat from Hildy's head and took her arm, turning to leave. Knowingly, Marie paused as the woman stopped her, holding out the hat.

Marie was pleased to explain, "You must experience, how you call it, 'haggling' when you search for the bargains." She counted out just 20 francs—not 23—which the woman accepted without a murmur.

Hildy was thrilled to have been the key focus of this international transaction. "I do thank you for my hat, Marie. And you have taught me how one must bargain as well."

Marie guided Hildy out of the current of the crowd into a backwater of clothing stalls. "And now, you must have a dress to go with the hat." They shuffled past vendors leaning over their counters and babbling seductive come-ons. Marie looked briefly at Hildy's hat and removed a lilac flowered frock from a clothesline strung between two trailers.

A woman in an identical dress in pink loomed from behind the counter. "Ah, *très belle, n'est-ce pas?*" She stood modeling what resembled an oversized apron with spaghetti straps.

"It does look cool," Hildy conceded as the woman removed the dress from the line and draped it over Hildy's shoulder.

The woman prodded her toward one of the trailers. A swarthy man wearing a single gold earring guarded the entrance.

"Oh, I'm sure it's too *petite*," Hildy protested, handing the garment back. But the woman pulled the bodice in several directions to demonstrate its stretch.

Hildy took an uncertain step, then thrust her tote at Marie. "Take care of this, will you, please?" Hildy cocked her head toward the man on the stool and whispered, "Would that person be a gypsy, Marie?" She looked quickly away as he winked at her elaborately.

The woman shoved her into a tiny changing cubicle curtained off in the trailer. She closed the curtain with a dramatic flourish, enclosing Hildy so snugly in the tiny space that she doubted she could turn around. The bottom of the flimsy curtain hung barely to Hildy's knees, the top sagging on its string to below the level of her shoulders. How was she ever to manage this maneuver?

Peering over the top, she met the leering eyes of the gypsy man and fought the impulse to bolt. She looked out the doorway for Marie who was nowhere in sight. Resigned, Hildy turned her back with an effort, dutifully slipping the frock over her head and working her tunic top down before removing her polyester slacks. Perspiration trickled down her face.

"*Combien?*" she called desperately over the curtain, determined to do whatever was necessary to escape this stifling confinement. Not waiting for an answer, she bundled her discarded clothing in a ball, clutched it under her arm and fled past the gypsy.

Marie reappeared and began negotiating with the vendor. "You like the dress, Hildy? We can purchase two for a bargain price, in different colors, of course."

Hildy hesitated. She wanted to take her friend, Charlotte, something more significant than sorrel seeds. "Ill take one in yellow, too, Marie," she decided, pleased to have that settled. She would tell Charlotte the frock was representative of native crafts.

A few moments later Hildy and Marie sipped *limonade* at a table in a packed café. "I feel like I've shed my former self, Marie. First, my *chapeau*, and now this charming creation. Next thing you know, I'll be stomping barefoot on grapes!"

Marie laughed. "Like Sophia Loren, eh?"

"Ah, *mais oui!*" Hildy felt a sudden wild abandon. Who cared what Alex was doing in Monaco? Let him enjoy his goodies; she'd enjoy hers. By plunging into the culture, Hildy felt fueled with a new enthusiasm toward *tout le monde*. Perhaps Consuela should become a gypsy!

"Before we go any further, Marie, may I ask you something?"

Marie was attentive.

"Should a person be frightened of these gypsies?"

Her companion leaned forward. "That one at the dress stall, he give you no trouble, Hildy?"

"Not really. It's just that I need to know more about them. For my novel." Hildy saw a way to probe for some answers, while at the same time fleshing out the multi-faceted Consuela. "Lescaut did warn me about them."

"Do not listen to her. She is obsessed."

Hildy pressed her question. "Victoria—Madame Helmsley—said that you suspected the gypsies might have had something to do with the death of André Dupres."

Marie sat back. "But that is nonsense! I say no such thing. André died of a heart attack, though we were at our castle when this happened. This Englishwoman, she decorates the truth, I think."

"Embellishes, yes," Hildy corrected. "I suspected she might."

"*Ooh-lah-lah*! By the time we return from Beaulieu, André is buried. I know only what Lescaut tells us. Why would his sister lie?"

Hildy hesitated. "Might I ask you something personal, Marie?"

Marie's eyes sparkled with anticipation. "But of course, Hildy. Anything at all."

"Would you say this André was attractive?"

The Marquise blushed. "A simple shepherd? Hildy, *ma chère*, he was of peasant stock. The aristocracy—," she paused, "it would not be *correct*." Then leaning forward, she added, "The man did have a certain…one would say…sex appeal. But as for me…" She shook her head.

"I hope you don't mind my asking about it. The man seems to have had such an impact on everyone. With his art as well."

"Dupres' death was very sudden and, for some, very sad." She looked quickly away. "But see what I have for you, Hildy." She reached for a paper bag at her feet. "I buy you a special anniversary present while you try on your dress." She laughed with delight, handing Hildy a small cardboard box.

Hildy stared at the unfamiliar words on the label.

Marie pulled open the lid to disclose several yellow plastic items shaped like small hand grenades. "You plug these into the wall socket. They make poison, so the mosquitoes, they sniff and fall over dead!" Marie lowered her head to the table to demonstrate.

"How unique! Alex just loves devices!" From what little Hildy could decipher from the label, the plugs were the French version of Contac capsules, dispensing time-released insecticide. There was one major difference: their purpose was to eliminate the complaint, not cure it.

Trying to make room for the box, Hildy burrowed inside her bulging tote. "I want to show you something, Marie." She fumbled in the bottom of the tote. "Now, where is it?"

"You lose something, Hildy?"

"I saved a piece of glass from the broken window." She emptied the contents of the tote on the table. "It was an especially pretty piece of the glass I found. I wrapped it in tissue." She rummaged through the contents on the table top. "And now it's gone!"

"But no matter, Hildy. A piece of glass, after all."

"I'd hoped to have a jeweler set it as a pendant."

"I take you to Cannes. We buy you real *bijou*."

Hildy felt a wave of disappointment over the vanished crystal. "But this *bijou* was special, Marie." She could hardly expect Marie to understand that it symbolized Hildy's revitalized creative aspirations for the entire last half of her mortal life. "It's hard to explain. You see, it was the Star of Bethlehem—from André's window."

"Perhaps you will find it again." The Marquise looked at her watch. "Come. We go now to the *fromagerie*."

Hildy gathered her things and followed Marie into the madness of the marketplace. Her elation had been replaced by a terrible sense of loss.

Chapter Twelve

When Marie dropped Hildy at her villa later that afternoon, Hildy saw Edmund spring from one of the lounge chairs
in the garden and disappear behind the wall of mimosa which
edged the terrace. Marie had evidently not noticed, but with
hurried thanks, Hildy stomped into the garden.

Edmund was busily clipping at the mimosa branches,
Alex's compact-disc earphones clamped to his head.

"What do you think you are doing?" she demanded.

Edmund gave her his most disarming smile as he lifted one
of the earphones. "*Pardon Madame*?

"Give me those earphones at once! That player belongs to
my husband."

Edmund put down the shears and carefully removed the
apparatus. "But I only borrow it because it helps me to trim the

mimosas quickly, as you wish me to. *Voilà*." He handed her the small black box and bundle of wires, pointedly eyeing her new frock. "Ah, Madame, you look so *français!*" He traced a finger over one of her bare shoulders. "You buy this wonderful *ensemble* at the market?"

Hildy drew back, her hand darting to cover the place he had touched. "Get back to your work, Edmund."

He dropped the shears and danced away, grinning back at her mischievously.

The man's audacity left her beyond exasperation. "And kindly bring in my packages from the courtyard. Put them in the foyer. Do it now, Edmund!"

Collapsing into a chair, Hildy fanned herself with her new hat. Her eyes fell on her journal lying on the table. What was it doing here? She was sure she'd left it in her bedroom. Or had she brought it out with her that morning when she inspected the terrace for her luncheon and forgot it when Marie arrived to take her to the market? Of what possible interest could her journal be to Edmund who could barely speak, let alone read English? She grunted. He was not to be trusted in any way, a creature of devious tricks.

Edmund strutted back to the hedge, gathering a clump of mimosa trimmings to dump ceremoniously in clear view of Hildy.

"Edmund!" she said sharply.

He looked up with an expectant smile, as if awaiting her slightest command. She held up the book. "What is my journal doing here?"

"I find it in your car, Madame. I keep it for you to be safe."

"I know very well I left the book in my bedroom, Edmund," she said firmly. "On my desk!"

"You do not believe me? Come, I show you where I find it." He extended a grimy hand and led her to Alex's car, gleaming from yet another of Edmund's perpetual wipings. "You drop it on the floor and it slide back."

Clutching her journal, Hildy bent to look inside the car. She spotted something shiny under the edge of the rear seat.

Her crystal! No. She picked up a gold drop earring, dangling it from her fingers. "Pray, what is this?"

"*Ooh-lah-lah*! This falls from my pocket. It belongs to Yvette. I give her a ride from the village today in the car of Monsieur. It is no problem." Edmund pocketed the earring.

Hildy was too tired to confront any more lies. She looked past him at the pool, thinking how lovely it would be to have a nice cool swim, but the pool was still covered with lumpy yellow algae. "I want that *piscine* cleaned, Edmund," she ordered, "and our gardens manicured, do you understand? I have a *fête* in le *jardin* in just three days?" She shook three fingers at him.

His brows furrowed. "Mon-ee-coor?"

"Oh, forget it! Go back to your trimming," Hildy stalked into the foyer. Let Alex handle Edmund when he returned.

She tucked her journal in the basket among the packages of *fromage* and fresh *haricot verts*, *artichaux* and *tomates*, and carried it to the kitchen where she found Madame Lescaut. The housekeeper offered a sympathetic nod, doubtless having observed Hildy's scene with Edmund. Why did she allow the man to wander in the house, take Hildy's things, her husband's disc player? Was she afraid of the oafish Edmund, for heaven's sake?

Hildy plopped the basket on the counter top. "Was there any call from Monsieur?"

"Au, oui. He call this morning when you leave. He return in time for *le diner*." The housekeeper continued to scour her already spotless counter top, moving Hildy's basket of packages aside.

"Did he tell you what train we should meet?"

The housekeeper shrugged. "I do not understand everything the Monsieur say. Nothing about the train." She carefully removed the fresh vegetables from Hildy's basket and rinsed them in the sink.

Hildy retrieved her journal from the basket. "Was Edmund in my room while I was gone, Madame Lescaut?"

"*Oui*, he say he must measure *pour les rideaux*—the

screens." She stopped, her face flushed with anger. "He is crazy. We have no screens for the windows in France! He lies! *Toujours! Toujours!* I can do nothing."

Hildy nodded, struck by the frustration they clearly shared in dealing with the churlish yardman. "Of course. I knew yesterday he had found no screens. Although he claimed he spent hours in my husband's car looking. More likely he was joyriding around the countryside."

"Joyriding, I do not know. But he does not do his work. This, I know." She removed a tall glass from the cupboard. "I have iced tea *avec citron frais* for you. You rest from the market now and have your tea, yes?"

Hildy felt a welcome comfort from Lescaut's concern. "That's a lovely idea. Thank you, Madame Lescaut."

Hildy carried the tea to her bedroom where she put her tote on the desk. She sipped the iced tea, then put it down to pull out her journal. Flipping through it, she noticed the last page had been torn out. She knew she had not written on it yet, but she was equally certain she had not torn it out.

Running her finger along the jagged torn edge, she wondered whether other pages were missing. She kept every entry she made, even if she later crossed it out, in case she might have set down a metaphoric gem she could later use. Flipping the pages, she remembered the map she had found in the hut and tucked in the journal. It was still there, folded along the same worn creases. Relieved, she shut the book. She could be wrong about this whole incident. Still she would never have dropped her journal in the car. She always knew the whereabouts of her journal.

And the crystal, so she had thought.

As for the earring, that was certainly not supposed to be found in the back seat of Alex's car. Obviously it belonged to one of Edmund's girlfriends, probably that sultry gypsy girl pretending to help Yvette at Victoria's villa.

But did this oaf actually make a pass at *her* back there in the garden—putting his disgusting finger on her shoulder? Or was this simply the way of the French commoner—the peasant way? Lord, she sounded like the Marquis!

Dare she tell Alex about any of this? He would go after the hapless Edmund with his bare hands.

Actually, she rather hoped he would.

She wandered about the bedroom, hearing the insistent chirping of the birds. On her tiny desk lay the stack of colored index cards. How much of what she'd detailed on those cards would now fit in her new story projection? She slipped off the elastic and thumbed through the cards.

The incident on this blue card—where she had Diego, the scurrilous gold prospector, follow Consuela to the desert cave—might not work in the Pyrenees locale. Suddenly the thought was pushed aside by the image of Edmund as Diego! She sat quickly, uncapping her pen to scribble on the card. She felt the exhilaration of sudden insight. Yes. This fix on Diego would open a number of story avenues, as well as intensifying the Consuela's emotional turmoil. Hildy's mind sorted through the complications such a devious scoundrel might engender. She slid out a fresh pink card.

She would amplify Diego's relationship with the character she called the Raven Princess in her story, a venal and ruthless temptress. The lustful Diego would be drawn to her wealth and power, but suffer rejection because the Raven Princess wants only Orlando, the stone carver. She subverts Orlando's creative talents to her own self-indulgent needs. How? Hildy's mind raced.

That was it! The Raven Princess would commission the artisan to make her a sculpture—a *statue* of herself. She would come every day to his work place to stand before him, posing seductively in the nude.

Hildy paused, her pen in mid-air. Of course, it was Edmund who had posed for Victoria, not the other way around. But Hildy let the train of thought carry her along. The Raven Princess would now be—who else, but Victoria? Instead of the Apache princess, she would be...an evil, calculating...Spanish *contessa*. Her pen flew across the pink card, filling both sides.

Hildy seized another card and considered new story directions. Yes, even though André Dupres had in reality died, in Hildy's story, the artisan Orlando would live and become world-renowned. It would be Diego who would die, that worthless scheming scum of a yardman. She corrected herself: Diego was a prospector. It would be death by drowning—in an algae-covered, slimy green swamp!

Chapter Thirteen

Hildy's thoughts were interrupted by the sound of a car crunching up the drive to the courtyard accompanied by hilarious laughter. Please, God, she thought, not Edmund committing some new outrage.

But it was Alex alighting from Victoria's red Citröen as she bid him profuse *adieux*. What was that all about? She wondered, only slightly relieved to see two other passengers in the car.

As she hurried down the stairs and out to the entrance archway, Alex rushed over. "You should have come with me, darling," he said, putting down his bag to hug her. "Monaco is like one of your fairy tale kingdoms—palace and all. And the hotel, perched above the rocks, overlooking the Mediterranean...you've never seen anything so colorful."

"Apparently you did manage to run into Victoria." Hildy waved her hand toward the car. "What is that all about?"

"Victoria wants you to meet her friends," said Alex, guiding her back to the car.

"Hildy, luv, how quaint you look," Victoria cooed.

"I went to the flea market with the Marquise," Hildy said in her defense. "She insisted on buying me this frock."

"It's smashing!" said Alex, spinning her around

Victoria turned to a young woman in the back seat, wearing a beaded turban and a spangly white sweater over black satin tights. "May I present Dawn Smith? Dawn, I want you to meet Alex's wife, Hildegarde."

"*Neato* name," said Dawn, leaning out the window. "Hi."

"And my adorable Peter Balfour." Victoria kissed him on each check.

"Lovely to meet you," replied Peter, shaking Hildy's hand.

"Peter is a film producer in England, formerly with the BBC," Victoria told Hildy. "Actually he produces all over Europe."

He was an attractive man in his thirties, dressed in white slacks and an open pink shirt. He wore an Egyptian ankh on a gold chain around his neck.

Hildy's nerves tensed immediately. Lord, an actual living, breathing producer! She desperately hoped she was familiar with his films. "I'm thrilled to meet you, Mr. Balfour."

"Call me Peter, please." He smiled.

"And Dawn…" Victoria paused a moment, "acts."

"Peter's planning to make a new film called *Petros*," Dawn said, brightly. "His films make people see beyond the *real*. Don't you agree, Vickie?"

"I don't really understand all that New Wave rubbish, but Peter's films are fun." She hugged his arm. "I've told you, Peter, all those Masters you have living in the Himalayas absorbing energy would be ever so much happier in a more agreeable climate." She called to Alex, starting into the villa. "Ta, Luv. See you."

Determined to somehow squelch Victoria, Hildy turned to

Peter. "How symbolic, Peter…producing *Petros*, the Greek word for stone. Metaphorically 'rock' signifies a solid, grand idea." She trusted he noted her perceptiveness.

"You must find time to talk to Hildy sometime, Peter," said Victoria, turning on the ignition. "She writes…what is it? I can't recall."

"Novels." Hildy shouted, above the roar of the engine. "Romantic adventure novels…easily adapted to the screen!"

Hildy's elation over meeting Peter subsided later when she confronted Alex in the living room. "I trust you enjoyed the Grand Prix," she said, backing away when he tried to kiss her.

Madame Lescaut glided in carrying a tray of iced tea.

"You must be psychic, Madame." Alex gave the housekeeper a genial smile, then turned to Hildy. "You got my message, I trust."

"Madame Lescaut did not comprehend all of what you told her, nor do I understand why you didn't call me last night when you knew I would be here." She thanked the housekeeper who nodded and quickly left the room.

"I would have, Hildy, but it was too late by the time we left the casino. I knew you'd be asleep." Alex tweaked her cheek playfully. "Did you get lots of work done on your novel?"

"We left the casino, did we? Was it 'we' for the whole two days, Alex?"

"What's that supposed to mean?"

"Why did you ride home in Victoria's car? I thought you were taking the train."

"I ran into her at the races." He wagged his head incredulously. "I thought she'd be off somewhere sketching, but there she was, hanging over a street barrier as excited as everybody else. So when she offered to spare me the mob scene at the train station today…"

"How accommodating of her." Could their meeting really have been accidental, Hildy wondered? "Well, things have been perfectly awful here, if you're interested. Some very odd things have gone on. Things with that clod Edmund, and things that probably involve these gypsies camped outside of town."

He removed his jacket and held her close. "Relax, darling. I'm here now to protect you. Come on upstairs. I brought you a present."

Hildy refused to budge. "Exactly how did you run into Victoria, Alex? Was this a tryst of some sort?"

"Listen, if running into her in Monaco had been a 'tryst,' as you call it, I would hardly come roaring home in the lady's car. I ran into her at a casino table. She saved me a train ride back, for God's sake."

"But you love trains. Almost as much as your Porsche."

"Look, Monaco was a zoo. When someone offers you a ride back after a long, hard two days…"

"Of what?" Hildy asked tartly.

"Jesus, Hildy. What's gotten into you?"

She avoided his look. "Well, you might be interested to know that while you were casino-hopping with Victoria, your gardener was carousing around God-knows-where in your car with who-knows-what kind of women. I found a gold earring in the back seat."

Alex's face darkened. "That nervy bastard! I'll kill him."

"Furthermore, while I was at the market today, he was helping himself to my journal and lounging around the garden, listening to your disc player."

Alex started for the front door. "Where is he? I'm firing him right now."

"Please, Alex, wait." She hurried to stop him. "I'm planning a *déjeuner* on Tuesday. I need him to deal with *les herbes*." She managed a weak smile. "It was supposed to be a surprise for our anniversary."

"What in hell is 'lay zerb'?"

"It means greenery. I'm planning to serve luncheon on the terrace."

"It'll take a machete to tame that wilderness." He loosened his ascot and turned to pick up his camera case and a shopping bag he'd deposited on the stair. "How do you know Edmund was out carousing in my car?"

Hildy told him about the incident at Victoria's that morning, about Nadia, the gypsy waitress, and Edmund's dubious account of the earring. "He claims it's Yvette's, but I find that must unlikely. Yvette's gypsy friend is an obvious sexpot, far more enticing to a half-wit like Edmund than gardening."

"I have never trusted that creep." Alex fumed. "What in God's name was he doing with your journal? Don't tell me he's interested in your notes. Hell, he can't even read English, can he?"

"Oh, he lies. About everything. Lescaut says the same thing. She has no control at all over what the man does. I think he terrorizes her when I'm not here." Hildy settled on the sofa to sip her iced tea. She realized her observations were somewhat circumstantial, but she knew she wasn't wrong about Edmund. And for some reason, she felt no regrets about wounding Alex with the horror story about his car. Her imaginings about Victoria and her husband were turning into real suspicions. Not that she couldn't have expected this. Hildy had recognized the Englishwoman as a "bird of prey in a froth of chiffon plumage" the first time they met at her villa.

"In any case," Alex's tone softened, "You'll be pleased to know that that Balfour weirdo came here to do a survey for his movie. You might have a chance to talk to him about your writing stuff."

"My 'writing stuff.' That's what you think of my creative skill, isn't it Alex? Well, let me tell you something. I'm not just your toy wife, dabbling in silly 'writing stuff!'" She plunked her glass down and stood up. "I am determined to write this book, and nothing is going to stop me. Not your condescending image of me as your corporate wife, not the insanity of this stupid, lying yard person, and," she looked straight at him, "not your having a B-movie fling with some bosomy bitch!"

"Oh come on, darling. Let's not be dramatic."

In the silence, Hildy felt her heart pounding.

"I brought you a present." Alex reached in the bag. "The minute I won a few francs at the crap table, I immediately rushed right out." He held out a slender, chic box.

"That was sweet of you," Hildy said flatly, removing the cover. Inside, nestled in tissue, lay an assortment of silk scarves in every color of the rainbow. She felt a pang of remorse at her outburst as she lifted out a pink one.

"Like the ones you dreamt about the other night." Alex wafted another scarf from the box to brush her check. "When you were looking for your patchwork robe." He kissed her gently. "For my favorite *Madame*."

Hildy adored the gift but could not relent. "I suppose Victoria helped you pick them out?"

"I chose them myself." Alex looked crushed. "After 34 years, I should know your favorite shades."

"I love them." Hildy fluttered another out of the box. She felt numb. Taking a breath, she rose from the sofa. "Stay here. I have a special gift for you from the Marquise." She brought the small sack in from the hall. "You'll never guess what it is."

"I hope not a can of Drano," he chuckled, opening the box and holding up the yellow bomb. "Lovely. What is it?"

"To kill *les Moustiques*. Since Edmund claims he can't.

Alex studied the instructions, shaking his head.

"You just plug it into an outlet, and it releases malathine, killing the mosquitoes on contact," Hildy explained.

"God, imagine," Alex sighed, "a bug-free sleep, at last."

"There is one very vexing problem, Alex."

"Can it wait until after my shower?"

"My crystal piece is missing." Hildy hesitated. "Edmund probably took it. Though I cannot imagine why. Remember, I showed it to him when I asked about a jeweler the day we went to St-Paul-de-Vence?"

"Have you confronted him?"

"To hear more lies? Why bother?" Hildy thought a moment. "Come to think of it, I haven't actually seen the crystal since I showed it to Edmund that morning. I wonder if someone did steal it when I was bumped in the cathedral."

Alex put the bug bombs in the bag. "Frankly, I think Edmund's a lot more likely to make off with the Porsche than a piece of broken glass. It'll turn up. You probably just mislaid it."

"No. I know exactly where it was. Wrapped in Kleenex in my tote." She thought a moment. "Lescaut also knew I had it. She saw me with it the morning after the storm."

"Why wouldn't she just ask for it?"

"As a matter of fact, Marie had my tote with her for five or ten minutes today while I tried on my dress at the flea market. Right after that was when I discovered the crystal was missing." Hildy shook her head slowly. "It seems impossible the Marquise would take me shopping, then steal…"

"I swear," he said, grabbing her around the waist, "you sound like Agatha Christie lining up her suspects, for God's sake. Put that novelist's imagination to rest."

"I am not imagining that someone took my crystal, Alex."

"I was kidding you. Listen, give me a chance to clean up and we'll find a quaint little *auberge* for a nice quiet dinner. How does that sound?"

"No, Alex. I've had quite enough quaintness for one day, thank you. Chunks of meat on wooden blocks, headless chickens with their feet still attached, the smell of blood…Right now, I need time alone, if you don't mind." She started up the stairs, hating the idea of inviting Lady Helmsley to her anniversary luncheon. She paused on the landing. Come to think of it, why not make the luncheon work to her advantage? "By the way, I believe I'll plan to invite Peter Balfour to my luncheon on Tuesday. If nothing else, it will be an opportunity to discuss my work with a professional. I'll have to get busy immediately to organize and transcribe my latest notes for him." Hildy paused meaningfully. "My *writing stuff*."

"I see." Alex turned away.

"Incidentally, Edmund made a pass at me in the garden today." Defiant, she waited for his reaction.

Alex's shoulders slumped. "Hildy, darling. Give me a break."

"You think I'm making it up because of that Helmsley woman, don't you? You can't imagine a man finding me desirable, can you?" She felt tears coming. "Hear me right now, Alex. You make me sick!" She fled up the stairs.

In her writing corner, Hildy tore the cover off the type-writer, placed Lescaut's prescribed rubber pad under it, and rolled a sheet of paper into the machine. Her fingers could not move swiftly enough to pour out the raw emotions consuming the confused but resolute Consuela. In the nightmare of her quest, the hapless half-caste would be forced to rally her passions anew in her struggle to realize her dreams. She would be more than a match for the Raven Princess, the new nemesis of her novel.

And God help her, Hildy vowed, so would she!

Chapter Fourteen

The first thing in the morning, Hildy detoured through the mimosas to Victoria's villa to borrow a flan pan. However outraged she felt, Hildy was determined to stage her *déjeuner sur l'herbe*. And more importantly, to get closer to the film producer, Peter Balfour. She owed that much to herself.

She was enormously pleased about the pages she'd completed on her novel the previous evening, despite her unsettling suspicions—or maybe because of them. The truth was, her emotional turmoil had proved a powerful creative impetus.

But writing was so endlessly difficult! Was she really destined to publish? God, she even had trouble getting her grandson Tim's attention to tell him a story. Maybe Alex was right. Why put herself through constant rejection? Losing the novel contest had been humiliating enough.

Yet, hadn't her writing given her a way to cope with the chaos of Alex underfoot, ever since that Monday he didn't go back to work? She surely loved him. She really did. But she needed time to herself. Her novel gave her a way to escape into a fantasy world often more rewarding than her own.

Hildy opened her journal to write, always a help to clear confusion.

I remember when I was a girl those summer afternoons I'd play paperdolls on the screened porch. Their home was a black and white composition book in which I pasted pictures of rooms clipped out of my mother's Ladies Home Journal. As I moved my paperdoll family from room to room, living out their fictional day, I wondered what would it be like when I got married? Now I know. Formidable! If I continue on my novel, against such incredibly distracting odds, does this mean I lose Alex to the first seductive female who comes along? What if I have to choose between our marriage and my goals? How unfair.

Her train of thought did nothing to diminish her antipathy toward Victoria Helmsley. What would this woman's *inner* motivation be in seducing Alex? Recalling her workshop lessons on characterization, Hildy could see clearly that Victoria was her 'nemesis,' whose outer motivation was money. But what exactly went on in Monaco with Alex? Did Victoria really think she could cash in her chips and win *him*?

Why was she letting herself go on like this? There was no way she could be absolutely certain anything at all was going on beyond a silly flirtation between this woman and her husband.

Besides, if nothing else, the luncheon would be a 'career move'—another term she'd learned from reading trade papers. She must decide beforehand how she might spark Peter's interest in her work. Would he be impressed, perhaps, if she read passages aloud from her journal? Possibly, but she must put all this aside for the moment and concentrate on borrowing a flan pan.

"A flan pan?" Victoria looked puzzled at Hildy's request.

"I really wouldn't know, Hildy. I rarely cook at all." She called toward the kitchen, "Yvette!"

Hildy steeled herself. "I'm having this little luncheon on Tuesday, and I'd like you to come." Hildy looked behind Victoria into the *séjour*. "And Mr. Balfour and Miss Smith, naturally. I understand they are visiting."

"What a wizard idea, Hildy! I've been at wit's end thinking how I might entertain my guests properly. Peter's an old friend I find terribly amusing, even when I don't understand a thing he says. Dawn...well she's new. Peter has such awful taste in women, after he and I...well, we've remained chums. Isn't that civilized?"

This hint of another untidy relationship was not reassuring. "Oh, terribly civilized." Hildy took a breath. "It will be our 35th anniversary, Victoria. A very special day."

Victoria gathered up the skirts of her filmy peignoir and ushered Hildy into the *séjour*. Actually, I was planning to invite you both down here for drinks that day."

"You knew about our anniversary." It was not a question.

"Naturally. Alex told me in Monaco. Do sit down, dear." She perched gracefully on a sagging ottoman. "It's so frightfully rare for a marriage to survive that long. Mine lasted—oh, much less time."

Hildy picked up a framed photo of a strikingly attractive man helping a curly-haired youth of about twelve mount a horse. Both wore English hunting attire. "What a handsome pair."

"That's Jeremy and our son." Victoria reached for the photograph and hugged it to her. "I miss Lindsay so. His father insisted on sending him to boarding school, so we have just the holidays together, really."

Hildy was surprised at the wistfulness in Victoria's voice. "I miss our grandson too. Tim's not quite old enough for horses yet, but he does love having his grandfather, Alex, take him on the train—sometimes just little rides to the next station and back." There was no reaction. "Tim is very close to his grandfather."

Victoria replaced the photograph on the table. "It's so dreadfully lonely for me back in England. I became a docent in the dreary Ashmolean museum only to give me some reason to get out of bed each morning."

How well Hildy knew the feeling! But unwilling to share her sympathy, Hildy said nothing.

"I prefer the life here in the south of France." Victoria tossed back her burnished coppery hair. "God knows, working with those medieval relics gives one nothing much more than the feeling of an above-ground burial."

"I would certainly agree one feels more *joie de vivre* here in France. It's a matter of pointing one's energies in meaningful directions, Victoria, wouldn't you say? Not just playing games with one's emotions—or other people's." Hildy stared at her pointedly.

Victoria's laughter shimmered through the room. "Hildy, you do put things so poetically! I can't think why nobody wants to publish you." She turned to Yvette, staring at them vacantly from the archway. "Madame Bigelow has need of a flan pan. Would you describe it to her, Hildy? Use French, if you can."

"*Oui.*" Hildy pinched her fingers in an imaginary circle, pantomiming the placement of a crust. "*Pour la quiche, n'est-ce pas?*"

Victoria giggled. "Really, Hildy! Your mimicry is a hoot!"

Yvette's eyes flickered vaguely, and she ambled back toward the kitchen, mumbling in French.

"Where is Peter, by the way?" asked Hildy with a tight smile. "He will be here for the luncheon, I hope?"

"Peter rose early to attend Mass in the village, then to chat up the Priest a bit. He may want to use the old church in his film."

"Oh, yes. *Petros.* Will Miss Smith be working with Peter on his film?"

"Who knows? One hopes she can act, even a little. I find her a bit of a simpleton, actually. She apparently sleeps until midday, whereupon she spends hours agonizing over what clothes to wear. Then she can't wait to find a beach—or any excuse for taking them off again."

"I'm afraid she won't find many reasons in La Roquette." Hildy gave a wry laugh. "Except, perhaps, at your pool. And there certainly are no *paparazzi* waiting to snap her firm little body for the trade papers, are there?" Hildy deplored the realization she was gossiping with Victoria.

Victoria plucked a cigarette from an open crystal container on the coffee table. "I don't propose to worry about Dawn at all." She flicked a lighter and blew smoke. "I suppose I'll have to think of some extravagant place for dinner—preferably one where Miss Smith can make a spectacular entrance in her leather, boots and beads. Lord, she dresses like Barbarella. Did you see the film? I'm sure she'll spend the entire day readying her costume for the occasion." Victoria rearranged the folds of her peignoir. "I prefer softer things, myself."

"You might try a lovely little *auberge*. We lunched in one the other day, in the countryside just outside Mouans Sartoux. Of course, you might find it a bit rustic…" Hildy thought of the waitress, Nadia, and wondered whether Victoria had learned about Yvette's impromptu pool party.

"I don't find those country places exciting at all, not like the cafés…" she took a long puff of her cigarette "…in Monaco."

Hildy stiffened. "Wasn't it too bad you didn't manage to get any painting done. Alex tells me you're quite an avid racing enthusiast. Or did he run into you in one of the casinos?" She looked toward the sound of banging pans in the kitchen. "I do hope I'm not putting Yvette to a lot of trouble."

Victoria waved an indifferent hand at the noise. "Peter spotted Alex practically climbing a lamp post to get his pictures. Dawn insisted we all get together for drinks later. She couldn't wait to change into another of her costumes."

"Really? Dawn didn't strike me as much of an organizer. And was it a fun evening?" Hildy wished she could refrain from digging, but could not.

"Oh jolly good fun. That, by the way, is how I learned one

must wait for Miss Smith to get her so-called act together. I think Alex and I waited over an hour for Peter and her to meet us on Friday night. The two of us managed to get quite awfully pissed at the hotel bar."

Hildy shifted uncomfortably in her chair. "Alex does enjoy his gin and tonic."

"My dear, we are talking about martinis. After all those dirty, noisy races! And nothing less than Bombay Gin for dear Alex, in the manner of a proper Colonial, if you please. Alex is a terribly amusing companion, isn't he?"

Hildy resented Victoria's invitation to share even this harmless truth about her husband. "Oh, yes. Alex is a caution, all right. And your dinner was delectable, when you finally got around to having it, one imagines."

"I really don't recall, Hildy. It was a totally wild evening at the tables, then a lovely brandy in the hot tub at the hotel. I do wish our landlord would install a Jacuzzi here, don't you?" She gave a bitter laugh, "Assuming they could possibly organize the plumbing up this hill, which is not at all bloody likely, is it?"

"Brandy in the hot tub. How congenial." Hildy felt her stomach tightening into a knot and rose quickly from her seat when Yvette appeared in the arch. "Ah, you've found something." She took the pan from the servant girl.

"Is okay?" Yvette inquired.

"This is *pour un gateau*, dear." Hildy recognized the cake pan from the pictures of utensils in Volume II of Julia Child's cookbook. "A quiche is much flatter than a cake, you see." She handed the pan back, anxious now to escape any further tales of jet-set Monaco.

"You could always buy your quiche at the *boulangerie*, Hildy," Victoria suggested. "I shouldn't bother cooking up fancy dishes, if I were you."

"Thank you, Victoria. I don't consider it a bother at all. Not for something as important as an anniversary." She started for the door. "You pointed out yourself how few people get to celebrate them, year after year."

Yvette suddenly shrieked and pointed at the pool outside the French doors.

"Good Heavens, Yvette, what…?"

Yvette had rushed to the edge of the pool, then backed away, yelping hysterically. Hildy followed Victoria to the patio.

The cat, Ariadne, floated, half submerged, in the water.

Hildy put her arm around the quivering Yvette, while Victoria grabbed the pool skimmer and knelt to reach for the bloated animal. "How long ago did this happen, Yvette! The poor animal's been dead for hours! Days, maybe…"

Yvette shook with sobs.

"Why don't I call Edmund," Hildy stared, horrified.

Victoria rose to her feet and handed the skimmer to Yvette. "You dispose of it, Yvette," she said cooly.

"Don't put it anywhere on the premises. Take it away, into the field up there. Just get rid of it."

Hildy released the trembling servant girl. "How odd. I always thought cats abhorred water."

"Ariadne was not swimming, for God's sake," Victoria snapped.

"But how do you suppose it happened, Victoria?"

"Does it bloody well matter? The cat is dead, *mort. Fini.* Who cares a farthing for a goddamned cat!" She swept into the villa.

Hildy's mind was spinning in her own emotional turmoil. Now, here was a drowned cat. She stared at the stricken Yvette. "I'm sure it's not your fault, dear. It was an accident of some kind."

"No accident, Madame." Yvette said in a broken whisper and crossed herself several times. "Someone has kill *le chat.* I know this."

"Who would do such an evil thing? And why?"

"*Pourquoi? Je ne sais pas.*" But Hildy sensed a hollowness in Yvette's denial. She looked at Hildy and shook her head tragically. "*C'est diabolique.*"

Chapter Fifteen

When she reached the curve in the lane on her way home, Hildy suddenly turned toward the village. Perhaps she'd find Peter and ask him about his film. Her emotions demanded a respite.

Why was it that people like Victoria Helmsley, whose lives were so thoroughly messed up anyway, seemed to attract other bizarre disasters as well, like having their cats drown?

And flaunting her silly little flirtation with Alex, by way of proclaiming herself irresistible. Despite the woman's attractiveness, her desperation was obvious—and hardly surprising. She had practically nothing else going for her. Even her art was tacky! Actually, the poor wretch was emotionally rootless. Like an airborne virus. Hildy stopped at once to write down: "Victoria—the voluptuous virus." It sounded to her like a circus act.

Hildy found Peter sighting down the alley beside the church. He wore long English shorts and an open white shirt. She noticed for the first time that beneath his luxuriant mop of brown hair, Peter had the thin face of an ascetic.

"Mr. Balfour, *Bonjour*!" Hildy called. "*C'est moi*, Hildy!"

"Capital!" he murmured, peering through a small viewfinder hung with ribbon from his neck. "Fabulous *chiaroscuro*!" He let the finder fall to his chest. "Madame Bigelow!" *Enchanté*. How are you?" He retrieved a slim black attaché case and approached with his hand out, then gave her a French hug instead, kissing both cheeks. His pale gray eyes were wide with excitement. "We missed you in Monaco. And how goes the novel?"

"It's progressing extremely well, Mr. Balfour. But slowly. In fact, I'm in the midst of refocussing my theme in an entirely new locale. I feel it will offer a more fertile atmosphere for my story."

"Ah, but how vital that is!" He took her arm and started along the square.

Some townsmen lounged on the rim of the trough circling the fountain. Apparently, no one did laundry there on Sunday, Hildy observed. "The square is charming, isn't it? We ran over a chicken here when we arrived. I think the old woman who owned it put a gypsy curse on us."

Peter guffawed. "You've not been having bad luck here, one hopes?"

"I'm not serious, Peter. I don't believe in curses." Hildy decided she would not tell Peter about Ariadne. "Alex was just driving too fast."

"Good," Peter said. "But how delightful to find a kindred spirit in this remote place! Will you join me for coffee, or a glass of wine, Hildy? I need to make some notes." His eyes darted restlessly about the slowly shifting scene in the square, fixing on one element, then another.

"Coffee would be delightful, Peter."

The young man hugged her arm, his eyes scanning the

faces of the townspeople in the square. "Quite frankly, I am desperate to talk about my film. To someone quite detached, but with artistic sensibilities like yourself. Victoria is utterly bored with me, I'm sorry to say, and doesn't in the least understand my ideas. Nor my films."

"She does paint," Hildy offered.

Peter merely cocked his head ambiguously. "And Dawn. Well, Dawn is essentially a performer, not really a visualizer, if you know what I'm saying. Though she's quite visual herself," he chuckled, "particularly on the big screen."

"Oh, I quite understand, Peter. One's vision is so key. But one does need a sounding board, I find. Alex isn't awfully interested in the arts, unfortunately, though he does relate well to things like ruins—or ramparts."

"You see, Hildy, what I'm trying to do is so awfully bloody profound! Cosmic, one might say, if that doesn't sound too pretentious."

"Indeed not. I might presume to seek your advice as well, actually."

"Marvelous! Let's nip in here and see if they'll give us something to drink at this hour."

The café was empty except for a stout Frenchman in an apron replacing a broom behind a dark wood bar. Peter dropped his case beside one of the small, weathered tables on the sidewalk outside and held a chair for Hildy. "I've been in the village since the Mass at seven this morning. I've no idea of the time." He ordered their coffee, his eyes minutely examining the proprietor's face as he did so. "*Quelle visage!*" he remarked to Hildy when the man left.

Hildy looked after the man, disturbed she might have missed something important. She debated placing her journal on the table, then reached for it. "I just feel more comfortable with my journal in sight. I hope you don't mind." She patted it fondly. "That way I know my visions won't slip away from me."

"Quite. My film, you see," Peter's eyes bored into hers, "is the Christ story, crafted as a metaphor for today."

Hildy opened her journal to a fresh page, her lavender ball-point racing to inscribe the date. *Christ metaphor*, she wrote, unable to avoid smiling. "I love it already, Peter."

"What would happen if Jesus were to appear in the world tomorrow, instead of two thousand years ago?"

"Why, I have no idea, Peter. I've never given it a thought."

"That's it, Hildy. *Petros*. My film."

"How compelling. Definitely high concept." Hildy sat back. "It's utterly fantastic you should be on that track, since, in a way, I've been preoccupied with a related subject this past week."

"But not as I will film it, dear lady." Peter insisted. "Despite the fact that we are all *one* with the *One*, my vision will be uniquely mine. You see that, don't you?"

Hildy reached to cover Peter's hand. "Please, Peter, don't be alarmed. My interest comes from an altogether different direction: stained glass. You see my point?"

"Actually, I don't. *Petros* is about Jesus Christ in the 21st Century."

Hildy laughed. "Sounds a bit like Buck Rogers or something, doesn't it?" Getting no response, she added quickly, "I'm sorry. My interest is quite serious, Peter. Stained glass, you see, is a religious archetype. A *Christian* religious archetype." She hoped Peter made the connection between her idea and his. "I feel stained glass symbolizes the hues of the infinite."

"Really? That is somewhat similar then, isn't it?"

"There was a stained glass window in our villa by an artisan named Dupres. It broke during a mistral when we first arrived."

Peter smiled. "My word! Your arrival has brought on a veritable bloody siege of mishaps, hasn't it! First the chicken…"

"But, the remarkable thing is, the window depicted a shepherd and the Star of Bethlehem! The beginning of the Jesus story, don't you see? The very thing you're doing as a film."

"Incredible! My Jesus is a farm worker, in a vineyard."

"A shepherd—," Hildy had to think a moment, "a grape picker. I suppose one could form a connection."

"It is actually quite extraordinary, Hildy." Peter hunched forward, his eyes steely bright. "Nothing like this happens without reason, of course. The divine energies have somehow shuffled the pages of our scripts together, that's what's happened."

"Peter, you won't believe this but I was just about to say the very same thing."

"It occurs all the time. A page of my script was Xeroxed and put in yours."

She withdrew her hand. "Isn't it wonderful? And I haven't even seen your script. Nor did I know until this minute what your film was about."

Peter recaptured her hand. "I'm not talking about my film script. I mean my personal script. And yours. The life-script we are acting out this very minute."

Hildy stirred from her confusion to scribble in her journal. "Yes, I see what you mean. It's quite an intriguing concept, though I'm not sure what it signifies. I've never thought about my life being Xeroxed, quite frankly."

Peter leaned his elbows on the table with the palms up. "A mere synchronicity, luv. You needn't worry about significance."

"That's a relief. I really would have to give it a great deal of thought, before deciding what it meant."

"My film, of course, will not depict archangels, walking on water, that sort of thing."

"Oh good. That must be very expensive to produce."

Hildy felt she ought to jot down Peter's approach. She made an entry: "miracles—costly." Pen poised, she asked, "Your story will take place in a contemporary setting then?"

"In a way, yes. I shall employ 'persona-parallels,' you see. The Jesus persona-parallel is the main one, but there are the persona-parallels of John the Baptist, Mary Magdalene, Judas—all the Biblical regulars. However, I shall not employ the traditional sandals-and-toga crowd—Ustinov, Lancaster,

Bellamy, that lot. And definitely not Chamberlain."

"I agree. I really didn't approve of his behavior at all in *Thorn Birds*." Hildy thought a moment. "My main character is Consuela. She's Hispanic. Lots of Hispanics work in vineyards in America. You've heard of Cesar Chavez?"

"My personas will be French."

"Oh, I see. Will you call them 'persona-parallels' in your film, Peter? I don't believe that's been done before."

Peter laughed. "God, no. Far too cumbersome, I feel. I use the term only to explain my concept to you. The characters merely parallel those of the Jesus story."

She nodded, then followed Peter's gaze to the square, where a bearded peasant was leading a donkey toward the fountain's trough. "Actually, this little rural village," Peter said, "it could be a modern-day Galilee, don't you agree?"

"I suppose it could, yes." Hildy felt she should offer artistic encouragement despite her impression of Galilee as primarily a desert. "But, of course, I've never been to the Holy Land."

In Peter's thoughtful silence, her mind went to the casting she might consider for Consuela when her book became a mini-series. Angelica Huston? Possibly. Definitely not Collins...

"May I tell you more about *Petros*, Hildy?"

"Pray, do, Peter." Hildy recovered her concentration. "Did you choose the title because of your name by any chance?"

"It might seem so, but no. *Petros* means 'rock'. The metaphor of Faith. The rock of the church, the rock the angel rolled away from Jesus' tomb. But my *Petros* is not about religion; it will dramatize the power of energy. Etheric energy. The ultimate stuff of the cosmos. Or you may think of it as karma, if you like—whatever."

"I see." Hildy just knew Peter was sharing a profound thought. "Speaking of karma, I'm having a luncheon on Tuesday. I hope you'll come. There's something I must show you, *à propos* of all this." She leaned toward him, lowering her voice dramatically. "The man who created the stained glass, André Dupres, actually was a shepherd himself. I've explored the little hut he worked in and in view of what you've told me, I must share an amazing flash of insight I had at the time." Hildy flipped back a few pages in her journal and read aloud, "The dismal darkness enfolds me here, the void of an *empty tomb*.' Like your Holy Sepulchre after the *petros* was rolled away."

Peter's eyes widened with interest as Hildy shut her journal and sat back, pleased to have found the occasion for reciting one of her better metaphors. It even had alliteration.

She found the similarity to Peter's tomb exciting indeed. But what was it about her short visit to France that had repeatedly brought her to a preoccupation with thoughts of death?

Chapter Sixteen

The morning of her luncheon, Hildy sat unhappily at the kitchen counter grating out her unabated hurt and anger along with two kilos of gruyère. She and Alex had barely spoken to one another after his gala arrival home from Monaco two days ago. What was there to say? She had no interest in discussing her visit with Victoria on Sunday, which if anything, confirmed her worst suspicions. And today—their anniversary— she felt compelled to send Alex on a series of errands for her party to guarantee his extended absence. The irony of the circumstances did not escape her: arranging the perfect anniversary celebration for a marriage now mortally threatened.

"*Bonjour ma chère*!" Alex sauntered into the kitchen and doffed his beret. "Happy Anniversary."

Hildy turned her face away when he tried to kiss her. "If

you would pour me a *chopine* of cream, please." She continued kneading the flour and butter together, most of it sticking to the bowl.

Alex thumbed through the cookbook to Julia's conversion tables. "Based on the Imperial English pint or the liquid ounce?"

"Look," Hildy glared at him, "my cheese won't even reach the runny stage if you don't convert Fahrenheit to Celsius. Just do it, please."

Alex loosened his ascot. "What's happened to Madame La Farge?"

"Lescaut was called to Grenoble to attend a sick uncle. I had no choice but to change her day off. Does it say in there how many *cuillères à bouche rapé* equals two cups? I can only conjugate up to *cuissez*."

"Why not serve one of your never-fail omelets?" Alex removed his calculator from his madras vest pocket.

Hildy glanced at the wall clock. "Right now my question is whether to go for the *vol-au-vent* or stick to *demi-feuilleté*."

"What would you do if you were in Arizona?"

"Buy crescent rolls and press them in a pyrex. However, that is academic, since I haven't the vaguest idea of how to turn on the oven."

Alex flipped some pages to "Temperature and Timing." Are we using solid fuel, electricity or gas?"

"Please stop clowning around, Alex. Just figure out how to get the oven going! And in the meantime, kindly measure me a half litre of anchovies for my *niçoise*." She slid the measuring cup across the counter.

"Let's see," Alex murmured, his calculator clicking, "if 178 *mille-liters* equals 1, and 3 *dls* makes one and a quarter cups…"

"Then we won't be having any salad." Hildy bit her lip, wiping the sticky dough from her hands on her apron. "I wish to God I were in my own kitchen."

Edmund strutted in carrying a basket of ruby red roses. "Madame Helmsley send you these from her garden. *Pour vôtre anniversaire!*"

"How thoughtful of Madame." Alex said, sniffing the roses.

"Tacky would be the more appropriate term. Put them anywhere, Edmund, or in the trash, if you like."

Edmund searched for a vacant spot on the counter, now a tapestry of cheese and anchovies. "Ah, Madame makes *le pizza, eh?*"

Hildy whirled around. "I would appreciate less frivolity and more serious solutions to these problems, if you don't mind." She was close to tears. "What I need is Simone Beck."

"Just calm down, Hildy," Alex said anxiously. "Where do I find her?"

"How on earth would I know?" wailed Hildy. "She's Julia Child's faithful assistant—the one she always summons in times of crisis." Hildy choked trying to laugh. "You can bet Simone could convert to Celsius in two seconds, and she wouldn't need a calculator either." Hildy slammed the cookbook shut, tears spilling to her cheeks.

"I get Yvette," said Edmund, dancing back and forth. "*Tout de suite! Madame! Soyez tranquille!*"

"By all means," Alex commanded. "Do that at once, Edmund." He pushed Edmund out the door.

"Stay calm," Hildy muttered to herself. "I should have just canceled this entire thing."

"There, darling. It's going to be all right." Alex paused. "You know something, Hildy? That is possibly the first efficient idea the fellow has ever had, although I don't doubt it will cost me."

Hildy dabbed at her face with the apron, leaving behind a patch of dough. "Don't give it a thought, Alex. You can use your jackpot money from Monaco." She threw off her apron. "If you'll *pardonnez-moi*, I'll go change. Our guests are due in less than an hour." She stomped up the stairs.

Half an hour later, Yvette shot into the courtyard on her Vespa, with the gypsy, Nadia, riding sidesaddle. Yvette wore a clinging Côte d'Azur T-shirt and jeans so tight she was barely able to swing her leg over the machine to dismount. Her friend, Nadia, looked like a cliché gypsy in an embroidered off-the-shoulder blouse, long woven skirt and thongs.

Observing their arrival from her bedroom window, Hildy groaned. How could she keep these slovens out of sight? She smoothed her new lilac frock, patted her hair and sped to the kitchen.

"*Ici, Yvette*." Hildy pointed to Julia's recipe in the cookbook, now soiled with butter and cream. "You make this for me, please."

Yvette nodded meekly, as she fingered the towering mound of cheese on the counter.

Hildy waved her arms helplessly toward the oven. "You can make hot the oven, no?"

Nadia smiled demurely at Hildy, as Yvette nudged the gypsy girl forward.

Yvette seized the dough from the bowl and slapped it down on the counter, flattening to fit the pan. Piling in the *fromage*, she pat it into position with practiced fingers. At the same time, Nadia bent over and deftly lit the oven.

When the gypsy girl straightened up and turned around, Hildy drew a quick, sharp breath. From the girl's ear hung a hoop earring like the one Hildy had found in the Porsche. She would have to deal with this alarming discovery some other time.

"I cook this nice for you, Madame," Yvette announced, lifting the plate of dough triumphantly.

"Marvelous, Yvette." Hildy backed away, relieved. "I think my guests are arriving." She gave Nadia a disapproving look. "Perhaps the gypsy…your friend, might make my *salade*. She can wash her hands right here in the sink." She handed Nadia a bar of soap.

Hildy gathered up Victoria's roses and plunked them in a pitcher. If nothing else, the ruby red would complement the flowered mats and napkins she'd managed to pilfer from among Lescaut's locked drawers. She'd had to settle for blue and white pottery dishes, which, she decided, along with the red roses would create a patriotic tri-color theme. On second thought, the last thing she cared to do right now was to further cement foreign relations.

Stepping outside to greet Marie and Léon de Musset, Hildy noted immediately that the Marquise's ensemble of Monoprix separates in clashing shades of magenta and fuchsia would argue with her patriotic palette. "*Très dramatique*," Hildy told her. "Alex, you must take a picture."

Marie patted Hildy's cheek. "Happy Anniversary, Hildy. Alex, he like your new dress?"

Alex turned from the outdoor bar he had arranged on the patio to put his arm around his wife. "Tell the truth, Marie," he asked in a Maurice Chevalier voice, "are we not *Français*?" He adjusted his beret.

The Marquise grabbed the camera. "We take the happy couple first!" Untangling her chain from her colored beads, she stood back to focus. "*Hoopla!*" She snapped the shutter.

"What you need is a drink," said Alex, helping the Marquis to the bar. "No need to stand on ceremony, sir, on this hot day." He helped the Marquis slip off his maroon blazer. "We dine, Arizona style, *n'est-ce pas?*"

If, indeed, we have anything to eat, thought Hildy. "I must check to see if my pastry is puffing." She endeavored to appear casual. "Madame Lescaut has gone to Grenoble."

The Marquise frowned. "To Grenoble? On this day? But how inconvenient for you Hildy." She turned to Léon. "This is outrageous, Léon!"

The Marquis shrugged. "Always she must go to Grenoble! You must speak to her, Marie."

Hildy realized in a fresh wave of frustration that neither of these people had any control whatever over their employees. Léon was "royalty", playing landlord. Her royal highness, sweet Marie, in her Monoprix separates, neither looked like a Marquise, nor commanded her vassals.

"Yvette is helping in the kitchen," Hildy said without conviction. "Alex, why don't you check on the wine?" She whispered to Marie, "She's brought that gypsy girl along, the one we saw at Victoria's."

The Marquise looked alarmed. "I do not permit gypsy in my villa."

"I know." Hildy patted her arm. "But there's nothing we can do about that just now. I'll have Alex get rid of her later on." Hildy started for the kitchen to check on Yvette's progress when she heard voices beyond the jasmine separating the pool lawn from the path.

"That's Victoria and her friends." Alex moved swiftly toward the gate to greet the arriving guests.

"Marvelous." Hildy murmured, gulping her wine. She reached over to pluck a ruby rose to fasten in her hair. "While we wait, we shall have more *vin*, yes, Marie? Léon?" She forced a laugh.

Victoria appeared in the stone archway, a vision in flowing green chiffon. She paused to polish her dark, designer glasses, her titian hair undulating over bare shoulders. "Beastly hot, isn't it, darlings?" She marched to Hildy with arm outstretched. "Our anniversary girl. Congratulations, Hildy." She pulled Hildy into a French embrace, spilling Hildy's wine. "Oh dear. Did that get on your frock? What a quaint frock it is. Have you been shopping with Marie?"

Hildy bristled and rushed to accept a hug from Peter. "Peter, dear. I'm so glad you came. And Dawn. I'd like you to meet Marie and Léon de Musset."

"*Enchanté de faire votre connaissance*." The Marquise adjusted the glasses on her nose.

"Speak *anglais*," her husband commanded, his eyes fixed on Dawn.

"Oh, I understand that," Dawn said. "And *au revoir*, of course."

Hildy took Peter's arm. "Peter is a motion picture producer. Isn't that exciting, Marie?"

"Actually, I may be filming here in La Roquette," said Peter.

"Here?" Léon's face lit up. "Ah, a filming will bring much money to our village."

"I have your Pimms for you, Victoria," Alex said, holding an opened bottle to pour her a goblet full, over ice.

"Anyone else for Pimms?" Hildy inquired. "I'm sure Alex has put in cases and cases to quench Lady Helmsley's thirst."

"It's such a hot day." Alex laughed dutifully.

"Scotch for me," Peter said, settling into a wooden lawn chair. "With a splash, if you please. No ice. And white wine for Dawn. Right, luv?"

Dawn nodded, perching on the arm of Peter's chair. She unbuttoned her black satin jumpsuit to reveal a gold lamé halter top. "I totally relate to midday *soirées*, don't you, Peter?" She bent her head, tightly wound in a beaded black scarf, to rest it against Peter's.

"A *soirée* is in the evening, luv." Peter gave her hand a reassuring squeeze.

Marie sidled to Victoria. "I'm so terribly sorry about your cat, Lady Helmsley. Such a tragedy." Hildy sensed Marie disapproved of her tenant's cat.

Victoria shrugged and lifted her Pimms to drink. "I've quite recovered, thank you. I'm afraid it was a ghoulish prank by some village person who resents your tenants' presence here. No matter. *Noblesse oblige.*"

Peter flinched as Dawn's bejeweled turban gouged his head. "Do mind your bangles, luv. They're quite lethal."

"Sorry, Peter." Dawn raised her head to gaze at the pool.

Peter accepted his scotch from Alex. "So, how about it, Alex, did you enjoy the races?"

Alex grinned. "The roar of the kerosene, the smell of the crowd! It was just great. And you?"

"I find the struggle for power those races perpetuate a grievous frivolity, Alex. Sorry."

Alex returned to the bar. "Fine with me, sport. Whatever turns you on."

Peter continued, "Although we did have one moment of convergence, unfortunately not bloody harmonious at all."

Dawn enthused, "One of the racers flipped over the wall into the sea!" Her meticulously accented eyes opened wide. "I expected the car to burst into flames."

"Good heavens, Dawn," Victoria said. "You sound positively disappointed."

"How awful!" Hildy turned to Alex. "You didn't tell me that."

"Why would I, for God's sake?" Alex asked.

"He didn't see it," Dawn said. "He and Vickie were off shopping when it happened."

"No one calls me 'Vickie,' Dawn. Absolutely no one," Victoria explained. "I would appreciate it if you would refrain from doing so."

"But why?" Hildy asked. "Vickie is quaint, don't you think so, Alex?" Hildy could scarcely believe she had said that.

The Marquis lit a cigarette. "The Grand Prix." He exhaled the smoke. "It has become an orgy of peasants throwing their money about. I regret to say, I find it incredibly decadent."

"*Ooh-lah-lah*," the Marquise protested, "But how many thousands of francs have you lost yourself on that stupid race, eh?"

"One day soon," Peter said, "we shall recognize that one need not compete for power; the power lies completely within ourselves. Right, old chap?" He looked at Alex.

"If you say so, champ. More wine, anyone?"

Hildy leaned over to whisper to Peter, "Have you read Shirley MacLaine? She talks about that."

Peter looked up at her, confiding, "Yes, I know. *Petros* obviously is another approach to the same idea."

Hildy was warmed by the shared insight.

"When you get right down to it," Peter addressed the group, "the Grand Prix is nothing more than a modern-day chariot race. They even wear helmets."

"But, darling, I loved Monaco," Dawn enthused. "It's so...I don't know..."

"It's hard for you to put into words, isn't it, Dawn?" Victoria said coldly. "One hopes you've kept clippings so you'll be able to communicate what you saw."

"Dawn prefers colored lights," Peter said, rising to allow Dawn the full use of the chair, since she tended to topple off the arm. "And Dawn especially likes to be around people. Appropriate for an actress, *non*? Someone to respond to her."

"Peter responds splendidly," Dawn smiled, staring directly at his crotch. "Am I going to be in this *Petros*, Peter?

How about your Mary Magdalene persona, or whatever you call it? She's so *neato*."

"You're too slim for a whore," Peter said. "But don't fret, luv. We'll find something. Maybe a townsperson."

"Whores can be slim," Hildy assured Dawn. "They come in all shapes and sizes." Her gaze rested on Victoria.

"So, you will shoot the film here, in our village?" the Marquis inquired, alert to possible business opportunities.

"I'm scouting pastoral settings here, yes." Peter acknowledged.

"Perhaps some of my properties you would find suitable, Monsieur Balfour?" He gestured toward the fields. "I have splendid pastures, and sheep rentals are possible."

Peter looked across the stone fence at the field. "Perhaps," he said. "Hildy, is that the shepherd's hut?"

The Marquis lowered his bushy eyebrows. "The shepherd hut also can be leased, should you desire. Naturally, I can make all of the official arrangements with the proper authorities in the village."

"I wonder if I might see the hut?" Peter replied. "Would we have time before our luncheon?"

The Marquis stepped forward. "I should be happy—"

"No, No, Léon," Hildy interrupted. "I will show it to Peter. Perhaps you can help Alex with the drinks." Peter stood up to offer Hildy his arm. "And Alex, why don't you tell Yvette we will serve the quiche in fifteen minutes." She put her arm through Peter's and led the way. "You'll find the hut a quite rewarding locale, I think, Peter. It's simply bursting with karma."

Chapter Seventeen

"Reeks of odd energies, doesn't it?" Peter stepped to the bull's-eye window inside the hut and forced it open.

Hildy sniffed the air. "I believe that's because it's kept closed up."

"Figuratively, I mean. You've heard of bad vibrations."

Hildy nodded. "I sense poor karma, if you want my opinion."

"Where is this Dupres, Hildy? He obviously has left his materials here."

"Didn't I tell you, Peter? André is dead. He died suddenly last year."

"How did I know that?" Peter looked thoughtful. "You didn't tell me the other day, but I knew the shepherd was dead when I entered this hut."

Hildy looked at him uneasily. "He was our housekeeper's brother. I'd have you meet her, but she's gone to Grenoble for the day."

"How did he die? It must have been tragic. He was a young man."

"Oh, I'm sure it was. A heart attack, I believe." Reflecting on Peter's odd comment, Hildy added, "I must tell you, Peter, I don't believe André just dropped dead."

"Really? What do you believe?"

Hildy shook her head. "I don't know. Something is being kept secret."

Peter grinned. "Or so the writer imagines, yes?"

"I suppose I may be looking for drama that isn't really there," Hildy admitted, "but I can't help it. He couldn't have been an ordinary shepherd."

Peter's eyes were on the stack of art boards. "These are the stained glass sketches?" He held the round mimosa sunburst sketch closer to the window. "You're quite right. This is extraordinary. Certainly not to be expected from a field hand."

"The colors vibrate," Hildy said. "It's uncomfortable to look at them. I've wondered whether he actually made a window from that sketch and where it might be. I found a funny sort of map in here." She wriggled the drawer of the table open, "along with this ugly pointed knife." She held it up.

"Probably used as a tool of some kind." Peter pushed the contents around, pausing to examine several of the colored glass shards against the light. "I can't begin to see how the man created stained glass pieces in this dismal light."

Hildy had taken the journal from her tote and unfolded the map. "See? These X's aren't at all precise."

Peter turned the creased paper over. "Do you suppose Dupres had contacts of some sort in these places, girlfriends, perhaps?" He smiled.

"Or marked where his windows are located?" She pointed to the X at the bottom. "That could be the one that broke in our villa. Or the one he restored at St-Paul-de-Vence. I saw it when I visited the cathedral there."

Peter scrutinized the writing. "Hard to imagine this child-ish scrawl is anything important, isn't it?"

Hildy replaced the map in her journal. "I'm quite certain Edmund, the yardman, made a copy of this map, Peter."

"Really? Why do you think that?"

Hildy recounted the incident of finding Edmund and her journal in the garden and her discovery of a page torn out.

"Is Edmund that simple-minded young man who's always playing with the hose? Who moves in that little jig-jig-step wherever he goes? Lord, I've wondered whether he was rowing with two oars, that one."

"I realize it hardly seems likely, but at the same time, I know he tore out that page. Why would he do that except to copy the map? Surely not to plagiarize my notes."

"Maybe he just needed a piece of paper."

"But why would he have my journal in the first place?"

Peter walked to a stack of sketches, flipping through them. "A bit of a mystery, what?" He looked back at Hildy. "Would that put Yvette in this web of intrigue as well, do you suppose?"

"His cousin and possibly that gypsy girl." Hildy sighed and stared up at the bull's-eye window above her eye-level. "Are you aware that Victoria is painting this Edmund person? I saw the canvas in her studio."

"Well," Peter said cheerfully, "It's her business after all, isn't it? I'm sure I've no place at all judging Lady Helmsley."

Hildy was reluctant to pursue the matter of Victoria's morals with Peter. "Victoria thinks of him as a 'tiller of the soil', a sort of man-of-the-earth or some such nonsense. But this gardener act could be a pose. He might be a foreign agent."

Peter clucked his tongue. "My dear girl, I really doubt he would have the necessary wit."

"I know I'm rather imaginative, Peter. Everyone tells me that." She looked off into space. "Sometimes it's a curse. On the other hand, it's probably why I feel compelled to write."

"Tell me more about your novel." Peter pulled out the chair and sat astride it, leaning on the back.

"Well, let me see. It's a romantic adventure about a peasant girl named Consuela and a stone cutter named Orlando. The third corner of the triangle is an unscrupulous opportunist I've called...Raven Princess. It's mere coincidence that my story involves an artisan like Dupres, but I've decided to use that. I'm picking up all sorts of ideas from my observations here—I don't mean just in this hut."

"Tell me about your observations, Hildy."

She considered her reply for a moment. "Well, take Victoria. She's a perfect prototype for my Raven Princess, I feel. Frankly, I sense a ruthless quality there. The Princess, of course, takes what she wants, without a qualm."

Peter grinned. "I couldn't disagree with that insight. With due respect to my hostess, Victoria can be quite the manipulative bitch when she decides to be."

Interesting that you see that too, Peter. The Raven Princess is not at all the type of woman you would trust—not for one minute." Hildy resisted saying more. "And I'm using that fool, Edmund as well. He makes a marvelous bandit."

"Wizard idea!" Peter rubbed his chin with one hand. "Your Raven Princess will not succeed in her scheme, one imagines."

"Oh, no. She won't win." Hildy thought a moment. "Actually, I've had this notion of killing off Diego—that's the Edmund persona-parallel," she smiled an acknowledgment of Peter's term, "but as I think of it now, I believe the Raven Princess will be the victim. Yes...perhaps gored at a *corrida*, since Spain is nearby."

Peter laughed. "Oh dear. Nothing too gruesome, I hope."

"I'll have to think about it, Peter," Hildy said. "I don't much care for bullfighting."

"And what is your novel's essential theme, Hildy?"

"The lust for gold," she replied simply, adding, "in today's metallic civilization."

"Interesting way to put it. Aren't we all enslaved by this 'metallic civilization,' as you call it?" He nodded slowly. "It's a time-honored kernel of universal truth you're dealing with,

Hildy. But utilizing your own canvas, of course. Excellent!"

"Do you really think so?" Bathed in the warmth of artistic recognition, Hildy busied herself pretending to neaten the stack of art boards. "And who will write your script, Peter?" She turned to stand with her hands clasped in front of her.

Peter smiled. "Lacking a modern day Matthew, Mark, Luke or John, I shall probably do the treatment myself." His eyes bored into hers. "But, as I explained the other day, the energy that fired those ancients still flows, and will forever, in the universe. I am in touch with it, Hildy. It flows through me. And you as well, my dear. In all of us, actually."

"Is the feeling heightened here, in this hut, do you think, Peter? I certainly feel as if I've crossed some sort of threshold in this place." Hildy stared at the circular sketch of the mimosa blossom. "It happened the other day when I tried to work here, and again today. But today it's a terribly positive thing_I'm feeling. Almost as if someone's arms are around me."

"That's wonderful," Peter said rising to his feet. "You were quite right. It's a place of intense mystical energy." He frowned. "I'm wondering if I'd be able to film here, actually."

"There isn't a whole lot of space."

"I don't mean that. You've surely heard the paranormal stories about photographs taken in some forbidden setting that come back all blurred from the processing lab? Or show things that weren't there?"

"Good heavens. No wonder I couldn't write here!"

They stepped outside the hut, and Hildy locked the door. "Do you think you might be willing to glance at my notes, Peter? When they're ready? I'm assembling them now—if you think you might like to see them."

"Of course. I should be honored. You have an extremely refreshing grasp of the creative process, Hildy. Undisciplined, but insightful. And that crucial eagerness—that compulsion—to write. It's clear you absorb—soak up everything."

"I suppose I'm quite obvious about it with my journal. I should be more clever."

"Mind your heels on the steps, Hildy."

"I'm so anxious for you to meet my Consuela. She might well be transposed to a Ruth persona-parallel. I may still have her raped in the Pyrenees, but by Diego, not Orlando. It's a bit complicated transposing all my Apaches into Spaniards."

She stopped, pointing to the field of lavender stretching toward Mougins. "I find that breathtaking, don't you, Peter? By the way, André's grave is just beyond that clump of oleander." She continued, "You see, Consuela's flaw is her negative approach to life, resulting in a sense of hopelessness."

"Nihilism is fascinating."

Hildy wasn't sure what the word meant. "I could see rocks fitting into her story, can't you, Peter? Metaphorically, of course, as obstacles."

"You can improve on that, Hildy. Remember the *Petros* that was rolled away to release the Christ spirit into the world."

Hildy took his arm and resumed walking back on the path. "I see what you mean. I'll think about that as I plunge ahead. The thing is, I expect the Pyrenees have loads of rocks."

"Do put your notes in order so I can look them over, Hildy."

"I'd be very grateful. I'm grateful to you already. Something wonderful is happening to me here in France." She paused. "Some terribly traumatic things, but some wonderful things with my writing. I shall absorb it all and piece the fragments together."

"Like stained glass?" asked Peter.

"I hadn't thought of that, Peter. Yes!"

He turned her face to him, holding her chin. "*On the earth, the broken arcs; in the heavens, a perfect round.*"

"Like a rose window. Was that Wordsworth?" Hildy asked.

"Browning." Peter was silent for a moment, then he said cheerfully, "I have a rather kinky notion for casting my Judas."

Hildy looked at him, waiting.

"I'm considering using a woman."

"Oh? I don't suppose she would be of Spanish extraction?"

Peter shook his head. "Sorry, no. I see her more as a Tammy Bakker. Would that not be rivetingly contemporary?"

"Brilliant! I would certainly be riveted." Hildy's thoughts churned. There was absolutely no reason Consuela could not be "born again," but with considerably less eye makeup.

Chapter Eighteen

"How lovely your table looks!" The Marquise fingered the sprig of mimosa Hildy had added at each place as a touch indigenous to the region.

Alex seated the guests at the outdoor table, as Hildy readied the presentation of her quiche in the kitchen. To her horror, she noticed a nearly empty wine bottle poorly concealed under a kitchen towel on the counter. Adding a cluster of parsley to the center of the dish, she told Yvette, "I'll help you with this. Nadia, it would be best if you serve the wine."

She steadied Yvette's elbow as the girl bore the steaming *quiche* to the table, to murmurs of admiration from all her guests. "*Voilà! Très bon.*" Hildy said, guiding Yvette's trembling placement of the platter. "And now, Yvette, *la salade, s'il vous plaît.*" Yvette reeled off, as Hildy dropped to her chair at the head of the table.

"Attention, please!" Alex rose with his wine glass. "To my beautiful wife, Hildy, on our anniversary!"

"Hear, hear!" Peter shouted. "A most remarkable lady, and an artist of shining promise!"

Dawn applauded, wine glass in hand, spilling on the Marquise. "Oh, sorry Marie."

Amid the clinking of glasses and wishes of congratulations, a cacophony of music sounded from the lane. Alex's glass stopped in mid-air. "Good God, what's that?"

"A parade of some sort?" Hildy suggested.

Edmund danced forward leading a band of four scruffy gypsies through the gate. One strummed a mandolin, another played a flute to the banging of a tambourine, while an elderly woman wailed what might be her notion of a haunting melody.

"That is possibly the most dreadful music I have ever heard," Victoria announced.

"I think it's festive!" Hildy smiled, her hand moving in time to the beat of the tambourine. "Wandering minstrels!"

Edmund bowed, stepping back with one arm raised to the musicians. "I arrange with Nadia to have them come make a serenade for you on your anniversary."

Dawn clapped her hands vigorously, first depositing her wine glass on the table.

"How very nice," Alex said. "Listen, Hildy. I think that's the 'Hawaiian Wedding Song.'"

"You might be right, old boy," Peter acknowledged.

Edmund nudged Alex, pantomiming a little dance with the bride-celebrant. "Oh, no, Edmund. I don't feel like dancing." Alex pulled his arm away.

"Oh, but I do!" Hildy leapt up. She twirled about, wistfully fantasizing Julie Andrews at the ball in *My Fair Lady*. She grabbed Alex, waltzing him awkwardly around the patio, curtseying elaborately at the end. She applauded the musicians.

"*Encore, Monsieur?*" Edmund held out his hand. "They have many songs."

"Here." Alex scowled, pulling some francs from his

pocket. "Tell them *merci* and to go away."

Edmund scampered to the gate, handing out francs. The gypsies faces were expressionless as they accepted the money and ambled away.

"Look there, Alex?" Hildy pointed to a figure in a black cloak who appeared from behind the wall to move off with the little gypsy band. "That's the man who's been following me! Do you see him, Alex?"

"How can you tell? These people all look alike. Maybe he's their road manager."

Returning to the table, Hildy was pleased to see that her guests were proceeding with their luncheon.

"The *quiche* is divine," cooed Victoria, "but then that's the one thing Yvette knows how to make."

"Yvette did not prepare the quiche," Hildy pointed out, staring at the Englishwoman. "I purchased and assembled the ingredients myself, with Marie's kindness in introducing me to the marketplace at Mouans Sartoux. This is Julia Child's personal recipe.

"*Magnifique!*" Marie said, touching a napkin to her lips.

"I just adore cheesy things," Dawn said.

The Marquis ground out his cigarette in the remainder of his salad as he drained his wine glass.

"More *vin*, anyone?" Alex said.

"Is this a local wine, Alex?" asked Peter. "It's nicely understated. Don't you agree, sir?" He addressed the Marquis.

"Ah, *oui*. We have excellent wines here. And in the Loire, too," the Marquis added, "where we have our fine, old castle. It could also be leased for your film, Monsieur."

Peter held up his glass to Nadia who had appeared from the kitchen with more wine. "I don't believe I'll have need of a castle, sir."

Nadia gracefully circled the table as she poured from two freshly opened bottles.

"Nadia!" Victoria cried, as she recognized the girl refilling her Pimms. "Is that you? What are you doing here?"

Nadia curled her lip insolently. "*Bonjour, Madame*. I

return to visit *mes amis* in La Roquette. "Madame is well?" She moved away to fill Alex's goblet.

"You know each other? I had no idea," Hildy said. "Marie and I saw Nadia the other morning at your house. We thought she was your guest."

Victoria watched the gypsy girl as she moved gracefully off to the kitchen. "She's no guest. I know her only remotely." She dabbed at her lips with a napkin. "Nadia used to live here. She posed for me once at my studio, stealing things from the villa when I wasn't looking. I should have had her arrested."

"I see." Hildy was jolted to have her misgivings about the gypsy girl confirmed.

Victoria smiled. "But tell us, Hildy, did you like the scarves Alex brought you from Monaco?"

Hildy took a sharp breath. "You were in on that, were you, Victoria? Yes, the scarves were lovely. Your choices were simply perfect."

"I picked those out, Hildy," Alex said quickly. "They're your favorite colors, remember?"

Hildy waved her fingers. "No matter. No matter at all."

Alex stood awkwardly. "Speaking of presents—" He sprinted across the courtyard and into the villa.

Dawn twirled her wine glass in her fingers. "It's no big deal that Vickie went shopping with Alex, Hildy. There was this darling shop right there in the hotel."

"Oh, you were all at the same hotel then?" Hildy's eyes were on Dawn.

"Of course," Dawn said. "We were together."

"Hildy," Victoria said, "*L'Ermitage* is the only place to stay in Monaco. One avoids the tourist traps."

Dawn leaned forward to address the group. "Did you see it on the *Rich and Famous*? Robin Leach says it's one of the top twenty."

Peter grunted. "Proper free-loader, that chap. Loves bathing in the pools of power."

Alex bustled back to the table with a package as Hildy lifted her glass. "Well, it's certainly nice to know you all shared a five-star experience." She looked pointedly at her husband. "Oh, yes. Including the hot tub." She drank the remainder of her wine. "I hope you've all left room for the *sorbet aux fraises*? You'll find it light but piquant." She called for Yvette.

Nadia hurried out for a whispered conference with Hildy. "Yvette, she is *malade*, Madame. She must go now."

Hildy heard the roar of the Vespa leaving the courtyard. "I'm sorry to report, Victoria, your servant has, I fear, become intoxicated and had to leave us. Nadia will serve our sorbet."

Alex thrust a small jeweler's box at his wife. "Happy Anniversary, darling." He bent to kiss her.

Hildy sat back, staring at the box a moment. Summoning what grace she could, she slipped off the ribbon and snapped open the hinged lid. There was nothing inside. "I don't understand this, Alex," she said.

Alex grabbed the box. "It's gone!" He knelt beside Hildy. "It was the crystal from the window. I had it set in a necklace for you in Monaco!"

Victoria rose and grasped her chairback. "But what could have happened to it, Alex? It was there when we left Monaco. I saw the jeweler wrap it."

There was an awkward silence as Hildy felt her guests' eyes on her. "And was it lovely, Victoria? Did you select the setting?"

Alex stood up. "This is awful, Hildy. It's not Victoria's fault. She went to the jeweler with me to translate, that's all. I picked it out. I wanted it to be the perfect—"

Hildy turned to Nadia who was bringing the dessert. "Just put it here, Nadia. I'll serve it. You have the large spoon? *Bon*." Her attention on the sorbet, she said, "Alex please sit down. I'm serving the dessert now."

Alex walked slowly to his place and sat miserably. "It was a gold setting with some filigree." His face suddenly flushed. "Edmund! God damn that bastard. I'm calling the police, Hildy. That sleaze bag's taken your crystal!"

Dawn looked stricken. "Or it could have been that gypsy.

You said she stole from you, Vickie. I'd search her right now if I were you. It's probably in her cleavage."

Alex started for the kitchen.

"Alex," Hildy said tightly. "I no longer give a damn about the stupid necklace, do you understand that? If you do find it, you can give it to Lady Helmsley." She lifted her chin as she rose and hastened toward the villa.

Dawn was suddenly on her feet bending across the table. "Vickie! What's wrong?"

Peter was on his feet as Victoria slumped sideways in her chair. "She's sick! I think she's fainted!"

Hildy turned back to the table. Marie rushed around it and put her head to Victoria's chest, listening. She dabbed at Victoria's lips where a dribble of liquid had appeared, calling to the Marquis. "*Le Docteur*! *Tout de suite*! Madame Helmsley is very ill!" She felt for a pulse. "I think she is very weak, Monsieur Bigelow."

"Help me get her into the Porsche, Peter," Alex ordered, lifting Victoria under her arms. "Where's the nearest hospital, Léon? In Cannes?"

The Marquis bobbed his head, helping the two men carry the inert form.

"Get in, Léon." commanded Alex. "You show us the way."

Hildy stood stunned, looking at the swirl of green chiffon heaped in the car.

Chapter Nineteen

As Hildy waited in the kitchen for her tea to brew the next morning, Lescaut bustled in with the obligatory *baguette* protruding from her net bag. *"Bonjour, Madame! Je suis lá!"*

Hildy sensed the housekeeper's high spirits were forced. *"Bonjour*, and how is your uncle?"

"Ah," Lescaut shrugged. "He rests well, *merci*. But what is this?" Her eyes were wide as she inspected the kitchen counters cluttered with unwashed dishes. *"Mon Dieu, Madame!"* Quickly she began scraping the leftover food into the garbage, scolding, "We will have rats!"

"I am so sorry, Madame Lescaut." Hildy's hand trembled as she poured tea from the teapot. "I simply could not cope with all this yesterday. I apologize."

Lescaut paused to stare at her mistress. "But what is

wrong? *Le déjeuner*, it was not wonderful?"

"You might call it a total disaster." Hildy attempted a smile, as she toyed with the Airline Guide she'd been looking at earlier. "I may change my plans to leave La Roquette, Madame Lescaut. Earlier than I'd expected. Something unexpected has come up." The stricken look on the housekeeper's face prompted Hildy to improvise. "*Le Monsieur* has…a virus. I opened the downstairs bedroom for him to sleep."

Lescaut trotted to the stove. "So? I make tea for him with honey. It is *l'influenza*?"

"No, it's not." Hildy straightened. "And he's not here. I don't know where he's gone." Hildy felt tears starting again, not believing there could be any left. "I'm sorry." She sat on the wooden kitchen stool and dabbed at her eyes with a paper napkin. "The luncheon was terrible. Yvette came to help with her gypsy friend, got drunk on wine and had to leave in the middle of everything."

"That one! A brainless child. I tell the Marquise she's no housekeeper." She asked, "This gypsy…?"

"Nadia is her name. She is visiting Yvette."

"Nadia!" The housekeeper's eyes blazed with recognition. "That gypsy devil! She is in La Roquette?" Lescaut banged down the can of scouring powder in her hand. "Ai! She, I blame for my brother's death! It is she who cause heart failure."

"André and this gypsy?" Hildy was aghast.

"An evil woman, this Nadia." She spat out the name. "But it is *fini* now. She will be destroyed as my brother was destroyed by her. May the devil take her to Hell!" She crossed herself, then took a step toward Hildy. "I am sorry I am not here for you, Madame. Never would I let this Nadia come near you."

"I don't blame you for any of this, Madame Lescaut. It couldn't be helped, any of it. Who could foresee Lady Helmsley would be stricken during lunch?"

"What is *stricken*? Something happens to her?"

"She got sick and fainted, passed out." Hildy illustrated by dropping her head sideways to her shoulder. "They took her to the hospital."

"*Mon Dieu!*" Lescaut halted her puttering. "*C'est dommage!*" It is no wonder Madame is upset." She wagged her head slowly. "But you must not leave here because of this. A luncheon only, it is, no?"

"No. It is more." Hildy struggled to explain. "*Le Monsieur*—my husband and I..." Hildy fought off a rush of emotion.

Lescaut tightened her hand on Hildy's shoulder. "*Un problème*? Ah, I think, yes. Something happen in Monaco, *peut-être*?" She shook her head and returned to put some dishes in the sink. She turned on the water. "Madame," she began, "I see them drive up from Monaco in Madame Helmsley's car, Monsieur Alex and this woman. I hear you shouting at him." She hesitated.

"I'm afraid I was rather upset. I'm not surprised you heard us."

"It is not my business, *vous comprenez* what I say now. This woman, she is not to trust. I see her with men before." She stopped to gaze out the window at the garden. "Yes, with André. And this jackass, Edmund." Lescaut turned back to Hildy. "*Toujours comme-ça!*" She pantomimed separating the top of her dress and thrusting her bosom out. "When a man is near. She must show herself, her..." Lescaut circled her own bosom.

"How perceptive you are, Madame Lescaut. Yes. You are right. In Monaco, there was *un liaison*." Hildy felt her control returning. "My husband is not, you see...he has always been..." She took a deep breath, "with *moi, comprenez vous*? Faithful."

"*Fidelement, non*?" Lescaut shot her a wry smile. "So, you poison the Englishwoman, eh?"

Hildy had to smile. "No, I did not poison her. Perhaps I should have, yes?" She sobered. "I really need to think about this. He may leave me for her. I don't know, but I will not wait for that."

"He will not leave you. You are a good, loving wife. This Englishwoman, she is..." Lescaut shrugged.

"*En Anglais*, a bitch." Hildy grew thoughtful. "Tell me something, Madame Lescaut. What happened to your husband?" Hildy saw surprise on Lescaut's face. "May I ask?"

Lescaut was silent a moment, then she turned to lean back against the counter. "I tell you this, because you must have a friend now. The Marquise, she does not know it. No one must know it." She considered a moment. "I have no husband, Madame. There was a man, Alain, we live as man and wife for nine years, when he was not at sea. We live in Marseilles, where he was merchant sailor. He never return one day. I wait. No Alain. No letter from him. His comrades tell me nothing." She turned away. "He find someone else, I think. In South America, Greece, or he is dead, perhaps. I do not know. I was left with…nothing."

Hildy went to put an arm around her, warmed by her admission.

Lescaut wagged her finger. "Do not let this *vache* steal your husband, Madame. Do not!"

The moment passed, and Hildy held herself erect. "Thank you, Madame Lescaut. You are a kind and understanding person." She looked at the Airline Guide in her hand, then picked up her tea and started for the door. "The final straw…"

"Final 'straw?'" Lescaut looked blank.

"To finish things, my piece of glass, from your brother's window," she paused at the archway. "My husband had it put in a pendant in Monaco for my anniversary. Someone stole it."

"Ah, the gypsy! She take the glass." Lescaut shook a finger at her mistress, "Did I not warn you? Never allow a gypsy in your house!"

Hildy nodded and wandered through the silence of the villa and out to the courtyard. The Porsche was still gone. She walked into the garden and looked at the disarray of the fateful lunch table, still strewn with glasses, half-full—except Victoria's, which lay on its side.

A sadness swept over her. Normally when she encountered cataclysmic circumstances, she dealt with them first in her journal, but this time, she had translated her distress into pages for her novel. In fact, she'd completed an entire chapter before falling asleep the night before.

She walked to a pool chaise where she could face the view of Grasse and sat gratefully. Taking a final sip of her tea, she opened the Airline Guide.

If she took the Concorde from Paris to JFK, she would arrive—could it be—before she left de Gaulle? Talk about expunging unpleasant times painlessly from one's life! What she really wished she could do was to leave today and arrive three weeks ago, before any of this had happened.

She looked down at her tote, resting at her feet like a faithful creature. She thought of the missing necklace she had never seen and smiled. Even if she did find the thief, she had no idea how to accuse him. She couldn't conjugate the irregular French verb "to steal."

Chapter Twenty

When Alex drove up, Hildy heard him first storm into the villa then, calling her name, burst out into the garden. "I need to speak to you, Hildy."

Hildy said nothing but blew on her sunglasses to clean them.

"I stopped down the hill to inquire about Victoria," he perched on the footrest of the chaise. "Peter says the doctor kept her overnight at the hospital after they pumped her stomach. She should be coming home this afternoon."

"I'm glad Victoria is better," said Hildy calmly. "Precisely what is wrong?"

"The doctor doesn't know exactly. He asked Peter if she was taking any kind of medication—whether she took drugs."

"Well, does she?"

"Peter says no. Whatever it was, the doctors say it was something she ingested immediately before passing out."

"You mean at my luncheon? Do they think it was the food I served, for heaven's sake?"

Alex shrugged. "They didn't say that, Hildy. Besides, none of the rest of us got sick."

Hildy offered a wry smile. "Madame Lescaut suggests somebody tried to poison her." She considered the possibilities. "Maybe Yvette? I'm only too aware the girl got herself bombed on wine in the kitchen. Maybe she laced Victoria's Pimms with something." She chuckled in spite of herself. "Or threw in a little Drano accidentally on purpose."

"Maybe we were just lucky—if it was a bacteria of some kind in the food."

"There's Nadia, of course. Lescaut blames her for her brother's heart attack. But I can't see what that has to do with poisoning Victoria. Of course, Victoria did say Nadia had once worked for her. I wouldn't wish that on anyone, but it's hardly a reason to murder her."

"Victoria said Nadia stole things from her."

"I'm afraid I believe very little of what that woman says. My Lord, if I'm right about the earring I spotted on Nadia, Edmund has been carrying on with her—as well as the *artiste* who has him pose naked in her damp little studio. Maybe Nadia discovered the nude sketch of her lover." She glared at Alex. "Sordid, isn't it Alex?" She turned her head away.

"At any rate," Alex sighed heavily, "Peter said it was a good thing we got her to the hospital. She'll recover."

"If anyone cares, whoever laced Miss Vickie's Pimms no doubt murdered her cat as well—the 'omen' Yvette hinted at that day we found Ariadne in the pool." She fanned herself with the Flight Guide. "It was an omen, all right."

"Peter's talking to the doctors about doing tests to identify whatever it was, if Victoria insists. She just wants to get the hell out of the hospital and forget the whole thing."

"How very stoic of Lady Helmsley."

"Of course, I reported the theft of the necklace at the local *gendarmerie.* That should stir things up."

"Really? I wouldn't bet on it."

"They have to do *something.* They can't just overlook a damned robbery! Besides, the two crimes could be connected."

"If they inquire, they'll discover a number of people knew Victoria drank Pimms." She looked archly at her husband. "Including you." Hildy sat back in the chaise. "Of course, except for stealing my own necklace, *I'm* the one with the best motive."

Alex gave her a laconic little smile. "Don't be silly, Hildy. They'll probably chalk the whole thing up to food poisoning—and blame the gypsies. That merry band of minstrels that showed up? Maybe one of them did it."

Hildy looked past the pool at the fields of lavender. "The fact is, I really don't care what you or the police think or do, one way or the other." She felt a wave of sadness sweep over her.

He picked up the Flight Guide. "What's this for?"

"It would seem quite evident. I am selecting my flight back home. If it's not a grave imposition, I'd appreciate a ride to Nice so I can catch a plane to Paris to pick up the Concorde. If that's inconvenient, I'll ask Marie to take me."

Alex grasped Hildy's arm. "Listen, darling. You're blowing this thing way out of proportion."

She pulled away. "While I'm in Paris, I shall, of course, visit the Louvre, so I'm not exactly sure when I'll leave for home. God knows, I'm not leaving France without at least one of my plans working out properly. You can remain here and nurse Victoria back to health."

"Hildy, please. I've been to Cannes to talk to International Villa *Vacances,* that half-wit agency that rented us this dump. Do you know what I told them?"

Hildy slid forward on the chaise, dislodging Alex. "No, Alex. What ever did you tell them?"

Alex stood with his hands on his hips. "I told them somebody had robbed us! And that this creep, Edmund, was milking us for everything he could get, and doing nothing to earn a dime."

Hildy was silent, waiting for him to finish.

"And I told them about Victoria."

"Did you now?" said Hildy, matter-of-factly.

"About the food poisoning, or whatever." Alex's voice was thick and unsteady.

"But not about sleeping with her in Monaco." Hildy's heart pounded with rage.

"How many times do I have to explain what happened, Hildy?" He glowered at her, then turned away. "You know what those fools at the agency did? They shrugged their shoulders. Like 'what else is new?' Can you believe that?"

"A typical attitude, I suspect. I'm apparently the only person in France who regards adultery as an outrage. Poor, naïve Hildy! Until now, I've been silly enough to trust you, Alex."

Alex went on doggedly. "I made it quite clear to the rental agency that this allegedly restful sojourn in the countryside was like vacationing in the third-world, complete with terrorists. I told them we'd never come back, nor would we recommend it to *anyone*!"

"Bully for you. You certainly told them off." She struggled to her feet. "I'll be leaving by Friday at the latest, Alex." Stiffly she made her way back into the villa.

Alex bolted after her. "Hildy! Give me a chance."

"What more is there to say about it, Alex? You slept with the bitch. Period. *Fini*."

He grabbed her arm. "All right! I slept with her!" His face suffused a bright pink. "It meant nothing. Nothing! Not a thing, darling. I was just being…," he attempted his continental smile, "European."

"Of course you were, Alex. When in Rome…" She shook off his arm. "Do you know how awfully trite that is?"

Alex sagged. "God, Hildy. You, of all people, ought to understand the fantasy of finding yourself in a place like Monaco, surrounded by glitz—nothing real…"

"And you were swept away by it, is that the idea? You forgot to mention an attractive younger woman throwing her bosom at you, getting drunk with you on Bombay Gin. Sharing a brandy in a hot tub! All terribly European and terribly tawdry. Frankly, I find it disgusting."

Alex made a move toward her and stopped. "Darling, please. How can I make you see I'm sorry? I wish it hadn't happened. I'll do anything."

"I'm sorry, Alex. It's not that easy to patch up a relationship of trust, thirty-five years worth, and of commitment. Not in Europe, not anywhere." She paused at the stairs to call out, "Madame Lescaut, might I have some tea whilst I do my packing, *s'il vous plaît?*" She turned to Alex, "If you'll *excusez-moi.*"

But in the bedroom, the feeling of finality brought on another flush of despair. She could not bring herself to summon Edmund to fetch her suitcases from the basement. The transition she faced now required acceptance of this crushing interlude in the south of France as an unavoidable stepping stone to her glorious future, a fresh page to be written. She sank to the bed. All she'd managed so far was the page about getting on a jet plane that arrived before it left. Did Peter Balfour's notion of the life-script allow for pages that made no sense?

The souped-up whirring of Edmund's pickup blasted her reverie. It was followed by Edmund's heated shouts from the courtyard. *"Madame! Monsieur! Venez-ici!"*

Hildy groaned and raised herself with an effort to trudge down the stairs and out the door. Alex stood already poised for a confrontation with the yardman. Edmund ignored him as he pulled a protesting Nadia from the cab of the truck.

"What's wrong now?" Hildy's heart sank at the prospect of yet another mad episode with the lunatic yardman.

"Nadia, she try to poison Madame Helmsley!" Edmund shoved the girl forward, as the wild-eyed Nadia turned to spit in Edmund's face.

"Oh, lovely," Hildy breathed, averting her eyes.

"You gypsy bitch!" Alex screamed. "Where is my necklace?"

"Yvette, she tell me everything, Monsieur." Edmund motioned to the cowering Yvette peering from behind the truck. "*Dîtes-vous*, Yvette! Tell them!"

Yvette trembled, convulsed with sobs and began spewing a stream of indecipherable French.

"For God's sake, Edmund. Do you expect us to understand that garbage?" Alex demanded. "What the hell is she saying?"

"Yvette, she saw Nadia grind up leaves of the oleander from the garden. It is poison to eat oleander. She make a potion on the stove, crushing the leaves, and she put it in Madame Helmsley's wine."

"You saw her do this, Yvette?" Hildy asked. Yvette bobbed her head, then turned away. "I don't wonder you're ashamed, Yvette—getting *swozzled* in my kitchen!"

"She doesn't understand a word you're saying, Hildy," Alex pointed out.

"Who cares?" Hildy said sharply. "For once I'll get no alibis! She does at least regret what happened."

Alex burst out, "And you think I don't?" He looked pained.

Lescaut strode heavily from the foyer of the villa to face Nadia. "Gypsy devil!" she snarled.

Nadia lurched sideways, struggling to wrench herself from Edmund's grasp. "Be still, *stupide*!" Edmund whirled her around. "I bring you for honest work and instead you try to poison Madame's guest!"

"Look who's talking about 'honesty,' eh?" Hildy said. "You're really something, Edmund."

"But she…" Edmund sputtered.

"That settles it, folks," Alex cut in. "Wait right here, everybody. I'm calling the *gendarmes*!" He stormed into the villa.

"No no!" Nadia screamed, pounding on Edmund. "Yvette—she was drunk. She lies!"

Edmund slapped the gypsy girl hard.

"Edmund! Stop that," Hildy commanded. "Do you hear

me? Now tell me why would Nadia do such a thing. I fail to understand any of this."

Edmund began a broken explanation. "She wishes revenge on Madame Helmsley. Nadia and the shepherd, Dupres, they were lovers." Edmund's unpleasant leer dramatized this revelation.

"I see." Hildy nodded thoughtfully. Lescaut had implied as much. "What's it got to do with poisoning Madame Helmsley?"

"Madame Helmsley and the shepherd," Edmund went on, "he come to her studio where she teach him to make the stained glass. She gives him books. She gives him tools." Edmund broke into a lascivious grin. "But that is not all she gives him. *Comprenez-vous,* Madame Bigelow?"

Hildy recoiled. "That hardly surprises me. Dupres and this 'painter' down the lane were lovers. Is that all?"

Edmund put up a finger to punctuate his words. "She go also to André's hut, in the field, to give the, ah, lessons, no? Soon André tells Nadia he no longer loves her. He is in love now with Madame Helmsley, yes?"

Lescaut gave Nadia a venomous look. "It was this gypsy's jealousy that makes my brother to die! His heart, it cannot bear the rage and curses of this gypsy devil, crazy in the head, screaming at him. 'Animal,' she calls André. She claws his face. I saw the marks!" Lescaut's face streamed tears as she pointed at the gypsy. "There is your animal!"

Hildy tried to picture the peasant shepherd she had imagined, romping in the hay field with Victoria. She squeezed her eyes shut against the depravity of it, then found her mind racing to a vision of Alex rushing into Victoria's arms, billowing yards of pastel chiffon into the winds. She shook her head. Her fantasy had turned into a Clairol commercial.

"Madame Bigelow," Edmund persisted. "It is Nadia who steals your necklace."

Nadia's face contorted with hatred. "Liar! Liar!"

As Alex stepped back to the courtyard, Hildy turned away feeling utterly depressed. "Tell *le Monsieur* what you have said, Edmund. About the necklace, and about our *artiste* down the lane."

"I heard what you said about the necklace," Alex told Edmund, "and I can assure all of you, the police are on their way." He advanced on Nadia. "When the police come, you will cough up that necklace, and if there is any justice in this stupid country, you will then go to prison."

Nadia dropped to her knees to wail at Alex's feet, Alex fighting to wrench her hands free from his legs. His calm suddenly evaporated. "Jesus! Where are the *gendarmes*? Let go of my legs, woman!"

Edmund pulled Nadia away from Alex and held her, wrapped in both his arms. She continued to shriek.

Alex rearranged his disheveled clothing and began to pace, his movements awkward. "Let me have your attention, please, all of you gathered in this courtyard. I've had it with this place. This rotten villa with its lousy furniture—not a decent chair in the place—and a shower that barely even gets you wet. Trees crashing through windows, mosquitoes feasting on you while you sleep! This garden which belongs in deepest Africa!" He advanced menacingly on Edmund, "And that pool—that sewer out there..." Edmund drew back, raising his arms defensively.

Seizing the moment, Nadia wrenched herself free and hurtled through the gate, Edmund charging after her. "*Arrêtez! Arrêtez!*" he screamed. Yvette sank to the cobblestones, weeping.

Alex's shoulders sagged in exasperation. "I give up. Let's bag this place, Hildy. Do you hear me? We're leaving."

"No, Alex." Hildy backed away as Alex tried to hold her. "While I could not agree with you more, I did not select this charming mecca of cultural enrichment, and though I've tried to make adjustments, your fairy tale French villa is a chamber of horrors." She swallowed hard. "Furthermore, there have been almost no amenities, little joy, and irreparable damage to my international good will. From now on, Alex, keep your surprises to yourself!"

Chapter Twenty-One

Hildy sat at the typewriter in the tiny alcove of the bedroom hurrying to finish the revised outline she would give Peter before she left for Paris. She reveled in the glorious feeling of control it gave her to gather the story into her grasp. And for the first time, she believed it could be good.

Alex came pounding up the stairs. "Marie wants to talk to you on the phone, Hildy."

Hildy banged the carriage return to the final paragraph. "Oh, dear! I really have no wish to talk to her just now." She pushed herself up from the chair. "But I suppose I must. What have you told them?"

"I haven't given them any details. Just that we're leaving and I have to see Léon to discuss terminating our lease."

Hildy picked up the telephone. "Marie. How are you, dear?"

"Ah, Hildy. I am devastated that you must leave. But you will still come to Beaulieu on your way to Paris, yes?"

"You're at the castle now?"

"*Oui*. We make ready for our summer here."

Hildy clutched the mouthpiece of the phone, desperately thinking. "I do so want to see it, Marie. I haven't really thought about it in all the confusion these past few days."

"You must plan on it. I insist. Alex and Léon will make their arrangements, and I will show you my wonderful castle."

Hildy shifted the phone to her other ear. "We'll let you know Marie. Will that be all right? Thank you so much." She held the receiver away from her. "Alex? Are you there? Please pick up."

When Alex appeared in the doorway a few moments later, she rolled the last page of her outline from her typewriter. Collecting the others with it, she stacked them together as she'd seen Angela Lansbury do every week on *Murder She Wrote*. She found herself humming the show theme.

Alex lounged against the door jamb. "What do you think, Hildy? I'm going to the castle anyway to meet with Léon. You might as well come with me."

Hildy stood to stretch, then taking her lavender pen, she carefully composed a note to Peter. She clipped it to her pages and slipped them into a fresh manila envelope. "I hadn't given it a thought frankly, Alex," she said finally. "I suppose the de Mussets were only too glad to escape to their castle after my luncheon fiasco."

Alex took a step into the room. "How about it? You want to see the castle, don't you?"

Hildy walked to the window and stared down into the lane. A few villagers ambled by with their baskets. She could see the tiny smudge of the Mediterranean through the pink roofs on the hillside. "I could rent a car in Paris and drive down myself, I suppose," she said thoughtfully.

"Come on, Hildy. That's stupid. Why fly to Paris and rent a car?"

Hildy's mind reeled at the thought of arranging a car and

attempting to drive in Paris. She hadn't the first idea how to rent a car, and the legendary Paris traffic…"You're right, Alex. It makes no sense at all."

Alex said, "Good," and squeezed her arms lightly, then sat on the bed to spread out the Michelin map.

She examined her hair in the mirror, pulling her fingers through the straggling dove-gray clumps. "Lord, I've got to do something about this."

"It'll be a nice drive. We could take our time and visit the wine regions on our way."

Hildy bristled. "I'm trying my best to be civilized about what's gone on here, Alex, but please bear in mind I am not interested in touring anything—anywhere—with you." She picked up the *Elle* magazine she'd bought in the village and thumbed through it, looking for a hairstyle. "I've wanted to visit the castle, as you well know, since I first heard about it. If nothing else, I will gather texture to enrich the stories I tell little Tim when I get home. Unlike his grandmother, Tim still believes fairy tales can come true."

Alex continued to study the map. "We could stop overnight in Beaune. There's an inn there near a huge underground wine cellar."

"I don't care a bit about exploring wine cellars, Alex. But if we must spend the night somewhere en route, please request twin beds." Hildy sat on the desk chair. "You will concede, I imagine, that our fairy tale adventure has come to a less than happy ending?"

"Well, Victoria did get the poisoned apple."

Hildy did not smile. "But not before she'd already bedded the handsome prince, unfortunately." She stood up and studied the magazine cover, finally tearing it off to fold it into her tote. "What news of the fallen damsel down the lane, by the way, not that I give a damn?"

"Edmund told Lescaut she's up and about. Recovered, I guess. He also reports Nadia is gone. Disappeared, probably back in Spain." He scowled. "With your necklace, no doubt. Talk about a fiasco."

"I've totally put it out of my mind. I suggest you do the same." She replaced the cover on her typewriter, snapping it shut. "I shall go with you to Beaulieu, Alex, but only because it suits my plans. You may cancel my flight from Nice, *s'il vous plaît* and notify the de Mussets we'll be coming. I'd like to leave tomorrow." Hildy picked up her tote. "I'm going to the village now to be coiffed."

"Terrific! I'll drop you off."

"Thank you, I prefer to walk."

He went toward her, standing at a cautious distance. "I'm really glad you're coming with me, Hildy." He looked at her earnestly. "Listen, you wouldn't consider a side trip to the invasion beaches at Normandy, I don't suppose?"

"No, I wouldn't. Not remotely. Hit any beach you care to, Alex, my love. I plan to fly home from Paris after I see the castle and complete my schedule for touring the Louvre, Notre Dame, the Tuilleries and possibly Montmartre. I'll appreciate your putting me on the Concorde when I finish Sunday or Monday next week."

Alex stared at the floor. "Whatever you say."

Hildy gave him a cold smile and handed him the manila envelope. "If you'd be good enough to walk down the hill and give this to Peter, I'd be grateful. Needless to say, I have no stomach for encountering your paramour again."

"For God's sake, Hildy, give me a break." He reached out and clutched her hand.

"I plan to, Alex." She disengaged his grasp. "An extended one." She stalked out of the room.

Strolling down the country lane to the village, Hildy looked forward to Peter's reaction to her outline and the chapters she'd done. Thank God for her writing. No matter what happened, she would have that. Her immediate concern, however, was transforming her Miss Marple look into a chic Yvette Mimieux, or at least Angela Lansbury.

She questioned whether she had selected the most likely place for this miraculous conversion when the only beauty shop she found turned out to be a shuttered hole in the wall, bordering the square. Sassoon need not feel threatened, she judged.

"*Bonjour, Madame!*" A pert peroxide blonde atop platform wedgies flung open the shutters, toppling a geranium pot from the ledge to the cobblestones.

Had the girl seen her coming and hastened to greet her first customer of the day? Of the year? Hildy retrieved the messy pot, handing it to the young woman. "*Bonjour, Mademoiselle. Je besoin de…*"

"*Entrez!*" said the girl, ushering Hildy in with a grip of steel. She politely plucked at Hildy's hair, demonstrating that she indeed knew what Hildy had need of. "Ah, *bon.* I make the hair *très belle!*"

Hildy fended off the girl's fluttering hands to observe with apprehension the primitive one-chair salon. An electric-wire permanent machine stood in the corner beside a rusted metal dryer. Hildy immediately deleted Yvette Mimieux from her fantasy, followed by Lansbury. With a little luck, she might emerge a slightly more presentable Miss Marple.

Hildy mustered a weak smile as the girl beckoned her to the solitary chair and adroitly draped a discolored plastic cloth about Hildy's shoulders.

"I like your frock," Hildy ventured, unable to think of the precise French for acknowledging the off-the-shoulder leopard print wraparound.

"*Merci*," the girl beamed. "*Je m'appelle Renée.*" Assuming a receptive stance, she awaited further instructions.

Hildy's palms sweat as she flipped through her phrase book to "Ladies Hairdressing," but found no mention of layers. "Would you *couper* my hair in layers?" Hildy asked. She lifted sections of her hair and pantomimed delicate snips in the air with an imaginary pair of scissors.

Hildy grabbed the *Elle* magazine cover from her tote and pointed to the model's tapered tresses, fringed with bangs.

"*Ah, oui! Comme-ci,*" the girl breathed reverently and removed a razor from the drawer.

Hildy stiffened. "Just *un peu*, please." She prayed she'd conveyed her point.

Towering atop her wedgies, the girl hummed softly to herself as she whacked away most of Hildy's hair below her ears.

"Please leave enough to use rollers," Hildy said, fighting her panic. She struggled to pantomime rollers with her hands trapped under the plastic.

Renée nodded and mumbled soothing French as she dramatically tossed an especially large hunk of Hildy's hair into the air.

Hildy watched it float to her lap. "Oh dear," she moaned, closing her eyes against the desecration. She'd be lucky to have enough hair left for pincurls.

The shearing completed, Renée reached for an unlabeled bottle and massaged it into Hildy's hair. Hildy hoped it was some sort of water soluble gel, or, please God, something removable.

"You are *fini maintenant*?" Hildy asked, attempting to break free of the girl's eager fingers.

"*Voilà!*" Renée spun her around to face the three-way mirror framed with gilded sconces. "*Très belle, oui*?" She held a hand mirror for Hildy to inspect the back of what remained of her hair.

Joan of Arc, Hildy thought. Before she was burned at the stake. She touched her hair. It had looked good on Ingrid Bergman. "*Bon*," she lied, anxious to depart.

Suddenly Hildy froze. "Good Lord!" Reflected in the mirror, she saw Yvette leaving the *épicerie* across the street. Hobbling along behind her was the gypsy with the black cloak. "I must go," she said, stripping off the plastic cover-up. She jumped up and grabbed her tote from the counter. "*Merci beaucoup*," she said, paying the startled Renée.

"Yvette! Yvette!," Hildy called as she fled across the cobblestones.

A guilty look seized Yvette's features.

"What are you doing here?" Hildy demanded.

"Ah, Madame. I shop for Madame Helmsley. Something is wrong?"

The cloaked figure had stopped and stared ahead, leaning on a cane, motionless.

Hildy took the girl's arm. "Yvette, please. Who is this person?"

The figure turned a withered face to Hildy and scowled at her.

Hildy gasped. It was the old woman they had encountered that first day when Alex ran over her chicken. Dear God! Was this witch some kind of insane gypsy avenger?

Yvette's eyes lowered. "She is my *grand-mère*, Madame."

"Your Grandmother! I don't understand. She has been following me for days now. Weeks. Why? What does she want?"

Yvette shrugged. "She is very old. I do not know what she do." She offered a sad smile. "Edmund and I, we take care of her, but we cannot be always with her."

Hildy felt anger sweeping through her. "What are you telling me? This old woman skulks around our villa looking in our windows, follows me to St-Paul-de-Vence, tries to steal my tote in the church!"

"No, no, Madame. You are mistaken. She is not evil." Yvette sighed with a helpless look at the crone in the cape. "Edmund and I, we give her diversion. We tell her she must follow the new strangers in our villa to see there is no trouble." Her eyes misted. "What can an old woman do in this village to be of use? *Ma grand-mère* is 84 years old! She thinks she is important because she must spy on you. She means no harm."

Hildy could hardly believe what she was hearing. This threat that had so terrified her, no more than a silly diversion to keep the old woman busy? "You let her travel alone? *She* is the one who needs to be watched!"

Yvette shook her head. "No, she is known everywhere. I send her to St. Paul many times. She follow the nuns in the streets, go to the church to pray. She believe it is good. She has importance, no?"

The old woman's eyes suddenly blazed. "You kill my *poulet*!" She raised a fist and spewed a tirade in French.

Yvette soothed her, stroking her twitching hand. "She does not trust *les étrangères*. I am sorry." She inclined her head to inquire, "You kill her chicken, no?"

"Yes, but it was an accident for heaven's sake. We gave her *beaucoup* francs to pay for it. We were very sorry. I told her that day in the square. Good Lord, we don't go around killing old women's chickens on purpose. Are you all crazy?"

Yvette spoke to her grandmother in frantic French, trying to calm her, but the old woman cackled on, spittle spraying from her cracked lips. With a final angry gesture toward Hildy, she hobbled away and disappeared into a doorway, her ranting mingled with a dog's incessant barking.

Hildy sighed with relief, then turned on Yvette. "I will tell you, young woman, I am not at all convinced that the conspiracy you and your cousin Edmund concocted to have that woman follow us was out of kindness for her—or as harmless as you wish me to believe." Hildy could see by Yvette's face that almost none of what she said had registered.

Yvette cringed from Hildy's reprimand. Quickly she moved across the square, finally breaking into a frightened trot.

Hildy stood watching her, wondering how much of what she had been told was true. The lies were incessant, she concluded. They flourished as abundantly as the flowers that choked her garden.

She held herself erect, feeling around inside her tote to determine that her valuables were still intact, then touched her hair lightly. Lord, it was short! She drew a breath and started across the square, imagining she was Ingrid Bergman as Joan—no. She revised that. Ingrid as Maria in *For Whom The Bell Tolls.*

Chapter Twenty-Two

On the morning of their departure, Hildy wandered for the last time through the garden. She inhaled, wishing she could bottle the sweet smell of jasmine to remind her of the beauty of this fresh summer morning, a kind she would never know in arid Arizona.

"*Bonjour*!" called Peter, stepping around the corner from the courtyard. He handed her an envelope. "I wanted to return these pages to you before you toddle off, Hildy."

"Oh, Peter, I hoped I'd see you before I go." Taking the envelope, she motioned toward the lounges near the pool. "Can you sit a moment? I'm so anxious to hear your comments on my material."

"Just for a sec, I'm afraid. We're off to Champigny-sur-Veude ourselves. Victoria insists I see St. Chapelle."

"Wonderful. Michelin says it has some stunning examples of Renaissance stained glass. The purplish blues with their bronze highlights are said to be beyond compare."

"Pity you can't arrange to see it, luv."

"Unfortunately, I can't. I must get on to Paris."

"Away from here, you mean." He gave her a sympathetic look. "I shall pay special attention to the stained glass, in any case, Hildy. Let me say, you really did open my eyes to its mystic qualities…the idea of energy transformed into colored light. I quite like that concept. In your case, of course, the energy is transformed into words."

Hildy felt pleased. "Well," she tried to say it modestly, "my poetry professor, Bernie, did say I was a word painter, though he suggested I needed a larger canvas for my strokes than poetry affords."

"Which leads me to your material, Hildy." Peter perched on the arm of the lounge. "I did find your pages stimulating. Bloody lot of action, isn't there?"

"It just seemed to flow, once I located my writer's voice." Hildy pulled a chair up to the umbrella table, uncapping the lavender pen to make notes.

"You have this remarkable ability to transpose what you experience into a larger-than-life panorama of incidents. Of course I recognize some of your characters—you've confessed to a bit of *roman à clef*, haven't you. But still, my dear lady, I simply loved what I read. It is an absolute proper romp—the best word I can think of for it. Outrageous, unlikely, bloody wild! It would make a simply marvelous vehicle for someone like Tracey Ullman—or Bette Midler."

Hildy was stunned. "A romp, do you think?" She thought about that. "Well, of course it's meant to be fun."

"Oh, it is, Hildy. It's wizard fun. Sort of in the style of James Bond, do you know? Serious, but great fun! My only criticism really is that you could relax a bit more with it. I mean, you've succeeded admirably in torpedoing man's lust for gold. But totally, I love it!"

She reveled in his words. "Isn't that funny. All my instructors have told me I write too outrageously. And you're saying, it's fun." She stood to hug him tightly. "Oh, Peter, I can't tell you what this means. I think I've been set free!"

"I must tell you, dear Hildy, the freedom of your spirit has quite infected me. There's truth in the craziness of your ideas, do you realize that?"

Hildy sank into her chair. "Really?" She fanned herself with her journal. "I like to think the outrageousness of life is archetypal in its way."

"Quite so. I must also tell you, your stained glass idea has put me in mind of fragmentation in a thematic sense for my film, *Petros*."

"Has it?" Hildy was unable to grasp a connection.

"*Petros* stone, don't you see, fragments glass. Yet glass itself is a kind of stone. I haven't got it quite worked out yet in my mind, but you see where I'm going with it."

"I'm trying to."

"You don't mind my toying with the idea, then?" Peter rose and started for the gate. "You really did inspire it."

"Heavens, I don't mind at all." Hildy trailed along beside him. "I feel flattered I may have contributed to your film in some way."

"Where will you be staying in Paris, luv?"

"I'll be at the George *Cinq* on Sunday. I've requested a view of the Eiffel Tower."

"That should prove elevating." He chuckled and kissed her lightly on the cheek.

"How droll of you, Peter."

"I couldn't resist it. Sorry. But I'm ever so grateful to you for your input, old girl. And I shall certainly see your name appears somewhere among the credits."

"You will? How exciting!" Hildy had never considered the possibility of her name appearing this soon on the silver screen.

"And I love the way you plan to dispose of Princess Raven!—having Orlando's sculpture fall on her when her pet jaguar attacks!" He chuckled. "But you might want to reconsider naming the animal *Ariadne*. Not an awfully good name for the jaguar, do you think?" He looked at her meaningfully. "And, of course, that was the name of Victoria's poor, drowned cat."

Half an hour later, Hildy took a last look at the *séjour*, decorated in its drab, jaundiced yellow. Was it her imagination, or did the ornamental devil guarding the hearth look smug?

"Madame is ready?" Lescaut appeared beside her at the doorway. "You must not worry about things *désagréable*, *non*?" She handed Hildy a thin box about five inches square and carefully removed the lid. "I give this little *fleur de lis* to you." Her eyes misted. "My brother, André, has made it last year." The housekeeper pressed the shining glass medallion into Hildy's hand.

"Madame Lescaut, I am overwhelmed!"

"You will give it to your grandson in America. A gift from Madame Lescaut and her brother, you will say."

"Hildy gave the housekeeper a hug. "Oh, I do thank you *beaucoup*."

Lescaut replaced the medallion in the box. "André, he would be happy." She wiped her eyes, then kissed Hildy on each cheek.

"I have something for you too, Madame." Hildy removed a tissue parcel from her tote. "For all your assistance."

Lescaut's face flushed as Hildy handed her the parcel. "Madame…"

"Open it," Hildy said eagerly.

Slowly Lescaut unwrapped the yellow frock Hildy had purchased at the flea market for Charlotte.

"Ah! *La même couleur* like the mimosa blossom!" Lescaut wiped her hands on her apron and lifted the dress by its straps. "*Merci, Madame*." Her face suddenly clouded. "*Mon Dieu*, I forget the picnic basket!" She clutched the gift and wrappings to her and dashed back inside the villa.

As Hildy approached the Porsche, Edmund looked out from under the hood where he was strenuously wiping off the engine block. He stood erect, stationing himself beside the car.

"All is ready *pour le Monsieur, Madame*."

"I gravely doubt it," Hildy murmured, placing her tote on the front seat. She noticed Edmund had donned a clean T-shirt, no doubt in anticipation of a generous tip from Alex.

Suddenly a police car rolled into the courtyard, and a plain-clothesman emerged carrying a notebook. "*Bonjour, Madame.* I come to speak with your husband. I am Jean Pascal, Inspector, Sûreté." He shook Hildy's hand.

"What's all this?" Alex tugged his hanging Hartmann over his shoulder. "Edmund, get the rest of our bags. *Maintenant!*"

Edmund slammed down the hood and scampered off.

The Inspector extended his hand to Alex. "As you know, we have been unable to apprehend the gypsy girl. We continue the search throughout the province, but we believe she has returned to Spain." He smoothed his pencil-moustache. "The necklace, it was a mere costume piece, *non?*"

"Of course, and the setting cost a mere two hundred dollars." Alex threw his bag into the trunk of the car. "And the poisoning, a mere attempted murder. But, naturally, such things happen here in your quaint provincial village at the drop of an oleander leaf, *non?*"

"I do not quite understand you, Monsieur." Pascal wore a bewildered smile.

"Alex, please," Hildy climbed into the car. "That's enough. Let's just leave. We've had enough scenes."

"If we find the necklace, we call the Marquis at once, *oui?*" Pascal backed to his car, tripping over Edmund's hose. "We are sorry for your misfortune, Monsieur." He got in and started the engine.

"Think nothing of it," Alex said. I still have my camera and my American Express Card."

Edmund trudged back into the courtyard with a suitcase in each hand, as the Inspector barreled off. "*Très* heavy," he panted. Without waiting to be told, he wedged the luggage into the trunk. Then, removing his beret, he strutted to Alex, handing him a scrap of paper. "Monsieur, you examine my bill, yes?"

Alex snatched it away and looked at it briefly. "Just one total figure, eh, Edmund? Nothing itemized?" He thrust it back in Edmund's hand. "Do you seriously think I'm going to pay this figure you pulled out of thin air?"

Edmund cowered. "It take many dollars to make villa nice, Monsieur."

Alex flung open the car door. "So true, Edmund. But you did *not* make the villa nice, *comprenez-vous*? Quite the contrary, your services have been terrible. I shall arrange with Monsieur de Musset to compensate you for whatever legitimate expenses we owe. Now, kindly step aside."

Edmund skittered backward to open the hood. "Look! I clean your engine perfect, Monsieur, like new!" He crouched to resume wiping vigorously.

"Get away from the car." Alex pulled Edmund away and slammed the hood shut.

"Just pay him something and let's go," Hildy pleaded.

Lescaut hurried out with a picnic basket and carefully arranged it on the floor of the back seat.

"*Merci, Madame.*" Alex said, his tone mellowing. He slipped a fat envelope into her apron pocket and gave her a tiny peck on the cheek.

Edmund clambered over the windshield with his rag, desperately polishing the spotless glass. "I must still check your tires, Monsieur. To be very safe for you."

"For God's sake, knock it off, Edmund! You will receive your legitimate wage, and not one lousy franc more." Alex climbed into the driver's seat and slammed the door. "Just get away!"

Edmund crumpled, then as Alex maneuvered the car out of the courtyard, chased after it, pounding on the trunk. "Monsieur! Monsieur! I take good care of your car! I wash it many times!" Edmund stopped, then raced into the outbuilding beside the courtyard.

"*Bon voyage, madame,*" Lescaut called from the courtyard, a rare smile spread on her face.

"*Au revoir!*" Hildy waved.

"I cannot believe that fool, Edmund," Alex marveled, shaking his head. "He actually expected…"

"Good heavens, Alex! Edmund's got an axe!" Hildy grabbed at the steering wheel, as Alex glanced quickly in the rear view mirror.

He accelerated. "We're not staying around to deal with that maniac—"

Hildy gasped. "My God! He's swinging the axe over his head, Alex! He's attacking the trees!" She watched in horror as Edmund furiously splintered the branches of the mimosa.

Chapter Twenty-Three

Alex drove in silence, determined to reach Beaune before evening as Hildy clutched at the dashboard to brace herself, trying desperately to take in the sights of fields and villages flashing by the Porsche.

It was five o'clock when they checked into their hotel overhanging a cobblestone street just outside the city walls. Hildy declined dinner to collapse into a steaming bath while Alex ventured off to explore the renowned underground wine cellars. Hildy was fast asleep before he returned.

In the morning she awakened to a summer day so beautiful, her heart wept at the realization that the magical trip to France was coming to an end—in a way she could never have envisioned.

They had been back on the road several hours when Alex

sniffed, remarking, "I believe something has died in the area."

"Oh!" Hildy gasped. "I forgot about the picnic Lescaut packed for us." She looked into the back seat. "What did you do with it, Alex?"

"I put it in the trunk when we checked into the hotel last night."

"Oh Lord, Lescaut told me she'd put in some Brie." Hildy rolled down the window to air out the car.

Alex automatically punched a button on the dash to ensure economy air-conditioning. "Why didn't you have her pack the stuff with ice?"

"You know perfectly well our refrigerator doesn't make ice. In any case, I see no reason why you should assume that I am in charge of provisions. Why didn't you have the hotel put it in the refrigerator overnight?"

"Why do you assume I'm in charge of refrigerating picnics?" He maneuvered the Porsche through the French countryside bordering the banks of the Loire.

"Lescaut also packed some *vin ordinaire*," Hildy told him.

"The *vin* will be *ordinaire*, but the Brie won't." Alex clenched his jaws as a group of Vespas, flagrantly unmuffled, screamed past in a huge billow of pink dust. "Damn those creeps! Shut your window, Hildy!"

Hildy sighed wistfully as the window rolled up. She had imagined the Loire river banks dotted with white cottages and bright flowers—not caravans of campers cluttering the road to find the perfect place to picnic, just as they were doing. "Perhaps we've come here 100 years too late."

"What's wrong is coming to France at all." Alex suddenly swerved off the road and bumped over the stony ground. "All right, pick a place to eat."

"Not here, Alex. This is not verdant enough." She pointed. "That knoll over there is much better."

"There's no shade," Alex barreled further over the rough terrain to where a huge cedar spread its branches. He stopped the car with a jolt. "Well, come on, get out."

Why was it Alex acted like a petulant child when he was

forced to do something he hadn't planned? As fast as Alex spread newspapers on the ground for them to sit on, the breeze blew them away, with Alex frantically chasing after them. It was clear from his entire attitude that this would hardly be a picnic, still she could not help laughing at how comic it had become.

Finally, anchoring the papers with rocks, he plopped down the picnic basket. "Are you going to sit down? Come on, let's have our goddamn picnic."

Hildy sat. The cedar boughs completely obscured any view of the famed Loire. She pressed her lids closed, wishing she'd never dreamed up this *Déjeuner sur l'herbe*. Was anything worth all this effort? "Why is it, Alex, you manage to ruin anything I relish? Couldn't you just this once go along gracefully with something that interests me?"

"This bread is stale," Alex announced, breaking off a crust of the *baguette* and batting a bug away from his face.

"Listen, let's just forget about the stupid picnic." Hildy struggled up from the newspaper which promptly blew across the meadow. She stalked down the hill to the car.

"Will you make up your mind, for God's sake?" Alex seized the basket and stood up, hurling the Brie as far as he could into the woods as he followed her to the car. "I guess I just don't know how to please you, Hildy."

She climbed back into her seat, moved the temperature gauge to a cooling sixty-five degrees Fahrenheit, twenty degrees Celsius, and removed her story notes from her tote. *Allons*," she said, "Let's move on."

Alex hurled the basket into the back seat and got in. He heaved a deep sigh. "What now?"

"To the castle, please." Hildy shook out the map with a loud crackle and studied it briefly. "Proceed ahead on this road to route D-955."

"Whatever you say, Hildy." There was a sadness in his voice. "From now on, you're in charge." The Porsche pulled slowly out of the woods.

Chapter Twenty-Four

Speeding west, they followed the winding Loire River for a time, neither speaking a word. Hildy stared out at the lovely scenery sweeping past her window, annoyed by Alex's petulance. If anyone should be in a foul mood, it was she—with all that had transpired in the past week. And trying to be civilized about it had been a mistake. She'd much prefer to be traveling alone, without Alex plaguing her at every turn about destinations. What Hildy wanted was to relish the spontaneity of the unfolding moment.

Why should she have to run away from the Riviera where the mere rays of pink sunlight sent her senses reeling with delight? Thank heaven she could sort out her feelings—fragments of her life—in her journal, the one place she felt in control.

It was this inner life she longed to share. Was that asking too much? At least Peter recognized her artistry. He had given her enormous reinforcement, possibly the first she'd ever experienced—from anybody. Certainly not from her husband.

Several kilometers later, Alex thrust the Michelin into her lap. "Since you seem to be an expert on France and its treasures," Alex said, "try giving me a clue as to where in God's name we are."

When they reached the traffic circle outside Bourges, Hildy was forced to speak. "I really cannot continue to read this map when you keep going around this circle. It makes me nauseous."

"I thought Marie gave you directions." He studied each exit spoke as they rounded the circle again. "Which goddamn turn do we take for Beaulieu?"

Hildy shrieked, "Not here! It says 'Orleans.' You'd better go around again and go *à droîte* somewhere before this."

"It would be extremely helpful if you would give your directions in our native tongue." Alex gave her an impatient look. "Why in hell don't they number their routes like we do in the States?"

Her hand quivering, Hildy tried to trace the route on the map. "I'm sure Marie said to take route D-955, but I cannot find it anywhere. Would it be anywhere near Brittany?"

Beads of perspiration had formed on Alex's lips as he circled for the third time, saying nothing.

"Honestly, Alex. I'm trying, really. This printing is micro-scopic, plus my head is spinning."

Alex stared ahead, navigating turn after turn around the circle. His eyes were squinted, as if he felt pain.

"Just get us off this circle!" she shouted. Anything to stop her dizziness. She clawed the dash as Alex careened around the circle again. What was wrong? He stared ahead, ignoring the exit signs.

"Alex, please," Hildy pleaded, "that's enough. Let's just ask someone."

Alex glowered at her. "Can't you read a goddamn map?"

"If you'd slow down, maybe I could."

"Screw the castle." shouted Alex, his face scarlet.

"Screw you!" Hildy shouted back. "And your damned English whore!" She threw herself back in the seat, breathing heavily. After a moment, she said more calmly, "Why is it we can't talk to each other without this anger…?"

"Simple enough. You hate me because I slept with Victoria. Case closed."

"For God's sake, Alex! Am I supposed to be thrilled?" She felt as if she was about to explode. "The mere thought of you in bed with her just revolts me."

Alex finally slowed and took the exit to Montluçon, even though it bore no route number. He continued slowly on the two lane road. "Hildy, I don't love Victoria. I love you. Won't you believe me?"

"That's just the point. How can I believe what you say, or trust you—ever again?" She turned away, refusing to let the tears come. "I think I should see a lawyer."

Alex banged his fists on the wheel. "God, that's just crazy, Hildy. This sort of thing happens to lots of people and they don't go running to a lawyer right off the bat."

"Well, dammit, it doesn't happen to me!" She drew a long breath.

"Listen, Hildy, Victoria Helmsley is a lonely, fairly attractive lady I ran into by some insane accident at the Grand Prix."

"So you took her to bed. I mean, there you were, and there she was—what else could you do?"

"Jesus. One night! That was all there was to this whole bloody thing."

"I wish you wouldn't use that word. Not now. Not ever."

Alex's eyes squinted under a pained frown. "I'm sorry." His breathing was strained.

Hildy decided to get it all out. "I don't suppose it's occurred to you, Alex, that dear Vickie might be after you for your lovely retirement bucks, not just your aging body."

"Say anything you want, Hildy."

"Face it, apart from sleeping with the hired help, and every possible man she meets, the poor wretch still can't even pay her rent. You can't say she isn't trying, though, can you?"

Alex swallowed. "I never saw myself as part of the lady's future."

"You're blind, Alex."

For what seemed like an eternity, Hildy watched the lush countryside slide past. Then, glancing at the map still spread on her lap, she announced, "We appear to be on route N-76, which leads where? I have no idea."

Alex was silent, then spoke in a tone as if talking to himself. "I'm beginning to realize something, now. Maybe for the very first time." He turned to her. "You used to be my anchor, Hildy. For all those years, when I went off to conquer the world. I could depend on you." His voice drifted off. "But you're not there anymore for me."

"Depended on me—or took me for granted, Alex?"

"That's not what I said, Hildy."

"Explain, then, Alex. I'm here. Always have been. I've never left you."

"No, Hildy, you're not the same," Alex said, addressing her softly. "I knew you had your hobbies, your Yoga, your writing workshops…"

"Don't you see, Alex? They were *my* anchor. They gave me a purpose, a reason to get up each morning."

"But this damn novel of yours…" he strained to find his words. "I always thought your writing was just another pastime, like playing mah-jong, or some stupid thing."

"I hardly call all the effort I put into my work, *stupid*." She turned away, smarting with the pain of being devalued.

"But that's what I'm trying to tell you." He grabbed her arm. "I realize now you are serious. You are actually going to write this book—and who knows what else?"

Hildy smiled faintly. "I've been telling you that all along, Alex."

Alex clutched the wheel as his body began to tremble. "Where in hell am I? Read the signs!"

Hildy watched the color drain from his face. "Alex, what's wrong?" She steadied his arm.

"You don't need me to be the chairman of our life together, do you?" He swallowed hard. "You don't."

"What I need is for you to understand that I have to express my talents, just the way you expressed yours in the marketplace. I need a place to be me."

Alex looked at her, then back to the highway. He said nothing for a long moment, then reached for her hand. "I'm trying to see that, Hildy. I guess I haven't made room for your dreams along with mine. Important dreams—every bit as worthy as mine. For all these years I've imagined my success was enough to keep both our dreams alive."

Hildy sat stunned. "Do you really understand that, Alex?"

"I want to. I'll try." There were tears slowly running down his cheeks. "Which way is it to Beaulieu? Where do we go next, Hildy?"

Hildy took a little breath and squeezed his hand. "Don't worry. We'll find our way."

Chapter Twenty-Five

Twelve kilometers later, a red light began to flash on the dash panel, and the car suddenly coughed and wheezed.

"Oh, no," Alex said in a small, helpless voice.

"We just need some gas, Alex. We'll stop and get directions at the same time." His hand still on the wheel, Hildy helped Alex guide the Porsche into a tiny gas station.

A fat, gray-haired woman waddled over to greet them at the pump. "*Combien?*"

"Fill it up, please. Super-unleaded," Hildy ordered, then realizing there was just one gas pump, she pointed to the tank, saying "Full," as she rubbed her stomach to pantomime a stomach full of food.

"*Enceinte?*" The woman laughed.

To lighten Alex's deep preoccupation, Hildy chuckled.

"The woman thinks I'm pregnant. Isn't that hysterical?"

Alex managed a faint smile. "A hysterical pregnancy?"

The woman reached her hand in through the window.

"I believe she wants the money first, Alex, like self-serve back home." Hildy rummaged through her tote, producing her Visa card.

"No *plastique*." The woman shook her head. "Only francs."

Hildy put the card back and fumbled out a twenty dollar bill. "You take, yes?"

Alex jumped out of the car suddenly, grabbing the hose from the woman and poking it into the gas tank. His mouth set in a grim line, he gave his wife a stern look. "I can still pump gas, Hildy. You never retire from that job." As he stared at the sky, gas began to overflow the tank. "Son of a gun!" Alex exclaimed. "This tank is not empty at all."

"You mean the computer lies?" Hildy asked.

Alex hung up the hose. "What the hell...?"

"Check under the hood," Hildy directed the woman, as Alex wiped around the gas tank with a paper towel. The two women stared into the maze of electronic circuitry.

"Maybe we need oil," Hildy suggested.

"I put oil in before we left," Alex told her. "It's nothing like that."

"Would you please hand me the owner's manual, Alex? In the glove box."

"I know where it is, Hildy, and I really appreciate your jumping in like this to help out, but," he pulled her away from the hood, holding her briefly to him, "the manual is entirely in German, if you recall."

Suddenly the woman straightened from her crouch over the engine. With a look of triumph, she handed Hildy a small plastic box she had retrieved from under the left wheel arch in the engine compartment. "*Fusée* gone! *Kaput*! She showed Hildy the melted metal strip through the transparent cap.

"Oh, I see," Hildy peered at it, uncomprehending. "It is easy to fix *fusée*, *non*?"

The woman had opened the box and probed inside. She

gasped. "*Qu'est-ce que c'est?*" The crystal necklace dangled from her oily fingers.

"Alex, lookl My crystal!" Hildy reached out to take it.

Alex looked dazed. "How in hell did that get under my hood?"

The fat woman eyed the Bigelows warily, backing off a step. "*Vous avez...*" She waved to her husband to come out of the office shed. "Dominique!" Her explanation to the man was a torrent of French, in which Hildy heard the word *gendarmes*.

"No, no, Madame," Hildy cut in excitedly. "This is mine. It belongs to me." She smiled demurely and posed with it against her throat, eyeing Alex with fluttering lids. "*Mon mari*, he *donnez-moi* for our anniversary, *oui*? Isn't that *très bon*?"

"Ah, *oui*. *Anniversaire!*" The woman's face cracked into a smile.

Alex looked relieved. "Happy Anniversary, darling," he whispered in her ear.

Hildy fingered the necklace, sunlight flashing across the crystal. "Lovely, isn't it?" She displayed it.

The woman bobbed her head, as she made change from her apron pocket.

Alex put his hand over Hildy's. "Let me help you put it on."

Hildy looked at the necklace and felt her pleasure drain away. "No, Alex." She crumpled the necklace into his fist. "Put it on Lady Helmsley. I'm sure she'll adore the setting she picked out."

Chapter Twenty-Six

The countryside was now a sea of green velvet dotted with grazing sheep. Hildy found it soothing to watch as she pondered her future.

The mystery of the necklace in the fuse box was perplexing, of course, but Alex's loss of control at the traffic circle troubled her far more. Was he having some kind of breakdown, she wondered? She'd heard that men often experience emotional difficulties when they retire.

Alex broke the long silence. "Why would that fool Edmund put your necklace in the fuse box?" He stared straight ahead as he drove. "It makes no sense at all."

Hildy shook her head slowly. "To hide it, I would imagine. I think when the police arrived, he was afraid they might search him and find it."

Alex snorted in disgust. "As if those morons would have the sense to do that. They think the gypsy took it."

"Edmund must have retrieved it from Nadia." Hildy's finger tapped on her journal. "If she ever had it in the first place. Frankly, I don't think she did. I think Edmund had it all along."

"God, Hildy. It's only a crystal—just a piece of glass. Why all this intrigue?"

Hildy pursued her track. "Edmund could have taken it anytime after you returned from Monaco on Saturday. You didn't discover it missing until Tuesday."

"I've lost track of all the lies these people told us. Didn't Yvette say…?"

Hildy opened her journal, finding a page of her notes. "Nadia denied stealing the necklace. Edmund is the one who said she did."

"Wonderful. If he said it, you can almost be sure she didn't."

"It was Yvette who said she saw Nadia grind up oleander and put it in the Pimms." Hildy looked up from the book. "Of course, Yvette could have put the poison in Victoria's wine just as well. She knew her mistress drank Pimms."

"They all lie!" Alex pounded the wheel with the heel of his hand. "You can't believe a thing they tell you."

Hildy was almost relieved to hear the familiar anger in his voice, but it brought her back at once to her uncertainties about their marriage. She looked off to watch the hills roll by. The bright green turned gray as dark clouds covered the sun.

It was almost three o'clock before they reached the turnoff to Beaulieu. "Watch for signs," Alex said. "We turn off somewhere before we reach the village."

"What kind of sign?"

"A castle sign. You know, 'This way to the Castle,' something like that."

The sky was becoming black with storm clouds. "I used to love storms," Hildy said softly. "Especially back on the Jersey shore when I was little. They're so dramatic." She thought back to how her life had evolved in fifty years. Had her dreams really changed that much? She thought of the glass *fleur de lis* Lescaut gave her for her grandson. For some reason, the thought of her family made her eyes start to fill. "Over there!" Hildy pointed, quickly brushing a tear from her cheek. "I think I see some turrets through those trees."

Alex swerved into a narrow lane, sending up a spray of gravel, then he slowed down as the woods closed over them.

"My God, Alex." Hildy sat straight up.

"What's wrong?" He braked the car.

"What if the poison was meant for me?"

"Please, Miss Marple. Enough sleuthing for now, okay?"

"I can't think of a motive, but wouldn't that be intriguing?"

A thin drizzle misted the windshield. Alex started the wipers and guided the Porsche through a tunnel of twisted cypresses ending in the clearing of the castle grounds.

"Why, it's huge," Hildy exclaimed. Silvery charcoal turrets loomed across a meadow of lush green. The car approached the massive stone wall surrounding the castle, passing through ancient iron gates. Hildy felt she had left all reality behind and was grateful.

"This is more like it. Right, darling?" Alex looked pleased.

"My goodness, I fully expected swordsmen to leap out at any moment and carry us off to the dungeon." She opened her journal, and scribbled a note, then shut it. "I'd better wait and do that later. I don't want to miss anything."

Ahead of them in a clearing of light stood a tiny stone chapel mantled with ivy.

"Oh, Alex, please stop. You must get a picture of that." She rolled down the window for a better view. "It even has a rose window."

Alex cruised closer and stopped the car. "It's almost too dark for a picture and it's starting to rain." He rummaged for his camera in the back seat.

Hildy jumped out and hurried to examine a plaque embedded in the stone beside a vaulted wooden door. "This is strange."

Alex looked over her shoulder.

"André Dupres' name is listed here, see?" Hildy pointed. "He can't be buried here. I saw his grave in La Roquette."

He backed off, aiming the camera. "Come on, Hildy. Smile. We're getting wet." He snapped off a picture and bustled her back into the car.

In the car, Alex reached into his pocket. "I'd like you to keep this." He reached over to drop the necklace from his fist into her tote. "It will never be for anyone but you, Hildy."

She tensed to protest.

"Just keep it," Alex insisted. "I might lose it."

Hildy stared at her tote, as Alex grimly started the car.

The pitted gray walls of the castle rose to a high pitched roof with several turrets jutting from the rough stone. Narrow windows of irregular old glass panes appeared as dark slots under gingerbread arches, flowering into crocheted spires.

"A real fairy tale castle," Hildy sighed.

Standing on a low flight of wide steps, Marie waved to her guests. "*Bienvenue!*" Above her, a gothic arch bore a stone carving of St. George and the Dragon.

Hildy trotted to the steps to receive a welcoming kiss on both cheeks from her hostess. "Marie, I am overwhelmed. Your castle is positively stately!"

"But the rain." Marie drew her face into a disapproving frown. "It is unfortunate." She ushered them into the marble-floored reception hall.

In the center of the room stood a carved refectory table bearing a huge bouquet of vermilion dahlias and crimson gladiolas.

"That is a Rubens in the archway," Marie pointed out.

Hildy studied the painting. "Oh dear, the poor thing has fallen off her horse, hasn't she. But what could one expect, when raped." Could this possibly be the original oil?

"Ah, *enfin*, you come." The Marquis entered through a tall door through which Hildy could see shelves of books. He looked regal in a dark blue velvet smoking jacket with a paisley silk ascot. Fringed tassels bounced on his patent leather evening slippers. "Welcome to Beaulieu." He kissed Hildy on both cheeks and extended his hand to Alex. "I regret you wish to leave us so soon."

"We're sorry too, Léon," Alex said.

"Have the police found your necklace?" Marie asked.

"It was—" Alex began.

Hildy cut in. "We found it ourselves, actually. It was…misplaced."

"I called Lady Helmsley," Marie said, "to make sure she is recovered. And Lescaut, she has explained about the gypsy girl. We can now, perhaps, forget about all of that, no?"

"*D'accord*, by all means. Let's do that." Hildy's eyes focused on an elaborate tapestry which hung almost to the ceiling of the room. "Isn't that magnificent, Alex?"

Alex stared dutifully. "Oh, yes. It's really quite an imposing place you have, Léon. I had no idea."

The Marquis offered a proud smile. "Such castles are not uncommon among the historic noble families."

"We should talk, Léon," Alex said briskly. "There are several things, as you know."

"But of course." The Marquis smoothed his satin lapel briefly. "First, you must fetch your luggage inside. I will wait for you in the library." He bowed slightly and returned through the tall door.

"I'll need just the two smaller cases in the trunk, Alex," Hildy turned to Marie. "I trust we won't need anything formal. Most of the luggage is strapped to the car roof."

Alex turned up his collar against the drizzle and sprinted out the door.

"Nothing formal, no." Marie led Hildy up the stone stairway. "We can no longer afford ceremony here."

Hildy's eyes were raised to a massive chandelier suspended by a thick chain from the darkness above them. "It must be hopeless trying to heat this place."

"A ton of coal daily in the winter," Marie told her. "That's why we go to the south. The *Midi*, we French call it."

Hildy followed the Marquise down a long corridor, her

heels clicking on the tile floor. The Marquise's thongs made an incongruous slapping noise. Hildy paused to examine a faintly burnished suit of armor gleaming beside a lit sconce in a shadowy corner.

"*Voilà!*" Marie flung open a heavy wooden door. "I thought Alex would find this room comfortable." She flicked on a lamp. "General de Gaulle slept here when he visited the castle some years ago." She smoothed the red velvet spread.

"Truly fit for a king," Hildy felt awed at the faded splendor of the room. "That canopy!" She marveled, pointing timidly at the velvet hung with gold-encrusted tassels over the bed. "I'm sure Alex will find this more than adequate." She looked down at the rug. "And this is an *Aubusson*, is it not?"

"One forgets; the rug is so old." Marie blew dust from the threadbare cushion of a side chair. "*Ai*, it is difficult to care for our furnishings with no servants. We hire students to help if we lease the castle in the winter, and Léon rents some of the property for campers. I hear them with their rock and roll." The Marquise trilled the words contemptuously.

"It must be hard for you now, remembering how it was at one time."

The Marquise smiled, lifting her chin slightly. "The Chateau de Musset remains for many generations, Madame. It will always be so."

They resumed their journey down the corridor. "So many rooms, Marie! I would get lost."

"And this, Hildy," Marie swung open another door, wincing when it squeaked, "this will be yours. You will find it suitable?"

"Oh, yes!" Her bed, like de Gaulle's was canopied but in a faded blue velvet. Above the matching headboard hung a religious triptych in gilded arched frames.

Relieved that the nobility provide separate guest bedrooms, Hildy walked to stand in the center of the semi-circle of tall, blue velvet draperied windows. "This is marvelous, Marie. Truly a fairy princess boudoir!" She looked up at the ceiling, painted into a sky and crowded with cherubs floating among the clouds amid swirling garlands of roses. "I do love the rococo."

"I am pleased you like it." Marie tugged at the heavy drapery cord, drawing aside the high draperies to reveal several enormous mullioned windows. Marie beamed proudly. "*Voilà!*"

Hildy looked out at rolling green meadows, dotted with clusters of trees. The storm clouds were broken at the horizon to let in a blue-green patch of sky and a declining sun. In the distance, a glow of lightning momentarily lit the billowing black storm.

After a minute, Hildy turned to place her tote atop the huge oval desk centered in the room. The parquetry of the top defined flowers and bouquets with ribbons in intricate mosaics.

"The desk once belongs to the Empress Josephine," Marie said. She moved the silver inkwell so Hildy could see the date.

"Exquisite."

Marie slid the inkwell back in place. "So, Hildy, tell me. Where did you find the necklace?" Her eyes were wide with interest.

"Edmund had it," Hildy said, "as I suspected from the beginning." She reached into her tote and pulled it out. "Behold." She dangled the necklace in the air.

Marie looked at it closely, cupping the crystal in her hand. "It's beautiful, Hildy. I'm so glad you found it."

"Alex's anniversary gift to me. It has caused me a lot of pain."

Marie scowled. "Edmund! Have the police arrested him?"

Hildy dismissed the question. "Alex will handle all that."

"I will tell Léon. I have never liked that young man."

Hildy considered telling Marie about the mimosas Edmund was hacking down when last seen and decided against it. His distressing antics no longer interested her in the slightest. "I consider the episode closed now, Marie. *Fini.*"

Marie patted her arm. "But everything is all right now, no?"

"I'm not sure, Marie." Hildy clutched the necklace into

her fist and dropped it back in the tote.

"But now, you will wish to freshen up, Hildy. The bath is down the hall. Then I show you a tour of the grounds."

The minute Marie left, Hildy pushed her thoughts aside and gave herself over to the enchantment of her surroundings. She pictured the lords and ladies drifting through torch-lit passages, a princess adjusting her Marie Antoinette wig in this very mirror on the wall.

She pushed open the door to the balcony outside the mullioned windows and strolled out to rest a hand on the pitted balustrade. She was the mistress of the castle, contemplating the grounds, the setting sun.

But she could not see the sun. The black thunderheads rolled toward her from the west. The drizzle had stopped, but the clouds would burst open with a deluge at any moment.

Damn you Victoria! This could have been our fairy tale ending. Alex's and mine, Hildy railed inwardly.

A sudden gust threatened to bang the door shut. Hildy grabbed it, catching sight of Alex, standing on his balcony seemingly miles away, looking out over the same scene, each of them viewing it alone.

Chapter Twenty-Seven

Hildy found Marie in the foyer a few minutes later. She had donned a rain cape and a wide brimmed gaucho hat. The thongs on her feet were wrapped in plastic bags.

"Take this, Hildy." Marie unsnapped a red umbrella. "In case it rains hard."

Hildy could hear the discussion taking place between Alex and the Marquis through the open library door.

"And this, Alex," the Marquis' voice proudly boomed, "a signature of Napoleon's aide, Marshall Pelletier. You can see the date here."

"That's really wonderful, Léon. But let's have a look at this lease. You see, since we've stayed less than a month…"

"It has been fully authenticated," Leon continued, "by the *Bibliothèque Nationale*."

Hildy would have loved examining the treasures the Marquis was obviously showing Alex, but she wanted no part of any negotiations concerning the villa.

"Naturally," she heard Alex's voice, "I want to be completely fair with you, sir. I wouldn't expect—"

"This could be another Versailles, Marie," Hildy said. "Let's do get on with our tour."

Marie guided Hildy through the front door, opening her umbrella as she pulled the heavy door closed. "Come, I show you where the hunters stay."

"You have hunters here?" Hildy hurried after her hostess across the glistening wet cobblestones. "What do they hunt?"

"Boars." Marie skirted a wide puddle. "We must rent rooms out in the winter to help pay expenses. Our taxes— *formidable!*"

As they passed a coach house adjacent to the stables, Hildy glimpsed the dark hulk of a carriage. She could not resist. "Please, Marie. May I peek inside?"

Horses whinnied a greeting—one of them was cream, two dappled, and one coal black. Hmm, Hildy noted, not a white charger in sight. She was amazed to see that the coach was ebony, trimmed with gilt, and bore the de Musset coat of arms. "Oh, Marie, this is marvelous!" She touched the dusty surface of the emblem on the carriage's side. "It looks positively regal."

"Ah," Marie laughed, "Léon's—how do you say it— great-great-grandfather, he use this when the castle is first built in 18th *siècle*."

Hildy was enchanted. "Two hundred years ago. It's hard to imagine."

By the time they reached the fringe of woods, it had begun to pour rain. "*Ooh-lah-lah!*" Marie huddled under her umbrella. "We must return now. But first, we feed the boars a little, yes?" She reached into her pocket for an apple.

An ugly bristled creature poked its snout from the bushes. "See? I give them apples." Marie clucked encouragement at the beast.

"Isn't that cute." Hildy was backing away and suddenly stumbled off the path into a deep puddle of mud. "Oh dear!"

"Be careful, Hildy," Marie cautioned, too late. "I am so sorry." She helped Hildy recover her balance.

"It's no problem, really. Just that my feet got completely soaked." Hildy smiled gamely to mask her discomfort.

"Come, we go back." Marie hurried Hildy along the path. "You must not take cold, no?"

Léon stood beneath the arch at the entrance, signalling wildly.

"What is it, Léon?" Marie ran up the steps while Hildy tried haplessly to scrape mud from her shoes on a stone.

"Telephone, Marie. Just now." He lowered his voice. "Madame Helmsley."

Hildy stiffened.

Léon attempted a genial smile. "She and the producer and the actress, they are coming here. They are close by Beaulieu."

"They come here?" cried Marie. "Do they not know we have guests?"

"I tell her that." The Marquis shrugged. "She apologized, but she cannot start the two day journey back to La Roquette. She does not feel well enough."

Hildy stamped her feet to remove mud. "Really! The woman's bad manners are beyond imagining, Marie. Anyone but dear Victoria would book a hotel." Hildy swept past her hosts into the foyer. "I feel the need of a brief rest now, if you don't mind."

"But of course, Hildy." Marie took her arm and offered a comforting smile. "I regret this happens, Hildy."

"Dinner at eight," Léon announced and hurried away down the hall past Alex.

"You must not let this unfortunate news spoil your visit, Madame," Marie whispered to Hildy at the stairway.

Hildy met Alex's gaze, recognizing the look of distress on his face. "Dining with my husband's mistress?" Hildy spoke with cool authority. "I can think of nothing more *amusant*."

Following a confining bath in the claw-footed tub, Hildy

bundled into the terrycloth robe and matching scuffies provided for Marie's guests. A crest like the one she had seen emblazoned on the old carriage was sewn to the breast.

Padding down the hall to her *chambre*, she met Marie, who was clutching a pair of cerise clogs edged in gold. "*Pour vous*, Hildy." She tucked them under Hildy's arm. "Your shoes are wet and muddy from the garden."

"Oh, *merci*, Marie. How very thoughtful." Hildy held up one of the clogs, noting the ankle strap was badly frayed. "Just the right touch of vivid color for the occasion." She had to say something.

"They are the right size for you? Good." Marie shook her head. "Three unexpected guests. *Mon Dieu!* I must hurry."

"Have they arrived?" Hildy asked coolly.

"*Oui*, they have arrived." Marie frowned. "I go now to see to dinner."

As Hildy shut her door, her hopes for a fairy tale finale at the castle faded. She would now feel obliged to wear Marie's clogs rather than hurt her feelings. Why did her tale seem doomed to an unhappy ending, with the wicked Victoria triumphant and Hildy's glass slippers transformed into a pair of clodhoppers even Cinderella's ugly stepsisters would reject?

Thank goodness she had brought her blouse-on silk that nicely concealed her waistline. Maybe the rainbow colors and plunging neckline would bolster her confidence. She held up the top and postured before the ornate oval mirror. Let the English bitch look to her laurels, she murmured, trying to feel worldly, but her face still reflected a doubting look.

Hildy tested the clogs on her feet and tried an unsteady step. They made her feet feel like lead, but she kept them on while she dressed to help get the hang of balancing. If she took small steps, she might manage to look regal—providing she didn't turn an ankle. She let the gown fall over her shoulders and smoothed the folds of the skirt. Whatever else, she was determined to make a grand entrance.

Lurching towards the oval desk, Hildy removed the crystal necklace from her tote. "By God, I'm wearing this," she said aloud, fastening it around her throat. She drew herself up, looking sternly at her image in the mirror. Then, raising her chin she put one hand on the crystal and fingered the facets. It truly was beautiful, more so than she had remembered, set off now in its gold setting.

And now her face. She lined up her makeup jars on the dressing table. First she splashed her face with soap drops and patted on toners I and III, unable to locate toner II. Then, she vigorously creamed on Visible Difference, praying it would work, before applying her foundation. Next, she brushed a softly glowing copper on her cheekbones and carefully outlining her lips with eggplant pencil, she filled them in with winery red.

Finally, her eyes. She squinted in the dimly lit mirror to define her lids with an olive gold pencil, nearly blinding herself in the process. Lord, she was nervous, all right. In an attempt to be doubly dazzling she bathed her lashes in a misty mauve mascara to complement her blue diamond eyeshadow.

Convinced she had given this her ultimate shot, Hildy turned her face from side to side to check the overall effect. Not bad. Lips moistened, eyes shimmering and cheeks aglow, she would give her ladyship a run for the money.

To release her tension, Hildy kicked off her clogs and walked out to the balcony. The rain had stopped, but the sky still threatened with torn black clouds spreading across the horizon. She breathed deeply as she'd learned to do in Yoga. A movement caught her eye.

Standing by the stream, partly masked by the high topiary shrubs that swept down from the castle, Alex gazed into the water from a little bridge. He looked startlingly handsome in his black pinstripe suit and paisley tie, more like the Alex she remembered before he had joined the jogging-suit brigade of the retired.

Suddenly, her breath caught in her throat. Emerging from the shadows, Victoria floated to his side, like a butterfly borne on wings of golden chiffon. A ray of sun glinted in the titian hair piled high on her head. Turning Alex in an embrace, she kissed him. Hildy could not believe what she was seeing. Was this real?

Alex dropped his hands from the rail, glancing about guiltily, then catching Victoria's hand, he led her into the shadows of the shrub-bordered path.

Groping for the balustrade, Hildy steadied herself. Alex's concessions about their life together, declared in an anguish of reckoning at the traffic circle, evaporated into nothing.

"Damn you, Alex, you lied!" She raised her voice. "Nothing has changed!" A rumble of thunder eclipsed her cry. "Listen to me Alex, forget the future. You and I have different dreams!"

Chapter Twenty-Eight

Trembling, Hildy returned to the room, letting the door bang shut behind her. She yanked savagely on the drapery cord to shut out her awful vision. "That does it!" she exploded, as the rod fell, tumbling the draperies to the floor in a dusty heap.

Hildy stared at the mess. Then, with angry determination she turned for a last look in the mirror. She touched her hair and lifted her chin defiantly. Flinging open the bed chamber door, she took a breath and marched into the shadowy hall.

At the top of the staircase, she paused to gather her composure. Suddenly a towering figure loomed toward her from out of the darkness, rivulets of shining matter running down both sides of its face. Hildy recoiled against the banister with a cry.

"Hi, Hildy," a voice said. "If this place isn't a total trip!"

"Gracious, Dawn. I saw this immense *thing* coming…"Hildy gaped. "What a striking helmet!"

"Isn't it outrageous?" Dawn adjusted the fan of beaded spokes webbed with bronze mylar radiating above her forehead.

"It's quite overwhelming," Hildy conceded, lightly touching one of the jewelled buttons fastened to Dawn's ears. The buttons trailed lengths of multi-hued bits of shiny glass to her shoulders. "But don't they hurt your ears?"

"I took an Excedrin," said Dawn, running her hands down the black satin sheath which flared at the knees. "God, if I ever get invited to the Academy Awards, this is my outfit. What do you think?"

"Indeed, why not?" Hildy felt invigorated by the girl's unbounded spirit. She took Dawn's arm. "Shall we go down together, dear?"

"*Quelle plaisir*, Madame Bigelow.'' Peter advanced to the foot of the stairs, holding a half empty wine glass. He bent to kiss Hildy's hand.

"How elegant you look, Peter," Hildy said, smiling.

Peter wore a pleated white shirt open at the neck under a soft, fawn colored leather blazer and jeans. Hildy noted he wore no socks with his tennis sneakers and for some reason felt elated with this flouting of Alex's Brooks Brothers tradition. She almost wished she had a bizarre helmet like Dawn's to wear, though perhaps without rivulets hanging from her ears.

The library was richly panelled in dark oak with a domed ceiling. A classic goddess sculpture flanked one side of the marble fireplace. Hildy observed immediately that neither Victoria nor Alex were in the room.

"Ah, Hildy, you look *ravissant*!" Marie was perched on a high-backed, carved Gothic chair. Her floor-length silk gown was striped in varying shades of crimson and cascaded to the floor about her throne. She looked completely the queen, receiving her courtiers. "*Mon Dieu!*" She stared at Dawn. "But how *trés dramatique*!"

Peter took Dawn's hand and stood away from her as she postured prettily. "Dawn is costumed for the ritual sacrifice of the virgins, as you can see. Pity there's no press here this evening, what?"

The Marquis kissed Hildy's hand. "We will drink to the visit of our friends at *Chateau de Musset, non, Madame*?" He kissed Dawn's hand, as she steadied her helmet. Hildy observed the Marquis had changed his ascot, no doubt to echo the royal crimson of the Marquise. "Where is Alex?" He poured champagne. "We must toast our settlement."

"I'm sure I wouldn't know," replied Hildy, accepting a goblet. "Do tell me, Peter, was St. Chapelle wonderful?"

"It poured with rain, actually. Still, I must say, I found the stained glass quite wondrous." He reached for a second glass of champagne and handed it to Dawn. "The idea of using it thematically interests me more and more."

"*Bonsoir*, everyone" Alex called from the doorway. "My God, Hildy. What have you done? You look fabulous!" He hurried over and kissed both her cheeks." And the crystal. *Magnifique!*"

Hildy turned to Peter. "You were saying about your film?"

"I really love your shoes," said Dawn, interrupting. "They're so ethnic. Are they from Arizona?"

"No, but aren't they unusual? I've borrowed them from Marie."

"But look here, Hildy." The Marquis motioned her over to a glass-panelled wall cabinet. "Here is a snuff box said to be of the French scoundrel Robespierre. Is it not extraordinary?"

After a lengthy dissertation by the Marquis on his various historic artifacts, a dark-skinned young man moved into the doorway. He wore a soiled white jacket over acid-dyed jeans and discreetly jangled a hand bell. "*Madame*," he intoned in a rich East Indian voice. "*Le dîner est servi.*"

Marie nodded and arose, gathering her striped silken skirt about her. "*Allons*. Peter, where is Lady Helmsley? Is she feeling all right?"

"Perhaps I should go and fetch her." Peter said.

Alex said, "I saw her a little while ago. She seemed okay then."

Hildy put her arm through Peter's and glared at her husband. "Why don't you go look in the bushes by the little bridge?"

Alex looked startled.

"She may still be savoring your most recent encounter," Hildy added, dragging Peter out of the library.

Murky portraits of long deceased ancestors, each with its own lamp shining above it, stared down from the wood-paneled walls of the cavernous dining hall. A vaulted ceiling glowed faintly from the island of candlelight on the dining table below. It was the longest Hildy had ever seen.

"Suppose you sit in this chair on my right, Hildy." Léon drew one of the carved, high-backed chairs out for her and Hildy slipped onto the rush seat, allowing him to slide the chair into place at the table. "And Peter—next to Hildy, please."

Her eyes marveled at the magnificent old room, some of it in dark shadow, giving her an odd sense of excitement, as if the mysterious castle held hidden secrets.

With the storm beating fiercely against the high narrow windows of the room, Marie took her place at the head of the table. "Thank you, Alex," she said, as he helped her with her chair. "Why don't you sit here on my right, and Dawn, dear, next to Alex." An empty chair next to Dawn remained for Victoria.

"Is your servant Indian, Marie?" Hildy asked, speaking louder than she wished. Her voice bounced from the wood walls with a slight echo.

The Marquis repeated in a clear voice, "Hildy wonders if Shivar is Indian, Marie." He turned back to Hildy. "Actually, he's not."

"Shivar is from Sri Lanka," Marie said loudly.

Dawn's voice piped, "Who is Sir Lanka?"

"How funny," Peter guffawed, turning to Hildy. "Is that a hoot?"

Hildy wasn't following the conversation at all. "What's

Shivar doing here in Beaulieu?" she called to Marie.

"He's a student we bring in on special occasions." Marie offered an apologetic smile. "A full-time staff is not possible."

Across the table, Alex lifted his champagne glass to Hildy. The soft candlelight touched the gray at his temples. "Hildy, darling, your wish to visit a fairy castle has come true. Shall we drink to that?"

The others smiled and drank. Hildy lifted her glass tentatively and leaned toward the Marquis. "Tell me about the chapel we passed as we drove in, Léon."

"Ah, it is picturesque, no? But seldom used now."

"Why is André Dupres' name on the plaque by the door?"

Marie answered. "I commission him to make the tiny rose window you see over the door. Is it not precious? It was one of the last ones he made."

Hildy thought a moment. "I wonder if it could be the round window from the sketch in the shepherd's hut. Remember, Peter?"

"We call it our *Mimosa* window," Marie said.

Hildy sat straight in her chair. "Then it is that window, Peter."

Peter spoke to the others. "The sketch we saw is really most original in concept—terribly vivid with color." He turned to Hildy. "We'll have to look tomorrow in daylight."

Victoria swirled into the room. "Darlings! I'm devastated that I've kept you waiting," she said, flinging her hand out in despair. "My hair simply rebels wherever there's the slightest hint of moisture in the air." Posing at the only empty chair, she waited as both Leon and Alex rose to seat her.

"*Permittez-moi*," said Léon, motioning Alex to sit down.

Shivar immediately entered with a heavy silver tureen on a tarnished tray. He began to serve the soup.

Victoria surveyed the table with a sweeping glance. "Stunning, Marie. Your taste is impeccable." Her gaze settled on Dawn. "What ever is that contraption on your head?"

"Don't you love it, Vicki?" Dawn smiled, steadying the headdress as she sat back to let Shivar serve her soup.

"The soup is superb, Marie," Hildy said as the servant vanished through the doorway.

"Thank you. It is Shivar's special *vichyssoise*." Marie looked around the table to see that her guests were enjoying it. "He adds some herb, I do not know what it is. But we were talking about André Dupres, Victoria." She looked at Hildy. "André never showed us a sketch of the window." Marie put a hand to her chin as she remembered. "It was entirely his own idea. We had suggested something religious, you know, like the shepherd window we admired so much. It was André who proposes the mimosa."

"Marie," Dawn said, "your *soupçon* is simply delicious." A tendril of glitter from Dawn's headdress trailed in her soup bowl. She lifted it out and patted it with her napkin.

"*Merci bien*, Dawn," the Marquise replied. "You are too kind."

"Hildy's very much interested in Dupres," Alex said, glancing around the table.

Hildy felt a surge of resentment at Alex's sudden willingness to acknowledge her interest in Dupres, as if he'd been supportive all along.

"You are feeling better, Madame Helmsley?" The Marquis smiled at her indulgently.

"Oh, ever so much, Léon. *Merci.* I had a lovely walk in the garden—frightfully damp it was, I'm afraid. The stream in your garden is lovely, isn't it, Alex? With the little bridge?"

Hildy stared intently at the tablecloth as Shivar whisked away her soup plate. Lightning flashed against the wood paneled walls followed by a series of thunder claps jolting the castle.

No one attempted to speak. "*Ah oui*," Leon said as Shivar ceremoniously served trout from another tarnished silver platter. These are from that same stream in the garden. Did you not notice the fish there, Alex?"

"Not really, but I had a fine look around while I waited for Hildy to dress."

Hildy sensed Alex was embarking on what he hoped would explain his rendezvous with Victoria in the garden. She felt her anger rising again at his tacky charade of innocence and Victoria's tasteless innuendo about their walk. She forced a smile. "Your *poisson* is marvelous, Marie."

"*Merci*, Hildy. I am glad."

Victoria applied her fish knife to one of the delicate morsels on her plate. "I'm afraid Alex is sorry he's leaving France. Cheer up, luv. Arizona won't be all that terrible."

"I don't consider Arizona terrible at all," Alex said, in a low voice.

"Oh, I'm frightfully sorry. I would never suggest Arizona is terrible. I've never even been there." She inquired of Marie. "Is that curry I taste?"

"Coriander, Madame," Shivar replied, offering her a spoon-ful of rice.

"I do apologize, Marie. I've become a tad paranoid about what I put inside my body since that awful gypsy tried to poison me at Hildy's luncheon."

It seemed to Hildy that every word the woman spoke was calculated to raise hackles.

Peter said softly, "I'm sure no one wishes to go into all that again, Victoria."

Suddenly, Victoria's knife clattered to her plate. "The necklace." Her eyes riveted on Hildy's crystal. "We all thought Nadia had run off to Spain with it."

"We thought that, but…" Alex began.

Hildy interrupted. "Do let's talk about something else, shall we? Dawn, tell me, what will your next film be?" Hildy covered the crystal with her hand.

A flash of lightning accompanied by a crash of thunder jolted the room.

"*Formidable!*" Marie shrieked in the tumult of sound. "I think the lightning comes very close now!"

The whooping of a car alarm pierced the air insistently. Alex jumped up, overturning his chair. "That's my Porsche!"

Dawn's helmet toppled forward and landed on her plate. "Oh, shit!"

"Good show, luv," said Peter.

Chapter Twenty-Nine

Léon got up and hurried after Alex. "The lightning maybe strikes the car!"

"Fetch Alex an umbrella," Marie shouted. "*Mon Dieu*, I never hear of a car struck by lightning."

"It wouldn't surprise me in the least." Hildy poked at her food, trying to sound cheerful. "The Porsche has been nothing but a bother, really. Our little Buick at home is perfectly fine, but Alex insisted on having this computerized wonder-car."

"It suits him, though, don't you think?" Victoria pushed her plate away, snapping open her gold case to extract a cigarette. "Your husband has the spirit of the adventurer."

Hildy bit back her irritation. "How perceptive of you, Victoria."

As no one made a move to reach across to light Victoria's

cigarette, she held it in the candle flame for a moment then puffed furiously to produce smoke. "Of course, Hildy has her writing, don't you, dear? How is your little book coming, by the way?"

Peter answered for her. "I find Hildy's ideas quite promising. In fact, she's given me some thoughts for *Petros*."

The car alarm stopped abruptly and Dawn removed her hands from over her ears. "What were we talking about? Vickie, would you mind blowing your smoke the other way, please?"

The front door slammed shut and in a moment Alex and Léon returned to their places at the table. Alex's hair was slicked with rain.

"Sorry," he said. "I'm not sure what the problem was. The fuse, I think. We had a problem with it earlier."

"That doesn't seem logical, Alex," Hildy said. "Surely an electrical storm is not supposed to do that."

Alex looked up at her. He seemed grateful to have something to say on a neutral subject. "Actually, the hood was unlatched as well. As I see it, we probably hit a pot hole somewhere and…"

"You mean the hood was open?" Hildy put her napkin down.

Alex shook his head. "You can't open the hood except from inside the car, but the latch was undone."

"Recalling our problem with the fuse box, Alex, I can't help wondering."

"I didn't know cars had fuses," Dawn said. "I thought they ran on gasoline."

"Do be still, luv," Peter said. "What about the fuse problem? What was wrong?"

"Well, actually…" Alex paused, looking across at his wife.

"I don't care, Alex," Hildy said with resignation. "Tell them."

Alex leaned forward, resting his arms against the table. "We did have some car trouble on the way here today. The computer was giving us false readings, telling us we were out of gas." He glanced at Dawn and nodded. "The Porsche does use gas, Dawn." He chuckled.

Victoria sighed. "I cannot believe we are discussing fuse boxes at Marie's glorious dinner party."

"Go on, Alex," Peter said.

Alex shook his head and grinned. "Believe it or not, when we stopped to check on the problem, we found a 'foreign object' in the fuse box." He sat back. "Can anybody guess what it was?"

Dawn placed her hands on the table. "Wait. How many letters?"

Victoria groaned. "Dawn, please. Finish your trout, for God's sake."

Shivar reappeared to remove plates and serve the *pièce de resistance*, a ghastly Floating Island in a glass bowl. The dinner guests offered restrained cries of pleasure, as Shivar ladled out the white meringue balls bobbing in caramel syrup. With a show of white teeth, he departed.

"So, Alex?" Peter asked. "What, pray, was in the fuse box?"

As Alex tried a mouthful of the dessert, Hildy observed his brave effort not to show his distaste. He hated fancy desserts, particularly runny ones.

Hildy spoke up. "What was inside the fuse box was this!" She held the pendant out from its chain where it caught tiny slivers of candlelight. "It seems our yardman, the esteemed Edmund, hid my crystal in the car to avoid having the police search him and find it. They arrived just as we were leaving yesterday." She scanned the table, and felt pleased she had everyone's attention.

"Edmund!" Victoria sat back, stunned. "But the gypsy wench. She was the one…"

"Since you were all there when it happened, you might as well hear the rest of it." Hildy paused. "Edmund stole my necklace after Alex returned from Monaco. He accused the gypsy, Nadia, and we had no reason not to believe him, since Yvette claimed she had seen Nadia put a concentrate of oleander in Victoria's Pimms."

Alex leaned forward, "But of course Edmund was lying. Obviously..." He stopped. "Go on, darling."

"Edmund lied about Nadia, having stolen my necklace himself, possibly even before the day of my luncheon. I suppose he planned to 'fence' it, as they say, to some dealer, possibly in Cannes, and get a few thousand francs for it."

"But that is incredible," Léon exclaimed. "Marie! You must discharge Edmund at once. I demand it."

"Of course, Léon." Marie's jaw tightened.

"Edmund is harmless, actually," Victoria said. "Just stupid. I would never leave anything around where any of those townspeople could find it. And that includes Lescaut, as well."

"Stealing is hardly harmless, Victoria," Hildy retorted.

"Oh, I don't mean it's all right. I simply mean one mustn't be careless with one's valuables."

Hildy swirled her goblet. "Or with one's husband, Victoria?"

Victoria's laughter echoed off the walls. "Really! How funny you are, Hildy. No one's talking about husbands."

Alex had gone gray in the face. "Why don't we talk about your book, Hildy? What's your opinion Peter? I understand you've reviewed Hildy's notes."

"I prefer not to discuss my book just now, Alex, if you don't mind."

"But why?" Victoria asked. "Come, Hildy, Alex is just being supportive."

Hildy rose and banged down her goblet. "I do not need you to explain my husband to me, Victoria. And I've had quite enough, a bellyful, by God, of your mindless, vicious, destructive game playing." She turned to Marie, "I do not wish to appear rude, but I simply cannot take any more of this."

Alex half rose from his chair. "It's all right, Hildy. Victoria's just being..."

Dawn said. "She's teasing, Hildy." She looked at Victoria. "You're awful, Vickie. God, the things you say to me."

"Shut up, Dawn," Peter said.

The Marquis coughed and cleared his throat.

"Sit down, Alex," Hildy commanded. "And please, don't try to interpret this woman to me. I am not a fool."

Victoria shook her head, "If I have offended you…"

"Everything about you offends me, Victoria. You are scheming, amoral and predatory. I find you positively—" she paused for the right word, "*toxic*!" She spat it out. "Like nuclear waste!"

Alex hurried over and put an arm around Hildy. "You have every right to be upset, darling. This past week has been a nightmare."

"Get away from me, Alex." She pushed him. "Just *get away from me*!" She marched to the door, nearly losing her balance on the leaden clogs.

Marie rose from her chair. "Oh, Hildy. Is there something I can do?"

Hildy stiffened her arms to stop the trembling. "What someone might do," she said carefully, "is *find Edmund*! That maniac has obviously followed us here to get *this*!" She brandished the crystal on its chain. "It wasn't a pothole that unlatched your hood, Alex; it was *Edmund*!"

She moved unsteadily across the marble floor of the foyer.

Peter ran after her and put his arm around her waist. "Are you all right, luv?"

"I'm really just fine, Peter. Thanks." She groped for the banister and started up the stairs.

"Let me go with you. It's frightfully dark. I insist." He guided her to the landing.

Another flash of lightning illuminated the sky through the mullioned landing window. Hildy drew in a deep breath as she paused to lean on the stone sill. "Did you see that, Peter?" She stared at the chapel across the garden while another flash of lightning created a glowing disc of the tiny rose window.

"What is it, Hildy?"

"The mimosa window."

Peter looked out, saying nothing.

"My fairy tale seems to begin and end with the mimosa." Hildy turned her face to him. "But the leaves of the mimosa—

that shut tight when they are hurt—open again and they go right on. And finally, there is another golden burst of flowers, and life resumes." She must remember to record that in her journal.

"Do you have that strength, Hildy?"

"That cosmic energy you speak about? That undying resource to continue?" She thought of Shirley MacLaine. "Yes, Peter. I have it."

She started up the stairs.

"Are you sure you can manage?"

"Quite sure. Thank you." She turned to look at him. "Peter, do see that the doors are tightly locked. If Edmund is out there, I would feel a bit safer." She blew him a kiss.

A gust of cold air struck her when she entered her room. The balcony door was wide open. Switching on the lights, she stepped over the fallen draperies to close the door, then looked for a key to lock it. There was none.

Shivering, she sank in the damask chair at the desk and pulled out the worn journal, her hand tracing the embossed cover. She sighed. As much as she would like to try to record her thoughts, there was no way she could unjumble her emotions.

Hildy stared out the window. The night had the clarity that follows a cleansing storm. Somewhere in the distance she saw the faint glow of a village lighting the broken clouds now scudding away from a clearing sky.

She felt exhausted and too chilled to undress for bed. When had she felt such a rush of emotion as what came over her at dinner? It had drained her. But she had no regrets whatsoever. She had only spoken the truth to Victoria Helmsley. But what difference did it make?

Kicking off the cerise clogs, she flung them across the room. She collapsed on the bed, hugging the blue velvet spread around her. The painted cherubs on the ceiling, weaving through their swirling garlands, made her dizzy, and she soon felt herself floating away, soaring among billowy clouds.

Chapter Thirty

"Hildy!"

Someone was shaking her, but the voice came from outer space.

"Hildy, please!" the voice implored. "What's wrong?"

But she was too groggy to reply. Her lips formed words, but nothing came out, like often happened in dreams.

"Good God, what's that smell?" It was Alex's voice.

She opened her eyes and squeezed them shut again. They smarted painfully.

Alex wrestled her to a sitting position. "What is it, Hildy? Wake up?"

She stared up at the ceiling at the cherubs. I have died and gone to heaven, she thought.

Alex pulled her to her feet. She reeled, her head spinning,

as he dragged her across the room and flung open the door to the balcony. His feet tangled in the draperies heaped on the floor. "What the hell happened here?" He wrestled her out the balcony door.

Her face and bare arms felt the shock of the damp night air. She tried to focus on Alex in his pajamas and robe. "What are you doing?" she groaned, her legs buckling beneath her.

"What is it, Hildy? Did you take pills?" He forced her forward and draped her body awkwardly over the wet balustrade.

She could feel beads of perspiration forming on her forehead. "Oh, God, I feel awful!"

"Take deep breaths, darling."

"I feel sick," she cried, her shoulders heaving.

"Easy, darling. I'm right here." Alex held her forehead.

"I don't understand why I feel so peculiar." Hildy suddenly straightened, steadying herself against the balustrade. "What are you doing here?" Her lips tightened. "I believe you have your own room."

"Listen, forget all that. I'm calling a doctor."

Hildy sucked in the fresh air. It tasted heavenly. "There is no need. I feel better now. Go back to Victoria."

Alex glared at her. "Will you cut that out?" His hand felt her forehead for a temperature.

She thrust it away. "Really, Alex. Trysting in the garden. How trite."

"We were not trysting. How many times do I have to tell you, what happened in Monaco is over. *Terminé*. That's what I was telling her down there in the garden."

"She apparently did not get the message. All that sly innuendo at dinner, as if I were a total fool."

"You're right, darling. The lady is mean. A shameless bitch." He whirled her around. "Can't we just forget about her now? Please?"

She looked at him, his eyes on hers. "I'd like to. I really would."

"I was stupid to get involved with her." He cupped her chin. "I never wanted to hurt you." His eyes held hers. "I am so sorry." He kissed her.

Hildy felt a pleasurable shock run through her. "Maybe that storm has blown away this nightmare. Could that be, Alex? They say the mistral purifies."

"I don't care what the damn mistral does. All I care about is you—that you're safe." He kissed her again.

She broke away suddenly, her hand to her neck. "My God, Alex, the necklace is gone!"

Rushing back inside, her legs numb, she fumbled through the folds of the pale blue velvet bedspread. "The clasp must have come undone."

Alex lifted the spread to poke under the pillows. "What happened to the curtains?"

"They just fell," she muttered. "Fairy castles aren't what they used to be." She lifted the edge of the fallen drapery to look on the floor, then peered under the oval desk and the damask chair where she had sat. "It's not here, Alex."

"What is that smell, Hildy?" He sniffed the air. "It's familiar."

"It's nauseating!" Hildy leaned against the balcony door and drew in another deep breath.

"A gas leak?" He threw open the bedroom door. "Léon!" His voice echoed through the stone corridor.

"Maybe someone tried to suffocate me like they do in James Bond movies." She searched the ceiling. "You know, Alex, one of those adorable little cherubs might be concealing an outlet to pump in carbon monoxide."

"Carbon monoxide has no smell, darling." Alex left the door open. "Anyway it's a little far-fetched in an 18th century castle, don't you agree?"

Hildy strained to remember her movements in the room earlier, but her memory was vague. She had felt cold and emotionally drained. "What time is it, Alex?"

He looked at his watch. "It's after one o'clock."

"If you hadn't waked me…" She put a hand to her throat.

His arms went around her. "I wanted to talk to you after what happened at dinner. I knocked earlier. You didn't answer. But I couldn't sleep, so I came back."

She smiled faintly. "It's good you did."

Victoria glided into the room wearing a nylon negligee, the same violet blue as her eyes. "What's wrong? I heard shouting way down in my chamber."

Hildy turned away.

"Just go away, Victoria," Alex said coldly. "Go back to your room. We don't need you here."

"But I want to be helpful," Victoria insisted.

Léon hurled himself into the room, a floor length gold satin robe flaring around him. Marie followed him, hugging a matching robe around her. Both bore the dynastic crest.

The Marquis sniffed the air. "Marie! You have used the insecticide here?"

"*Ooh-lah-lah*." Her eyes went to the fallen draperies, then to Hildy. "What happened, Hildy?"

Alex still had an arm around Hildy. "I could barely wake her. If I hadn't come back…"

"I think I'd have died," Hildy said. "Somebody drugged me and stole my necklace."

"It was Edmund, of course." Victoria's lip curled. "It was inevitable he would find a way to recover the necklace he hid in the car."

"*Mon Dieu*!" Marie cried, peering out on the balcony. "Did he climb up? It is very high."

"He didn't have to climb up, darling," Victoria said. "He simply broke into the castle." She turned to accuse Léon. "These locks are two hundred years old, are they not? Or are they *plastique*, *Monsieur*? From the *Monoprix*, Marie?" Victoria snorted.

Peter appeared in the doorway. "What's going on?"

There was a crash of metal from the corridor and Dawn's voice. "Oh, shit!"

"Dawn, for God's sake…" Peter rushed back out.

Marie put a comforting hand on Hildy's arm. "Léon, you must call the *gendarmes tout de suite*!"

Dawn emerged from the gloom of the corridor, helped by Peter. She looked spectral in a voluminous black velvet robe, its hood encircling her face. She was rubbing her hip. "I'm sorry. I fell over the armor."

"Dawn," Peter soothed, "run along back to your room now. You need your sleep."

"What is this thing?" Dawn held out an orange bug bomb.

Alex joined Léon as he took the object from Dawn.

"Marie?" Léon looked a question at the Marquise.

"I know nothing of this, Léon. The insecticide I keep in the kitchen until it is needed, in the summer."

Dawn pointed over her shoulder. "There are more out there. They fell out of the armor when I knocked it over."

Peter came into the room with two more bombs. "They look like proper grenades, don't they?"

"*Formidable!*" Marie looked at Léon. "Three of these in this room, *très dangereuses!*"

Hildy thought a moment. "The balcony door was open when I came back here earlier. He must have plugged them in, then when I was unconscious, taken my necklace and disposed of the bombs in the armor."

"But that's diabolical!" Peter said. "The man must be completely unhinged!"

Hildy was stunned. "He could have been right here in the room—under the bed, or on the balcony—when I came back!"

"Or concealed in that mess of drapery on the floor," Victoria said.

Hildy shuddered, then cupped the bombs in both hands and carried them carefully to the desk. "We really must not handle these. They will probably yield fingerprints."

"How long for the police to get here, Léon?" asked Alex.

"They are within two—three kilometers. I must call them directly."

"This is all too much for me, really." Victoria sagged against the desk. "It's bloody frightening with that insane pervert skulking about."

"Do not fear," Marie raised a protesting hand. "Léon, get your pistol."

Victoria hurried toward the door. "Listen, Edmund and

that gypsy tried to poison me, and now he's tried to suffocate poor Hildy." She shot a look of contempt at Alex. "I'm leaving, and I advise all of you to do the same."

A car engine gunned to a roar outside. Alex sprinted to the balcony, with Peter and Hildy behind him. Headlights suddenly illuminated the chapel then swung into the tunnel of trees beyond.

"It's the Citröen!" Alex shouted.

"Your car, Victoria," Peter leaned over the balustrade for a better view. "Edmund's making off with it!"

Victoria pushed next to Peter. "Good God!" she screamed. "Léon! Get the police! Peter, *do* something!" Her shoulders sagged. "Bloody hell! I'm marooned in this bloody awful place!"

Hildy shook her head. "If the police are like the ones in La Roquette, I haven't a hope they'll recover my necklace, or the car, or even apprehend that madman, for that matter."

Peter consoled Victoria. "There's nothing you can do but wait for the police, luv."

"Alex," Victoria wailed, "help me, can't you?"

Alex moved next to Hildy. "I'm very sorry, Victoria." He led Hildy back inside.

Victoria tugged on Alex's arm. "At least get me out of here, Alex. You owe me something…"

Hildy whirled to face her. "Actually, Victoria, my husband owes you nothing at all, unless of course you charge for your sexual favors, which wouldn't surprise me, to tell you the truth."

Victoria's eyes blazed. "Oh, shut up, you old biddy!"

Hildy went rigid, her voice controlled. "You listen to me, Victoria. You have been nothing more to my husband than a European adventure, do you understand that? A stop-off in the Michelin Guide—not even a two-star, at that. You are a loser. Do you understand what I'm saying? A pathetic, desperate *loser*! Now, please, just leave us alone. For good!"

Victoria glowered at Hildy for one long moment, then tore her hand from Alex's arm and ran from the room.

"*Regardez!*" Marie called from the balcony. "I saw a light in the chapel."

Hildy rushed out. "I see nothing, Marie."

"It is strange. It came and went, just now."

Léon charged in, brandishing a German Luger. "The *gendarmes*, they will come at once."

"My God, man." Alex shrank back. "Don't you have a little Derringer or something?"

Dawn had been observing from beside the oval desk. "Peter, should I go with Vickie? I think she's upset." She turned wide-eyed to Hildy. "I'm sure you hurt her feelings, Hildy. Even if she did deserve it."

"I know, dear," Hildy said. Dawn's innocence was almost touching. "Why don't you run along and help her. I believe she may be packing."

"Good idea, Dawn." Peter said.

"No," Dawn said, sinking to the bed. "Let her pack herself." She examined the rust on her velvet robe. "From that blasted armor. Would you have any carbolic acid, Marie?"

Peter went to Dawn and hugged her. "Later, pet. Let's just be quiet now, shall we? There's a good girl."

Dawn shook her head slowly. "God, I hate this place."

"You know, Alex," Hildy chose her words carefully, "the necklace with André's glass in it, and the coincidence of a light just now in the mimosa window he made for the chapel…" She picked up her journal. "The explanation will be found in the chapel. I'm convinced of it."

Alex glanced at the journal and back to her face. "Why? Is there something in your journal?"

"Not exactly. But I saw a map in André's hut." Hildy decided to say no more. She replaced the journal in the tote and took it from the table. "Marie, we'll need a flashlight."

"But of course." She scurried for the door. "And I get you a cape for your shoulders."

"Peter, you're coming, aren't you?" Hildy pulled her tennis shoes from her Hartmann and hastily slipped them on. "The time has finally come to have a look at André's mimosa window."

Chapter Thirty-One

Outside the chapel, Hildy shone the flashlight on the darkened circle of the rose window above the arched entrance. "We must all be quiet," she whispered. "We have no idea what may be lurking inside."

"Silence!" hissed the Marquis. He crabbed slowly forward along the path, the Luger held stiffly in front of him. Suddenly he leapt through the chapel door. "*Hallo! Attendez!*" His voice echoed in the stone interior. Waving the gun, he motioned the others to follow.

"Lord," Hildy groaned. "If that's what he calls sneaking up."

"Léon," Marie whispered, "be careful, *chèri*."

Hildy flashed the light on some timbers partially blocking their way inside the door.

"What is this?" she heard Léon say. "Marie? Who puts this scaffolding here?"

"I know nothing of it. The chapel has been closed all winter."

Votive candles near the altar flickered in the darkness. There was no sound but the drip of rain from the trees outside.

"*Hallo*!" Léon repeated.

Hildy winced. Colombo he was not. Anyone inside the chapel would scarcely be unaware of the Marquis' commando-style entrance.

"Wait," he said. "I light the lights."

There was a clicking as Léon threw a switch several times back and forth. "*Zut alors*! They do not work."

Hildy crept down the aisle, flashing her light. Three rows of wooden pews on each side would accommodate perhaps thirty worshipers. A finely carved communion rail separated the congregation from the modest altar, flanked by unlit iron candelabra.

Dawn's voice piped in the gloom, "My shoes are totally soaked, Peter."

Hildy hurried to one side of the altar where a woman clung to a loosely robed figure, reminding her of the Pietà. "Madame Lescaut," she gasped, letting the light flicker across the housekeeper's stricken face. "What on earth?"

"And who is this poor, young man?" asked Marie, pointing to the wispy-bearded figure. His face appeared ravaged with fatigue. His eyes darted about apprehensively as the housekeeper pulled him closer.

"Madame, Monsieur, forgive me." She raised a hand against the light. "I did not know what to do." She encircled the man's shoulders, forcing him upright. "I must explain. This is André Dupres."

"Dupres?" Hildy was stunned. She took a step forward and stared at him. Could these be the eyes whose intensity—even in a photograph—had magnetized her that day at the grave near the hut?

"What do you mean by this, Lescaut?" Léon demanded.

"Please, Monsieur, I will explain. André is not well." Lescaut wiped his face with her shawl. "He has been in hospital, suffering from great depression."

"But you told us he was dead," said Marie.

Lescaut bowed her had. "No, Madame. André did not die that night."

"Then what did happen?" Hildy asked gently. "Why have you lied about it?"

Lescaut got up slowly, her hand caressing the man's neck for a moment before she walked slowly to one of the pews and sat down. "A year ago when he was healthy and strong, André, he comes to know Lady Helmsley. She sits in the garden and makes drawings of him while he works. He is proud she wishes to draw his picture." Lescaut had slid a rosary from her pocket and was working the beads through her fingers.

"You see," she cast a loving glance at André, "he is a simple person, a dreamer. He accepts what seems to be. He thinks the *light* has much power and his colored glass makes the light more beautiful."

Peter coughed. "Sensing the energy, possibly. Some of us are particularly receptive."

Lescaut looked at Peter briefly. "Sometimes, I think André is, perhaps, alone in his special world."

"In company with many great geniuses," Hildy added, hoping to ease the woman's obvious anguish. "But why have you let us believe he died?"

Lescaut continued. "André sits for Lady Helmsley in her studio for her to paint him. She pays him a few francs to do this, and André needs the money."

"Victoria *does* fancy painting from life, I gather." Peter turned to Hildy. "You said she's doing a canvas of that gardener chap."

"André must be nude for this painting, she tells him." Lescaut's face became grim. "And soon, she takes him to her bed. It is not so extraordinary, *oui*? Not for this English-woman! I have seen her with men."

Hildy nodded. "Yes, you and I talked about that." She felt

Alex's hand on her shoulder.

"What of this evil woman's attentions to André?" Lescaut sighed. "Well, he is, after all, a man. But André is only a simple shepherd. He shows her his work in stained glass, and she tells him how marvelous it is. She buys him elegant tools for his work and finds him some restoration of stained glass to do in the village cathedral and some other places where a craftsman is needed."

"St-Paul-de-Vence?" Hildy asked.

"*Oui*, that was one." Her face darkened. "But there is this gypsy, Nadia, a friend of his cousin, Yvette. Before André becomes *le protégé* of Madame Helmsley, André and Nadia, they have *une amourette*. They are both young, *non*?"

"A serious romance?" Hildy sat down near Lescaut on the pew. "That day in the courtyard, you blamed her for hurting André. I thought that meant she had something to do with his death. But he is alive." She smiled at André. "Thank God for that."

His face softened in response. He continued to stare at her.

"I tell you everything now," Lescaut said. "After André has become quite skilled making the stained glass, he tells Nadia he and Madame Helmsley, they are in love. André tells Nadia he is finished with her and Nadia goes away to Spain for many months, but," Lescaut shook her head silently for a moment, "what kind of love is this with the Englishwoman?"

Marie spoke up. "Did Madame Helmsley ever speak to you of this…*liaison*?"

Lescaut snorted. "André is a simple toy for her amusement, nothing more."

"I am blind, Léon." Marie looked at her husband. "I saw none of this."

"What happened that night in the shepherd's hut?" Hildy asked.

"The gypsy, Nadia, she comes back that night last year in October, heavy with child. André is with Madame Helmsley in the hut. It is…intimate—very bad." Lescaut raised one of her hands as if to push away the memory. "Nadia has come back to tell André she is pregnant with his child!"

Hildy drew in her breath, then looked at Peter. "The creator of the divine windows fathers a child."

Peter reached for Hildy's hand and pressed it.

Lescaut's eyes blazed. "But the Englishwoman thinks Nadia lies to make André return to her. She pushes the gypsy from the hut. There is a struggle, and André tries to make them stop, but then—" Lescaut's shoulders began to shake. "Then the baby comes."

"Dear God," Hildy reached over to take Lescaut's hands in hers.

"Too soon. The baby is born dead." She stopped, then said with mounting anger, "The Englishwoman is in panic. It is no game for her anymore, *non*? She fetches me at once to take care of the baby and make things right. Nadia is in great agony. I leave André and run quickly for the priest. He send for the gypsies to take Nadia away. Madame Helmsley is gone, back to her villa. Very soon she returns to England to forget all of it. But the baby…" Lescaut shook her head. "And André is beyond help. I hide him in the tower at the villa for a time, but his spirit is dead. His mind sees nothing."

Alex's voice was soft. "And Nadia came back to La Roquette last week to kill Victoria."

Hildy looked at him for a moment. "Then the dead cat, Ariadne, was a gypsy warning." She asked Lescaut, "The grave marker I saw in the meadow?"

"For the baby. The priest gives the rites and we bury the child, a boy, as the new day breaks. I mark it later with André's name. Then the priest helps me take André away to Grenoble, the *Institut*." She shrugged and turned to Marie. "You and the Marquis were here, at your castle. I make up a story when you return. André is dead. What does it matter now?"

"So it is your nephew in the grave I saw," Hildy said.

Lescaut looked at her, tears filling her eyes. "No, Madame. Not my nephew."

"Then who…?"

"My grandson."

Hildy repeated the words to herself slowly. "Are you saying André is…?"

"Yes, Madame…my son."

Hildy enfolded Lescaut in her arms. "Oh, my dear woman." She reached a hand toward André, and he took it to come sit beside his mother, looking at Hildy with unblinking eyes.

After a moment, Hildy straightened, wiping her eyes with her fingers.

Léon's voice had an edge. "It is the way of peasants to tamper with the truth."

Lescaut braced herself upright. "When André came to your villa with me, Monsieur, you think he is my brother. I think, why not? To you, he is only another peasant. It makes no difference. Then, after what happened, there is still no reason everyone must know the truth. I keep this ugly tragedy to myself."

"Ah, but Léon," Marie protested, "we have never had a gardener like her son. Your villas gave you great pride then, *non*?"

Lescaut added, "You know this is true, Monsieur."

André's face brightened at Marie's praise.

Léon nodded his agreement. "You are absolutely correct, Madame. The gardens were *magnifique*." He scowled. "Then we hire this Edmund!"

"Why did you come here tonight to the chapel?" Hildy asked.

"Why?" Lescaut shook her head. "André talks always about his windows. *Three* windows, always these three windows. They let him try at the *Institut* to make new stained glass to make his mind calm again, but always he must find these three."

Hildy looked at the rose window. "Is this one of them?"

Lescaut pulled André to his feet. "I follow him here. He has run away from the *Institut*, and we must return. But, I must tell you…"

Hildy waited for the housekeeper to continue.

"The shepherd window…" Lescaut said.

"Yes?"

"It is not the mistral that breaks the window. It is André."

Hildy's hand went to her throat where the necklace had been. She shot a glance at Alex. "I can't believe this."

"*Oui, Madame*," Lescaut said. "It is true."

Hildy shook her head. "But I saw the mimosa branch!"

"*Non, Madame*." Lescaut stared at the rough stone floor. "He finds the fallen branch from the storm and smashes it through the window himself."

"The man in the cape I saw from the window that night." Hildy glanced at her husband. "It was André."

Lescaut struggled to explain. "In this madness, he must destroy it. I believe he destroys the Englishwoman in this way." She offered a sad, bewildered smile. "What is in his heart, I must guess. She gives him some very special glass and tells him to put it in these windows. Now he will destroy this hated glass. This glass of *hers*!"

Peter nodded slowly. "I can see the mystical connection he might form in his mind, Madame. In despair, the artist revolts and desecrates his art."

"After the mistral, I hide André again in the tower," Lescaut said, "then I must go to Grenoble on the day of your luncheon. A relative is sick. It is not true. I must take André back."

Hildy thoughtfully pulled her journal from her tote. She turned to where the map from André's hut had been folded into the pages.

André's eyes moved to focus on the map. Suddenly he jumped to his feet. "*Ici!*" He seized a candle and ran to climb the flimsy scaffolding he had erected under the rose window. "*La mimosa!*"

A moon had risen, throwing a pattern of light through the open arched entrance door. André's candle flickered against the icy blue disk of the rose window.

"No! No, André!" Lescaut gripped the scaffolding.

He picked up a tool and began to chip away at the masonry surrounding the window.

"André!" Hildy called. "No, please! Don't do that!" She

grabbed Alex's hand and ran closer.

"*Vic-tor-i-a*! *Vic-tor-i-a*!" His voice was anguished as he punctuated the cry with blows on the chisel.

"Tell him to stop, Lescaut!" cried the Marquise. "André! You make this window for *us*. You must not destroy it!"

"I will shoot him," Léon edged down the aisle, raising the pistol.

"For God's sake, Léon!" Peter seized the Marquis' arm.

Dawn's head rose from behind a pew. "Get down, everyone. Léon's going to start shooting!"

Alex looked at his wife. "God, what do we say to Dupres, Hildy? He's absolutely out of it."

"He's acting out his truth as he sees it, Alex. God help him, maybe it will help him cast his demons out."

"André!" Lescaut clutched the timbers of the platform. "You must come down now, my son."

André stared down at her. "*La mimosa*," he whispered. "I use the glass of Victoria, *non*?" His thin lips curled in an oddly mischievous smile, then contorted into a snarl as he leaped from the platform and dashed out the door with the mallet raised.

"Dupres!" the Marquis shouted. "I have a gun!"

Peter seized the gun from Léon's hand. "Let me take charge of that, sir, if you don't mind." He rushed out the door. "André! No one will hurt you!"

Suddenly there was a crash of glass as the mallet hurtled through the window and the colored glass showered to the stone floor. From outside, André's voice wailed, "*Vic-tor-i-a*!"

Moonlight through the vacant hole in the wall cast a blue pallor over the debris. Hildy swept the flashlight beam toward the door as André ran back in and knelt to examine the fragments.

"André, you will cut yourself." Lescaut tried to pull him away. "See, your hand bleeds."

Hildy brought out a handkerchief and tried to wrap it around his hand. "André. Look at this, please." She unfolded the map and shone the light on it.

He hesitated and looked at the torn paper. "My map," he said in a shaking voice. "*Ici, ici et ici!*" His finger left a bloody smudge on the map where he jabbed at the three X's.

"And your words here," Hildy pointed to the minute scribbles next to the X's. "What does this say?"

He peered at the map then turned wide eyes to his mother. He stammered out a gibberish of French.

Lescaut translated. "He says these are the three." She pointed. "The chapel, here, the villa in La Roquette and this one, St-Paul-de-Vence."

André plunged back to his search among the pieces of glass surrounding him. Suddenly a look of triumph spread across his face as he held up a small piece of amber glass. He turned to his mother, then to Hildy. "*La mimosa!*" he whispered.

"Were you calling me, André?" Victoria's commanding voice penetrated the chapel. She stood silhouetted against the moonlit door pointing a gun. "I have Hildy's diamond. Now give me my topaz, André. Do it now!"

Chapter Thirty-Two

"A diamond?" Alex looked at Hildy. "Hildy, did you…?"

Hildy shook her head. "Frankly, I'm stunned. I've heard crystals have hidden power but to turn into a diamond? You need a fairy godmother to do that." She tried to make sense of the mystery. "Of course, I realized tonight there was something very special about the necklace…" She hesitated.

Madame Lescaut started toward Victoria. "Do not hurt André. Please."

André looked around at the litter of glass, then slowly extended his hand with the amber nugget toward Victoria.

"Thank you," Victoria said, clasping the topaz in her fist. "I wish you could see your face, Hildy. The great American writer with her tiresome little notes and her boring insights. No wonder your husband strays, the poor man."

Hildy's chin went up. "Tell me something, Victoria. Just to make my tiresome little notes complete, when did you *first* learn I'd found my... '*crystal*'? Did Alex tell you in the garden tonight?"

Victoria looked directly at Alex. "He told me he had recovered the necklace *and* his marriage again. Isn't that sweet? Did you compose that poetic thought for him, Hildy?"

Hildy shot Alex a faint smile, but said nothing.

"He dumped me, Hildy," Victoria said flatly. "Are you pleased? I'm afraid it left me feeling rather desperate, maybe even a tad reckless. Remember, you called me a loser at dinner? The fact is, I've very little left to lose."

"So, having learned I had the necklace, you contrived a plan to asphyxiate me by planting the insect bombs."

Alex took a step toward Victoria. "Is that true, Victoria? I can't believe you'd—"

Victoria swung the gun at him. "The jewel is mine, Alex. Your wife stole it from André's window!"

"I must concede, Victoria," Hildy continued, "your improvised plan was quite clever. You waited for me to leave my room for dinner. Then, knowing that many bombs would become deadly when I closed the balcony doors and went to sleep, you could easily steal my necklace."

Victoria laughed. "You make it sound a better plan than it was. The bug bombs were just handy, that's all. And everyone would think it was an accident. I thought it a rather expedient scheme, actually."

"Incredible!" Peter looked stunned. "Are these pieces of glass really precious gems?"

"Oh, Peter," Victoria admonished him, "not all of them."

"But was it you who stole the jewels from the Ashmolean?"

"When I was docent there. Of course." Victoria pointed the gun at him. "Is that so unthinkable?"

"Actually, it is, old girl. How did you manage it?"

Victoria laughed. "Dear Peter. Who would suspect Lady Helmsley, wealthy part-timer at that doddering old museum, indulging her taste for the arts? When questioned, I merely wept a great deal and kept asking for the smelling salts." Her smile vanished. "The truth is, I needed money. I still do. You're so preoccupied with your silly films, you don't pay attention, Peter. I've told you Jeremy gives me practically no money at all."

"God knows you'll never get by on your painting, *n'est-ce pas*, Victoria?" Hildy said. "But why would you entrust the gems to André? Surely that was a great risk."

"Where does one hide a million dollars in jewels? I could not have them about if the police became suspicious. And André would do anything for his *patronesse*, is that not so, *mon chèri*?" She reached out to caress his cheek, which he turned abruptly away. "I never imagined he would hide them from me in his bloody windows."

Dawn's voice was heard from the shadows. "Vickie, you ought to be ashamed of yourself. You're nothing but a crook."

"Who asked you?" Victoria said harshly. "The point is, André, *chèri*, there is one jewel, the ruby, unaccounted for." She pointed the gun at him again. "Where is it?"

Hildy crumpled the map in her hand. "I should think it's clear, Victoria, this poor man had no idea your pretty pieces of glass were famous gems."

"André," Victoria snarled, "Where is the ruby! Tell me. Now!"

André looked at her vacantly and raised his empty hands. Reflecting a growing understanding, his eyes turned to Hildy. "I make many, many windows."

Hildy carefully pressed the crumpled map into a ball in her fist. "The ruby could be anywhere, Victoria."

"André does not know these are gems, Madame," Madame Lescaut protested. "He is a simple shepherd."

Suddenly, Victoria slapped André. "Fool! Where is the other stone?"

André put a hand to his cheek.

"Really, Victoria," Hildy said evenly, "There's no point in abusing the poor man any more than you already have."

Hildy saw Léon's eyes dart to the door, and followed his

gaze to see headlights flash against the trees. She sucked in her breath. "I should imagine that will be the police, *n'est-ce pas*, Léon?"

Victoria looked fiercely around the chapel for another exit. There was none. In panic, she raced out the arched door.

"Come on, Peter!" Alex bolted after her, Peter behind him with Léon's gun.

A police car idled at the end of the path. Two men had jumped out, one of them advancing down the path. "Stop!"

"That woman!" Alex shouted, pointing.

"She's gone off the path," Peter pointed the Luger at the thicket of shrubbery. "Get a light over here, chaps, can you? Mind, she's got a gun."

A beam of light swung around and stabbed through the wet foliage, stopping on the white face of the terrified Victoria.

Hildy hurried up the path. "Alex, don't go near her. She's got that gun!"

"I'm all right, darling," Alex took her arm. "The police have her now."

"Ah, Lieutenant Janvier," Léon said jovially. "We have a little excitement here tonight, eh?"

"*Bonsoir, Léon. Oui.* Is it this one who attempts to kill a guest of yours?" The disheveled Victoria struggled in the other policeman's grasp. "Madame, I suggest you cooperate. Things will go easier."

"It is not I, you idiots," Victoria cried. "There's a maniac loose out there! He stole my car!"

As the lieutenant started to speak, two pairs of headlights blinked through the trees along the winding road to the castle. In a moment the red Citröen purred to a stop, followed by another police car. "Ah, *voilà*! Here is the stolen car, *non*?"

Behind a steel mesh in the back seat of the second police car, Edmund glowered through the window.

Hildy took a frightened step back. "Alex!"

"I'm right here, darling." He hugged her waist and moved her away.

"*Mesdames et Messieurs*," Lieutenant Janvier said crisply,

"I shall wish to hear precisely what has gone on here tonight. Sergeant?" He turned to his colleague who was rigging a tape recorder to document the proceedings.

"*Oui*, Lieutenant." The sergeant plugged in a small microphone and spoke some words into it.

Hildy immediately groped for her journal and uncapped the lavender pen. "I suppose I could just get a transcript of all this, couldn't I?"

"I'm sure your notes will be infinitely more descriptive, darling," Alex added.

Peter had moved next to them. "Did you have any idea all this intrigue was going on, Hildy?"

"I was suspicious, as you know, Peter." She looked at her husband. "Of course, as a novelist, I tend to romanticize things, don't I, Alex?"

Alex grinned. "You could say that."

"But one thing is quite clear," Hildy said, completing a note in the journal.

"What's that?" Alex asked.

Hildy smiled. "Victoria is the one who wanted the diamond from the beginning. Edmund is merely a double-crossing confederate."

"*S'il vous plaît, Madame*. Wait." He took the microphone from the sergeant and held it in front of her. "Speak clearly into this."

Hildy cleared her throat and looked at the sergeant. "One, two, testing. Is this all right?"

The sergeant pressed thumb to forefinger to signal okay.

Hildy paused a moment to gather her thoughts. Should she use a casual Barbara Walters approach in her remarks or go for Diane Sawyer? After all, it wasn't inconceivable that excerpts from the tape might end up on the six o'clock news, or whatever it was called in France.

"Whenever you're ready, Madame," prodded Lieutenant Janvier.

"Oh, yes. Thank you, Lieutenant Janvier and good evening ladies and gentlemen—*Mesdames et Messieurs*. This is Hildy

Bigelow at Chateau de Musset in Beaulieu, France. A violent storm broke over the Chateau here tonight, leaving in its wake an international jewel theft and an attempted murder..."

Chapter Thirty-Three

As Hildy went on, setting the scene for her commentary, Janvier interrupted to hold the mike away for a moment. "I believe we can skip over some of this detail, Madame Bigelow. We need only the important facts now, please."

"I understand, Lieutenant." Hildy took a breath. "To give you a brief overview of this heist, the woman here is Lady Victoria Helmsley, a title she may have assumed. I can tell you, she does tend to gild the lily, as they say." She covered the microphone with her hand. "Do you understand that expression, Lieutenant? It means…"

"There is no need to explain, Madame," said Janvier curtly.

"In any event," Hildy continued, "there were three important jewels—a ruby, a topaz and a diamond. I believe you will find they were all stolen from the museum where Lady Helmsley was employed as a tour guide."

"I was a *docent*," Victoria snapped. "And an authority on the Medieval. Remember, Léon? You tried to sell me your family's moth-eaten tapestries."

The Marquis stiffened. "These were treasures, Madame. You know nothing of such things!"

Janvier held up an impatient hand. "You were saying, Madame Bigelow, you believe this woman who attempts murder here tonight also stole these gems? How do you know this, if I may ask?"

"If you will look in Lady Helmsley's purse, Lieutenant, I'm quite sure you will find a diamond necklace. The diamond is stolen—the setting belongs to me. If this seems at all confusing, I can…"

"With your permission, Madame Helmsley." Janvier fumbled in Victoria's purse and pulled out the necklace. "So!"

Hildy spoke *sotto voce* into the microphone. "Lieutenant Janvier is now displaying the diamond. I would judge it is about the size of a quite large M&M." She took a step toward Victoria. "I believe, Lieutenant Janvier, you will also find Lady Helmsley has a topaz. It may still be clutched in her hand."

"You Yankee bitch!" Victoria breathed, as Janvier pried the jewel from her fist.

"This accounts for two of the jewels, as you have no doubt discerned, Lieutenant." Hildy looked at Victoria. "There is yet the third—a ruby. You will find it in the cathedral at St-Paul-de-Vence, in the crown of *La Virgine,* a stained glass window near the sacristy. Are there any questions?" Hildy glanced about at her attentive audience. "Any questions at all?" Feeling oddly at ease, she waited.

"*Bravo*, Hildy!" The Marquise applauded lightly.

"Thank you, Marie. None of this would have been possible had it not been for our stay at your villa." She bestowed a smile on Léon.

Alex gave Hildy a laconic smile. "You can say that again, darling."

"Do you mind, Lieutenant?" Hildy held up the diamond. "Look how beautiful, Alex. See how the facets throw off subdued moon-embers, illuminating the night?" She fondled it in her palm. "I almost wish it were not a famous diamond."

"You have finished, Madame?" asked the Lieutenant.

"Perhaps I might describe the metaphoric significance of the diamond for the tape. You see," Hildy took Peter's arm, "Mr. Balfour, is doing a film called *Petros*, a contemporary story about Jesus. This stone—*Petros* means stone—this diamond was found in a window depicting the shepherds abiding in the fields by night. In the sky, we see the Star of Bethlehem…"

Janvier reached over to shut off the machine. "It is not necessary, *merci*. I think we will rely on our notes, eh, Sergeant? You may make a full statement later and give all your metaphors, and, of course, tell about the Nativity then, if you wish." The Lieutenant handed the necklace to the Sergeant who folded it into a glassine envelope. "There are indeed some details to be cleared up here."

"I do have my own notes for you as well, Lieutenant." Hildy held up her journal. "But suppose I give you the broad strokes of the caper as I see them. Shall I? You're quite sure you won't need an on-the-spot tape of this?"

Janvier shook his head, his expression somewhat pained. "No. I shall try to manage with just notes. Do continue, if you please. Briefly."

"As you wish." Hildy resumed, "Edmund, that rogue you have apprehended in the car there, was supposed to steal the jewel from me and give it to Victoria. They would share in its value. But when Victoria became ill at my luncheon and was carried off to the hospital, Edmund saw a chance to keep the necklace for himself, and did so." Hildy turned to Alex. "It occurs to me that Edmund may have had Nadia put the oleander in Victoria's Pimms, Alex." She made a new note.

"Of course," Alex nodded. "It would have gotten her out of his way for sure."

Hildy said to the lieutenant, "Unfortunately, Edmund

secreted the necklace in the fuse box of our Porsche to hide it from the police who arrived unexpectedly the morning we left, and we drove off with it."

"So," Léon mused, "the car alarm earlier, it was Edmund trying to retrieve the jewel, *non*? Hildy said it was he."

"Lying thief!" Victoria spat at Edmund.

"You never tell me it is *diamond,* you bitch," Edmund cried "I steal for you and then you plan to cheat me!"

"We subsequently found the necklace ourselves when we developed engine trouble," Hildy smiled. "So Victoria was forced to steal it all over again."

"I see," Janvier said. "And so the attempt on your life?"

"Fortunately, it failed," Hildy said, "but the woman's M.O. might be of interest to you, Lieutenant." She smiled at him expectantly.

"M.O.?"

"*Modus Operandi.* Her method, Lieutenant. It's a television term." Janvier was intent on his notes. "In any case, when Victoria found I had recovered my necklace, she improvised a plan to drug me with gas fumes from the insecticide bombs you French use in your light plugs, *three* of them. I'm sure she fancied it a lethal dose. You will doubtless be able to lift her fingerprints when you examine the insect bombs. We have the bombs. She dropped them in a suit of armor, which Dawn here fortunately fell against and wrecked."

"You'll never find them." Victoria snapped. "When you left for the chapel, I…" She stopped. "I think I should have a lawyer present."

Janvier said, "If you wish to make a statement, Madame, it is your right to counsel."

Hildy waved a hand impatiently. "She probably disposed of them in the stream off the little bridge, the obvious place."

Victoria gasped. "No, no! It was Edmund. He climbed through the window and tried to kill her."

"I'm sorry, Victoria," Hildy said. "You are the one found with the diamond, *n'est-ce pas*?"

Léon had lit a cigarette and blew smoke into the center of

the group, wheezing briefly. "I do not understand. If Madame Helmsley did not know André had put the jewels in his windows, how did she know this—crystal of Madame Bigelow is one of the gems? Eh?"

Hildy turned to Alex. "Victoria helped you select the setting in Monaco, isn't that so, darling?"

Alex hesitated.

"Come now, Alex," Hildy said softly. "I'm not angry about that anymore. She did, didn't she?"

He faltered. "My French. I couldn't…"

"Of course you couldn't," Hildy said. "But I'll bet Victoria understood quite well when the jeweler's eyes lit up and he told her the stone was a magnificent diamond."

"He did seem enthusiastic, as a matter of fact," Alex said. "I assumed he was just making a big deal, because he thought it was for…"

"For her," Hildy finished. "Of course. What else would he think, a handsome man and his attractive companion?"

Léon puffed on his cigarette. "Ah, *oui*. It would be entirely natural to assume this."

"In France, I'm sure it would be, Léon," Hildy agreed. "Of course, Victoria knew the glass had come from the shepherd window, and naturally, when she learned it was a diamond, she understood at last what André had done with the pieces of 'glass' she had asked him to hide for her. Then, when she thought André had died…"

Peter said to Victoria, "You did think that, didn't you? Everyone did, except Lescaut. And the priest, of course." He shook his head. "Bummer, old girl, what?"

The Lieutenant took handcuffs from his Sergeant and took Victoria's arm.

"Mind my dress, luv. Chiffon is frightfully thin—and delicate. I'll want to telephone my solicitor at once, of course. My word, but you do seem young to be a lieutenant."

"Oh, dear," Peter whispered to Hildy. "It's gotten a bit dicey for the old girl, what?"

The Sergeant stood Victoria against the car as he searched

through her purse. Her lids were closed, as if the incident had simply become a trying interruption.

"Your perceptions are fascinating, Madame Bigelow," the Lieutenant said. "But I have several questions still."

Alex smiled at him. "Of course you do, sir, but if we could get the ladies back to the castle now, and out of this dampness, I'm sure my wife can fill you in on the other details. She has kept meticulous notes in her journal, as you see."

Hildy displayed it again for the lieutenant.

"*Oui, oui*," Janvier frowned. "I am fully aware."

Peter turned to Victoria. "Exactly how were you planning to escape, Victoria? This fellow Edmund had your car…"

"The Porsche, of course." Victoria's lids remained closed. "How else? Alex would have given me the keys, wouldn't you, luv?" She looked up at him. "I did have the pistol, remember?"

"I wouldn't have bet on it, Victoria." Alex's voice was steel.

"My dear Lady Helmsley," Hildy added. "If you thought for a moment my husband would hand over the keys to the Porsche, you gravely underestimated his priorities. Poisoning me would be a whole lot easier." Hildy rearranged the cape Marie had provided her. "Now before I conclude my remarks at the castle…"

Victoria's eyes suddenly widened in horror as a figure burst from the shrubbery, her dark hair flying wildly. The glint of metal flashed in her hand as she rushed at Victoria, screaming curses. "Now, Englishwoman whore, I avenge my child!" Nadia stabbed the knife again and again into Victoria before Janvier and his aides could pull her away. "Murderess!" The gypsy shrieked. "And Dupres is alive! I watched you in the chapel. I will kill that pig who abandons his unborn child for a slut!" She strained against the Lieutenant's grip, shaking with rage.

"Someone, quickly! Léon! Alex!" Hildy rushed forward as Victoria backed away with a cry. "Marie! Call a doctor!"

Victoria collapsed to the wet earth, her body heaving slightly. Then she lay motionless.

Hildy saw blood spreading across the gold chiffon of Victoria's gown. "She's not moving!" Hildy's voice felt stifled. Behind her, she heard Nadia's voice as the police loaded her into the police car with Edmund. "You! You filthy lying bastard! You would blame me for your evil thievery with the whore! The witch who murdered my child!"

Hildy felt giddy under the explosion of such hatred. As Alex's arms went around her she let herself melt against him. "Thank God you're here with me, Alex."

"It's okay, darling. It's over now. Finally. We'll leave for Paris tomorrow."

Marie put her hand in Hildy's. "Ah, *formidable, Madame.* Such a night of horrors!"

"It's all right, Marie. We must go see what has happened to the others." Glad to leave the scene, Hildy hurried along the path back to the chapel. Behind her, she heard the Lieutenant giving orders on the police radio.

"Ah, the mimosa window," the Marquis moaned, peering up at the round hole above the chapel door. "I will have to replace it with *plastique, non?*"

Lescaut, who had stood quietly next to her son watching the proceedings, now turned to Hildy with her arms out. "Ah, Madame. I think it has changed everything for André to see this woman again—to know at last the truth of her scheming…"

"I'm so glad." Hildy hugged her.

"But of course they will arrest Lady Helmsley, *non*? It is right. She is an evil woman—and a thief!"

Hildy suddenly felt overwhelmed with weariness. "Why don't we all go back to the chapel and sit a moment. It's been such a tragedy for both you and your son, Madame Lescaut."

"But he is able to speak to me now!" Lescaut's face broke into a smile. "It is a miracle!"

Dawn sat in the pew beside André, attempting some primitive French. "*Vous êtes* OK, baby *non?*"

Andre's boyish face turned to her with a faint smile.

Hildy took André's hands in both of hers. "I am sorry I did

not know you except through your art, André. I wish you great success with it and with your beautiful glass. Your understanding of *la lumiere* has brought light into my life." She looked for a long moment at Alex. "Into both our lives."

"I am happy this is so, Madame," André said, a new sparkle in his eyes.

Hildy reached for the *fleur de lis* in her tote and unwrapped it. "You see? Your mother gave this to me when I left La Roquette to remember you always."

He reached for it and turned it over in his hands for a moment, then smiled and kissed it, handing it back to Hildy.

She put it back in her tote. "Come, Alex." She led him out of the chapel. "It seems the Raven Princess received her comeuppance after all, though my gypsy, Consuela, would never have sunk to murder."

"You really were quite wonderful, darling. I believe your journal may become a national archive of the *gendarmerie!*"

"Wouldn't that be nice? I suppose now I must finish explaining to the Lieutenant about Nadia and the various figures in black cloaks and about Edmund copying the map from my journal and..."

"Fine," he said. "I hope it won't take too long."

"I'm too exhausted to be anything but brief."

"Is that a promise?" He hugged her to him as he led her back up the path. "Look up there, see? There's a full moon." He kissed her lightly. "When Janvier leaves, what do you think? Shall we join General de Gaulle or Marie Antoinette?"

Chapter Thirty-four

Six hours later Hildy opened her eyes to find herself staring up at the ruby velvet canopy over General De Gaulle's bed. She and Alex had spent what remained of the night cuddled together in utter exhaustion.

Her glance moved slowly along the wall, striped with glorious gold by the morning sun. The nightmare was over, and as her eyes focused on Alex's sleeping face, she felt an overwhelming sense of renewal—and compassion.

Tiptoeing across the room to the desk, Hildy opened her journal and uncapped her lavender pen to write:

> *How stupid of me not to recognize Alex's need for nurturing. Cast adrift on an unfamiliar lake of leisure, he had no idea how to use it. Without the emotional*

gratification his job afforded him, he sought it some-
where else.

And where was I when he needed me? So preoccu-
pied with Consuela's lust for Orlando that Alex made
a perfect target for Victoria's charms. Ironic...that
the freedom Alex worked for so diligently could cripple
him when he finally achieved it.

The day was pleasant enough to breakfast on the terrace, but the sun promised feverish heat for the new day.

Clutching Alex's hand, Hildy greeted Léon, seated at the glass-topped wrought iron table. "Such a beautiful morning, Léon." She surmised the night had taken its toll, for he was still in his robe and pajamas.

Across the sloping lawn, the wind stirred the olive trees, exposing the silvery underside of their leaves. Hildy breathed the air.

Léon whacked the paper with the back of his hand. "*Rien!*" He scowled as he gulped his coffee. "Not a word of the affair last night at my chateau."

"I'm not surprised, Léon." Alex helped Hildy into a chair. "Lieutenant Janvier has scarcely had time to file his report."

"I hope he's able to include the dramatic details I furnished him." Hildy unfolded her napkin, noting it was soiled, and folded it up again.

Marie bustled out the kitchen door with a tray. "I have heated some croissants and there is *pamplemousse* juice for you in the pitcher." She placed the tray on the table. "I have no servant this morning. Unfortunately, Shivar must attend summer classes at university."

A distant telephone sounded its double ring.

"I go." Léon jumped up from the table. "Marie, warm up the *café*." He handed her a large brown coffee pot and an empty carton of cream which she carried toward the kitchen.

"So, darling, when shall we leave for Paris?" Alex munched hungrily on a croissant.

"No more deadlines, remember dear? It's playtime from

here on." She covered his hand with hers.

"*D'accord*," he smiled. "I'll call the George *Cinq* and tell them we'll arrive late."

Hildy strained to hear Léon's animated conversation on the telephone, but was unable to follow his rapid French.

A few minutes later, Léon burst back on to the terrace, his tartan robe flying unbelted behind him. "But this is extraordinary! Marie!" he bellowed. "You must hear this!"

Marie trotted back with the pot of coffee.

"On the telephone, Lieutenant Janvier. He confirms that the jewels are, in fact, as we surmised. The police have been in touch with the museum where Madame Helmsley was employed and they are sending someone immediately to identify the missing gems. Janvier says the diamond alone is worth over five million francs!" His face was radiant with excitement. "Eh? Is that not as we suspected all along?"

"I was sure they were stolen," Hildy lowered her eyes to her cracked coffee mug, endeavoring to appear modest, "but I never imagined they were that valuable."

"Your writer's imagination served you well, my little...mimosa blossom," Alex grinned as he spread a dollop of jam on a croissant.

"But wait!" Léon stood with both his hands on the table, presiding over his next revelation. "That is not all. The jewel at St-Paul-de-Vence!"

"The ruby?" Hildy asked.

"*Oui*," Léon seated himself. "They have found a red stone in the window of the cathedral, exactly where we knew it was to be found!"

"Where Hildy told them," Alex amended.

"They have not yet time to examine it to make sure it is truly the stolen ruby, but no matter." The Marquis beamed at Marie. "So, it is historic moment, *non*?"

"The news people will want many pictures, Léon," Marie said eagerly. "The public will wish to see the famous chapel, without doubt." Her face clouded. "*Mon Dieu*! I will need Shivar to tidy up."

Léon lit a cigarette and blew smoke in the air. "Perhaps it is best I leave the glass of the mimosa window exactly as when the mad peasant destroyed it, eh? There is plenty of time to repair it next winter."

Hildy mused aloud, "Might the public be interested in viewing my boudoir, do you suppose? For a fee, of course. It is, after all, where the attempted murder took place."

Léon's eyes widened with interest. "But *naturellement*."

"You could get hold of one of those little velvet ropes, Marie, to put across the door," Hildy suggested. "I think royal blue might complement the bedspread rather nicely."

"*Ooh-lah-lah*, the draperies!" Marie's hand flew to her mouth. "Shivar must rehang them at once."

"Actually, Léon," said Alex, "with proper marketing, you could draw hundreds of admissions to the castle. People flock to the Loire in season. We saw the cars and vans on our drive here. The proceeds might just heat this old castle all winter."

Léon's eyebrows went up. "And the taxes! *Peut-être* we lease out some of the *chambres*, *oui*, *Marie*? Construct *un terrain de golf*? and we arrange boar hunting for the winter…"

"*Bonjour*, everyone!" Peter strode out on the terrace in jeans and the same pink shirt he had worn earlier. "Isn't it a simply super morning!" He dropped into a chair as Marie poured juice for him and Hildy recounted Janvier's report.

"That's wonderful!" Peter gulped down his juice. "But Hildy, luv. I've had the most marvelous idea for developing the theme for my film. I was just explaining it to Dawn."

"Really?" Hildy put down her cup.

"What started me thinking was your observation last night that the diamond was a precious stone. Are you sensing the synchronicity?"

"Not exactly, Peter." Hildy glanced at Alex who looked totally baffled.

Peter leaned his elbows on the table. "And *Petros* means *stone*!"

Hildy smiled. "Yes, I did think that was worth noting."

Peter's eyes narrowed as he gazed off. "The film opens

with the shepherd, turned artisan, etching jewel-like shards of glass for the window which will be his stained glass masterpiece…"

"Your 'Jesus,' of course," Hildy murmured. "Yes, I can see it."

The Marquis waved an encouraging hand. "And you will need the pastures and the hut and *peut-être* some sheep, *non*?"

Peter ignored the Marquis, his eyes on Hildy. "My Mary Magdalene—are you quite ready, luv?—a *gypsy* wench!"

Hildy's mind shot instantly to Consuela, voluptuous vessel of Orlando's earthly passions—mysterious, tragic. She touched her napkin to her lips, scarcely daring to breathe. "Could Mary possibly have had savage beginnings, say of an *Hispanic* nature?"

Peter grinned. "Your Consuela, of course!" He tipped his head to one side and sipped thoughtfully on his coffee. "At any rate, I'd like to consult your notes on all this, Hildy, for my film." He looked at Alex. "Would that be all right with you, old chap? Hildy will be paid, of course."

Alex leaned back and smiled. "That's up to Hildy. She makes her own decisions." His hand found Hildy's under the table. "Naturally I'd be happy to negotiate the deal, if she wishes."

"Yes, Peter. You can draw up a deal memo and fax it to Alex." Hildy thought a moment. "Alex, we mustn't allow my journal to be subpoenaed."

Alex borrowed the lavender pen to scribble a note. "I'll talk to our lawyer about it."

"We may have a deuce of a job casting the shepherd," Peter said.

Hildy thought a moment. "You'll want someone with a beard, I imagine. How about Kenny Rogers? He might make an album of your theme music."

"Too old," Peter said without hesitation. "I want an absolutely unknown face."

"Oh dear. I won't be able to suggest an unknown person, I don't think."

Peter gazed into space. "I want a face that's pure and unsullied by passion, unravaged by the tempests of life..." He shook his head. "I'll have to think about it."

"Yes, of course." Hildy hesitated to interrupt Peter's thoughts. "Have you any thoughts at all as to who might play the gypsy Consuela?"

From the archway came the tinkle of metal bracelets as Dawn appeared in a frilled peasant skirt and blouse, a woven shawl draped across one bare shoulder. Giant gold coins dangled from her neck and ears.

Alex squeezed Hildy's hand. "There's your answer, darling."

"No contest." Peter grinned at Dawn.

As Consuela sprang into being at last, she stamped her sequined thongs and rattled her bracelets in a brief *flamenco*. "*Olé!*"

Dismissing all concern for her heroine's future, Hildy could now concentrate on her own.